I0615972

OPEN

Marisa Rae Dondlinger

Moonshine Cove Publishing, LLC

Abbeville, South Carolina U.S.A.

First Moonshine Cove Edition December 2021

ISBN: 9781952439230

Library of Congress LCCN: 2021923943

© Copyright 2021 by Marisa Rae Dondlinger

Cover and interior design by Moonshine Cove staff, cover images public domain.

CAN AN OPEN MARRIAGE SAVE A RELATIONSHIP? OR DOES IT SPELL THE END?

When Alex and Lila married, they dreamed of having a big family. Fourteen years, two children, several miscarriages and a stillbirth later, Lila is devastated when Alex torpedoes that dream by getting a vasectomy without telling her. Alex, a doctor, doesn't believe another pregnancy would be safe for her health or her heart. Lila shuts down—her body, mind, emotions—unable to cope with her guilt from the stillbirth, Alex's betrayal, and her unrelenting ache for another child. They grow apart, functioning as little more than co-parents.

Trust broken, intimacy extinct, Alex proposes an open marriage. A proposal he quickly regrets. Guilt, frustration, and heartache shadow him after each hookup as he realizes there is no substitute for Lila. But it might be too late. Time apart from Alex drives Lila closer to Geneva, a dynamic, yet haunted woman who helps awaken Lila's passion and voice. Secrets, sex and lies come to light, causing Alex and Lila to reassess their motives and desire to save their marriage.

What People are Saying about OPEN

"Family secrets are given a whole new treatment in Marisa Dondlinger's new novel, *Open*. Dondlinger's skillful manipulation of characterization leads to a glorious and dizzying flip-flopping of good guy/bad guy, causing the reader to jump from backing one character to the next. This is an amazing representation of the reality of marriage – both husband and wife are hurt, both feel betrayed, and both are guilty of their own sins. You won't be able to set this book down as you watch this relationship wax and wane like a candle in a breeze, and your loyalties shift just as quickly." — Kathie Giorgio, author of *If You Tame Me* and *All Told*

i

"Dondlinger writes characters you cannot help but fall in love with, even when you don't want to, making this story all the more relatable. Like family, you root for them and want to knock some sense into them all at the same time. I was hooked from the first page and didn't want to put it down." —Nora Murray, author of *Kingdom Come.*

"In Marisa Dondlinger's *Open,* the range of emotions pulled me hither and yon, raising empathy first with one character, then with another, sometimes with abandonment. Alex and his ego, according to Lila; Lila and her cold apathy, according to Alex; Geneva, hurting from her own problems and trying to push her way in. What a circus to watch these people interact and judge, all the while trying to hold themselves together. Secrets upon secrets drew me in deeper and deeper, clear to the end." —Mary Ann Noe, author of *To Know Her*

Excerpt

"I'll pick up the kids," he said, always Mr. Fix-It. "Take them over to Nick's for dinner and then drop them off when we're done."

How seamlessly we transitioned into separate lives. A de facto divorced couple. Did he realize it? Did he see how easily we could lose everything? How an open marriage would become a break and ultimately a divorce?

Did he care? Was this step one in a plan to ultimately leave me? "Fine."

"Fine." He didn't say goodbye.

My phone switched back to the lock screen, a picture of Levi and Charlotte smiling with chocolate ice cream on their faces, holding the cones up like souvenirs. I couldn't have it both ways. I had to agree. For them.

For Andy. Your support makes my dreams possible.

About the Author

 Marisa Dondlinger lives in Wisconsin with her husband and two young daughters. A graduate of the University of Wisconsin Law School, Marisa practiced law for several years before devoting herself to writing fiction. She's also the author of *Scenes From a Bar* and the forthcoming *Gray Lines.* When not writing, she enjoys reading, going for walks, and watching her daughters play sports.

http://marisaraedondlinger.com

Acknowledgment

Many, many people went into making this book a realized dream. While I write alone, success was only possible with my "team" behind me.

Thanks to the publishers and editors at Moonshine Cove Publishing. For picking my book among the countless high-quality submissions, for believing in the strength of my story, and for being receptive during the publishing process.

Kathie Giorgio at AllWriters' Workplace and Workshop, LLC for the mentoring and coaching. To the brilliant and insightful women in my Tuesday night writing group. Your support carried me through the writing and editing process.

To Rachel Anderson at RMA Publicity for her guidance in marketing this book.

To my parents, who always encouraged my love of writing. As life threw me curveballs, my mom would always respond, *Write about it.* She believed every experience, both heartbreaking and exquisite, was fuel for my writing. She was right.

Lolita and Harlow. You two are everything. Your numerous interruptions when I'm writing—asking for a snack, to tell me about your day, a story, or just that you're bored—always brings a smile to my face. Each day I wake up excited to see what new adventure you'll go on in this world. I am your biggest fan.

Andy. For giving me the time, space, and support to develop my craft. For encouraging me to join a writing group, sign up for classes, attend writing workshops, and giving me Saturday afternoons to write uninterrupted. You always believed, and didn't just say the words, but put that belief into action with your sacrifices. Love you always.

OPEN

CHAPTER ONE
LILA

Alex proposed an open marriage on a Wednesday night. It was a little after nine; Levi and Charlotte were in bed, hopefully sleeping, but, at least, no longer demanding fresh water, another book, or a monster exorcism. The breeze coming through the window held the chill of fall and smelled faintly of charcoal from our earlier BBQ. I sat on the couch, knees pressed to my chest, trying to fix the pedicure Charlotte slopped on my toes to make me look "fancy," while listening to a couple on *House Hunters* argue about the style of house they wanted. As if living in a refurbished Victorian was the key to marital bliss.

"I'm exhausted," Alex said, flopping down next to me. His hair was damp from the shower, while his cheeks held a rosy glow from his twilight run. "Back-to-back patients all day."

"Mmm." I worked faster, going from one nail to the next. This, right here, was the reason I usually went to bed right after putting the kids down. We functioned well as a family, as co-parents, but when it was the two of us? That required talking. A concerted effort to pretend we hadn't become strangers. After spending the afternoon with the kids, staying engaged, emotive, *happy*, I had nothing left to give. To myself. And certainly not him.

"Wouldn't it be great to get away for a few days?" He ran his fingers down my leg. *Healing hands,* his mom quipped, as if he were Jesus instead of one of Wisconsin's top pediatricians. "Relax, eat some good food..."

I shifted my leg away. "The kids can't miss school."

He sighed. "I meant us."

The silence between us hung heavy. To think, we used to bask in this hour after the kids went to bed, before exhaustion claimed us too.

We'd snack on popcorn, exchanging stories from the day, always landing back on something cute the kids said or did.

At the next commercial break, he grabbed the remote and flipped off the TV. "Listen, I was thinking—and I know this sounds...unconventional." He cleared his throat. "What about trying an open marriage?"

I flinched mid-swipe, spraying dots of slate-blue nail polish across the couch. Somehow, he managed to shock me again. My heart; my poor, tortured heart, zapped my brain awake. A hot, metallic taste filled my mouth as I remembered that awful afternoon last December, the one that set us on a path to this moment. I'd come home from Christmas shopping to find Alex on the couch, an ice pack atop his groin, a beer in his hands, an inscrutable look on his face.

Tell me you didn't, I pleaded. We lost Milo a mere eight weeks before. A stillbirth. Existing felt like walking around with an open wound. With the doctor's permission, Alex and I started having sex again. We clung to one another, seeking to fill the eternal well of despair. From that grief, I hoped, we could create something beautiful. Another baby. It shocked me to find out that Alex didn't agree. That he thoughts the risks were too great to try.

He stood up. *A vasectomy was the only way.*

I told you no. Tears spilled down my cheeks. We'd argued fiercely the past couple weeks, me lobbying for another baby, him talking to me like I was a patient that needed to accept a fatal diagnosis. He mentioned a vasectomy, but never did I think he'd go behind my back, without my permission, in direct contradiction to my wishes, and get the procedure done. *How could you do this to me?* I said, enraged that he could be so calm in the face of his betrayal. *To us?*

Because I love you, he said, trying to embrace me. *Because I can't lose you.*

You just did. I pushed past him and walked into the bedroom.

I started packing a bag, unsure of my intentions, but knowing I couldn't be near him. He continued explaining, twisting our history— five miscarriages, one stillbirth—to support his position, giving me a tutorial on the risks of another pregnancy, but never once apologizing. I screamed at him—profanity-laced sentences, abrasive, cutting words that belonged to my mother. Not me. But I was no longer me. I was outside my body, watching myself, my marriage, my future, crumble.

When the kids got home from school, I explained that I had to visit my mom for a couple days. A plausible explanation given her problems. Instead, I drove to Chicago, walked the streets where we met, fell in love, married. Back then, it was easy. We shared the same dreams. Interests. Values. Sure, we argued occasionally, but always came out on the same side. Lovers. Friends. Parents. I challenged myself to see it from his perspective, drew upon our sixteen years together, but came up empty. Nothing could excuse his duplicity, his callousness.

When I returned home, I was dying. Not physically, but emotionally. I would not leave him; at eight and four, Levi and Charlotte idolized their father. And I cared far more about their happiness than my own. Instead, I numbed myself, syphoned my anger to a dull ache. But numbing didn't leave room for any emotion—forgiveness or love or growth.

Alex jerked me back to the present, handing me a roll of paper towels. I soaked the towel with nail polish remover and dabbed the couch.

"Lila, say something."

"An open marriage," I said, tasting the words, letting them penetrate, hating that he found a way to break through my defenses. Hurt me again.

"I miss you." He nodded once to himself, curt and determined, a quarterback psyching himself up before a big play. "I miss talking to you. Joking around. Going out on dates. Just—" He barreled his crystalline eyes into mine. "—being close to you. I mean, Christ, Lila, it's been months since we've had sex. Months! You won't even let me touch you."

His plea for sex was old news. He'd all but taken out a billboard inside our bedroom, advertising his needs. And it wasn't only physical.

He craved intimacy. A real partnership. Like before. But this, proposing an open marriage, was new. An unsettling development that sank to the bottom of my stomach like an anchor, heavy and unmovable.

"You're a ghost of yourself," he continued when I said nothing. "It's like you died with Milo." He squeezed my limp hand. Alex believed I suffered a breakdown after Milo's stillbirth and never recovered. A self-serving conclusion. While the guilt immobilized me at times, especially when I saw a baby or woke from a nightmare, I directed that pain inward. Never at Alex. It was my fault, after all, that Milo wasn't upstairs, sleeping with his brother and sister. "I've tried to be patient, give you time to grieve, help you, but nothing I say or do factors." He sounded exasperated. "You don't want to get better."

I pulled my hand away. *See a therapist. Take anti-depressants. Join a bereavement group.* Those were the ways he offered to "help." But what was the point? Would I get my marriage back? Another baby?

"What if there is no better?" I asked, voicing a fate I already relinquished myself to. "What if this is me?"

"This isn't you," he said, adopting the gentle, yet firm tone he used with patients. "I know you. The you that's kind and passionate. That loves to laugh. This woman, the one's that so entrenched in grief, she doesn't see me?" He shook his head. "That's not my Lila."

"But why an open marriage?" Alex never struck me as the type to cheat. Then again, I never believed him capable of secretly getting a vasectomy. "Sex is that important to you?"

"Sex used to be important to both of us," Alex said, proving he had a selective memory when it came to what was "important" to us. "And I thought an open marriage might take some pressure off you. Give you time...to find yourself again. Figure out how to be happy." He tipped his head back against the couch and laughed, more out of despair than any real joy. "Maybe a break is what we both need, to remember why we fell in love. To come at this marriage with fresh eyes." He sat back up. "Either way, something has to change. We can't go on like this."

Fresh eyes. What a joke. If only Alex would look inward. Take a beat, reflect on the last year, reflect on the dreams we once shared. But Alex never second-guessed himself—an occupational hazard. When I returned from Chicago last winter, he tried reasoning with me, but then moved on. He was too busy with work, the kids, running, to look backwards.

While the vasectomy was a footnote in Alex's life, for those first few weeks, it held me in a stranglehold. My period taunted me, the visual reminder that my body was ready, craved more. I'd watch Levi and Charlotte and felt nauseous, thinking about what could've been if Alex wasn't so rash. Cried in the shower; great, wracking sobs that left me hollow and shaky.

Shutting down was a matter of survival. I knew all about the dangers of becoming incapacitated by grief, unable to rise from bed. The way it destroyed a child's spirit. My mother taught *that* master class.

"How would this work?" I ignored the whisper in my ear, the old Lila, the one that loved and trusted Alex. She told me to speak up, tell him the truth. That I tried to forgive him, but I couldn't. That I wanted another baby, that I would never stop wanting one. But why try? He didn't listen last time. He didn't care. I'd end up worse off, furious and spiteful—none of which was healthy for the kids to witness.

"You tell me," Alex said. "I wouldn't do anything you're not comfortable with."

I glared at him. "Is that supposed to be funny?"

"No, of course not. Fuck! I can't believe we're at this point. Discussing this." He rubbed his temples. "Doesn't this piss you off?"

Rage burned my tongue like acid. A flicker, quick as a lightning bolt, tore through my veins. Yes, I was pissed off. Pissed off at his refusal to apologize. His endless seduction attempts. His me-me-ME attitude. Was he always this oblivious? Self-centered? Had love blinded me to his faults or had Milo irrevocably changed him too?

"You brought it up." I kept my face placid. Growing up with the emotional circus that was my mother taught me not to react. To shut down instead of scream.

13

"Because I don't know what else to do!" He looked at me, his jaw tight. "I've reached my limit. How much rejection can one person take?"

I flinched. A subtle threat to leave. He betrayed me once, what was to stop him again? Renege on all his other promises? Had I sacrificed my happiness for nothing? Would he leave us anyway?

I had to agree. Protecting the kids was all that mattered. Levi and Charlotte would never sit at their bedroom windows, waiting to see if today was the day Daddy returned home. They wouldn't wake to find Mommy in a pool of vomit, unable to meet another lonely night without alcohol. They would always feel loved. Home would be their sanctuary. If I failed them in every other way, at least I would not repeat the mistakes of my parents.

"You can't have sex with anyone we know," I said, sealing my fate. Alex would have no trouble finding volunteers. He rounded forty last year, jokingly posing like Michelangelo's David in his boxer briefs, chiseled abs and all. Combined with a full head of dark hair, enhanced by a hint of gray, a disarming smile, and a weekly medical TV talk show, he still earned the full head-to-toe onceover from women in the coveted eighteen to forty-nine demographic. "So, if this is about some crush—"

"That's not it." He scooched closer, tucking my long hair behind my ear. "I'd choose you, every day and twice on Sunday, if you were willing."

His smile carried the affection of a greeting card. It reminded me of our love, but it didn't stir me anymore. Before Milo, our sex life was healthy, hot, enviable. But my desire for him died with the vasectomy. Trust was my aphrodisiac. And the trust was gone.

I closed my eyes. Inhaled deeply. The turnstiles in my mind wound at a frantic pace, trying to process the complications of this new life. I hadn't done this much thinking in months. I actively tried *not* to think.

"When are you planning on doing this?" Between Levi's soccer, Charlotte's gymnastics, and Alex's volunteer work, board commitments, and half-marathon training, there wasn't a lot of free time. Three days a week, he was at the hospital before dawn and, thanks to his show, *Ask Dr. Alex*, his private practice had a waitlist longer than for season Packer tickets. "After the kids go to bed? On weekends?"

"I don't know," he said slowly. "We'll figure it out."

I dug my nails into the palms of my hands, willing myself not to care. More nights alone. Maybe it would be a blessing in disguise. But his announcement worked like a shot of adrenaline, making it impossible to detach. I thought about him coming home late, another woman's fingerprints marking his body. Reeking of sweat and saliva and cum. Giving me an embarrassed smile. Or worse, acting like nothing happened. The barbeque chicken we ate earlier churned in my stomach.

"Lila." He wrapped his arms around me, pulling me close. My head instinctively rested in the crook of his neck, inhaling the smell of soap. Of home. "You're the one I want. If you were ready to try..."

The words hung in the air, an olive branch I couldn't quite snatch. "I can't."

"You can."

I swallowed. Hard. His breath was warm against my ear, the subtlest of comforts. This was Alex. My husband. My best friend. My *person*. How could I endorse him having sex with another woman? How could he ask? Everyone knew introducing a third party inside a relationship was like mixing alcohol and opiates—danger lurked in the unknown. *Stop this!* the old Lila shouted. *Before it's too late!* "Maybe we—"

"You have to trust me, babe," he said. "Being together, physically...it's the best way to help us heal emotionally."

I froze. The sentiment, similar to his justification for the vasectomy— *Trust me. This hurts now, but give it time. You'll see, it's for the best—* vanquished any affection. This wasn't about what we needed. It was about what he needed. Again.

I pulled away, whispering so he couldn't hear how my voice shook. "Let's try the open marriage."

"We don't have to decide tonight," he said, his mouth weighed down with disappointment. A familiar look. "Just, think about it."

I retreated to bed, unable to keep pretending that his request hadn't sheared the tangled vines of apathy that circled my heart. I lay there, breathing in and out, reassuring myself that I made the right choice. The only choice, really. I would endure this, as I endured all the other losses, with a brave face and a silent heart.

Nothing could touch me, as long as I buried it deep enough.

CHAPTER TWO
ALEX

I watched Lila behind the brim of my Notre Dame coffee cup, studying her movements like an anthropologist, looking for any impact from last night's conversation. She bustled around the kitchen, swiping peanut butter and jelly on bread, applauding the gigantic stilted letters Charlotte printed, and using her hand like an iron to press out the creases in Levi's homework. She moved on auto-pilot, one task to the next, as if her brain would spontaneously combust if she stopped moving.

It was better than the alternative. After Milo died—I say died because that's what happened. I despised the phrase "lost the baby." I didn't lose my baby. I goddamn knew where he was. After Milo *died*, she woke to kiss the kids goodbye, her hair oily and lank, the smell of sweat, sleep, and misery wafting from her body. She returned to bed, ignoring phone calls and the doorbell, until the kids came home. Still in her pajamas, she cooked dinner, her eyes as glazed as Snoop Dogg's, despite not having taken a single drug, prescription or recreational, before returning to her lair.

Yes, definitely better than that. But still, not my Lila.

I hoped proposing the open marriage would work like a defibrillator, rebooting her system. Jump-start her out of this funk. Make her realize that the lack of intimacy went from critical to life-threatening. But she agreed. Agreed! As if I proposed switching from Coke to Pepsi. The stillness of her body, the unblinking stare, the gnarled fists, told me she didn't like it. Somewhere in the recesses of her brain, an alarm sounded, but Lila either ignored it or shut it off.

From afar, our marriage looked solid. We attended soccer games, birthday parties, fundraisers. She accepted hugs, occasional kisses.

Innocent, friendly touches that affirmed we were committed, on the same team. But this public façade masked our private estrangement: Lila refused to have sex. Refused to be intimate. And I'm not talking about fobbing me off because she was tired or had her period or felt fat. I'm talking about months of rejection. No apology. No moment to consider whether she could get in the mood. No promise to make it up to me. Nothing. Complete utter indifference that our sex life was extinct.

It wasn't always that way. Lila used to make me feel like the center of her world, that she not only wanted me, but needed me. Not just at the beginning either, when it felt like we invented sex. Passion fueled our marriage. It elevated the highs, jolted us out of monotony, and helped us endure the devastating lows.

Living with Lila was like being on a diet and working at a doughnut shop. I could look, but never, ever consume. I saw her naked in the shower, mindlessly rubbing soap over her breasts. I watched her practice yoga, holding poses that made me flash back to our apartment on Bleeker Street. Back then, sex was an embarrassment of riches. I'd show up for rounds, still semi-erect, wearing her sweat like a perfume. I marveled at the way her ass defied gravity, her jean-hugging curves reminding me of those Guess ads from the 90s that served as my first anatomy lesson. But if I dared to touch, her eyes glazed over, her body went rigid, her voice monotone, as if her soul took a vacation.

The roar of the bus's engine echoed inside the kitchen, causing last-minute pandemonium. We each chose a kid, rubbing on sunscreen, stuffing lunchboxes inside backpacks, and giving kisses.

We stood at the front door, watching as the kids marched into the mouth of the bus. It was an ordinary moment, one of thousands we shared in creating this family, but it still gave me chills. I was so lucky...except. *Except.* My thoughts homed in on what was missing like a missile and hit its target. Ka-boom!

"I thought of some rules," Lila said, walking back to the kitchen. Her voice was flat, her shoulders hunched. Now that the kids were gone, her body deflated like a balloon. God forbid she put an ounce of effort into wooing me.

"Rules?" Lila loved rules. It was one of the first things I learned about her. Boundaries made her feel safe. In control.

"For the open marriage."

My stomach tightened. I hedged my bets all wrong. The night to reflect on my proposal hadn't changed anything. She was as remote as ever, choosing to pass me around like a Thanksgiving dish, rather than have sex with me.

The idea for an open marriage originated out of loneliness and desperation. Our lives resembled *Groundhog's Day*—different day, same suffocating lack of intimacy. She refused to talk. Refused to acknowledge there was a problem. Divorce was out. She emerged from a broken home, whereas I had the pressure of domestic bliss, my parents happily married over forty years. Either way, that document was inked in blood. Beyond abstinence and a deft hand, I had no other options.

Then I came across an article about how an open marriage can rekindle a marriage. Supposedly, it reminded you of how desirable your partner was, why you fell in love. Unlike an affair, which was shrouded in guilt and secrecy, open marriages promoted communication.

Best-case scenario, obviously.

"You can't have sex with the same person more than three times," Lila said.

I raised an eyebrow. Lila's mind was like a cave; there was always a new tunnel to explore. How did she land on three? What made four the point of no return? "Why three?"

"That way no one falls in love."

The sun filtered through the window, highlighting dried mascara sprinkled like mouse droppings beneath her eyes. This tiny detail symbolized the tumor in our marriage: Lila's apathy. Why couldn't she make an effort? Try to feel good about herself again? It's like she thought happiness would be a blight on Milo's soul.

19

"And you can't talk about us. Have sex if you must—" She whispered *sex* with the distaste of an elderly blue-haired lady in church. "—but don't turn them into your best friend."

I enjoyed meeting new people. Hearing their stories. And people *liked* me. Lila, who'd fly to Australia without saying a word to her seatmate, socialized only when necessary. It was a constant bone of contention. She claimed I overshared, campaigned for friendships like I was running for office, but Lila would have a hard time trusting a priest. She refused to let anyone in until they had been properly vetted.

Very few passed the screening process.

"I have to tell them we have open marriage," I said, popping the collar of my shirt and wrapping a Batman tie around my neck. At Superhero Pediatrics, with great power comes great responsibility. "I don't want to lead anyone on. Didn't you see *Fatal Attraction*?"

I mimed stabbing myself. Lila's face remained a blank slate, one of those stick figure diagrams Charlotte brought home from school, ready for her to humanize with a gigantic smile, oval eyes, and button nose. "Third—"

"How long is this list?" I had patients starting at nine. Paperwork beforehand. Calls to return. I poured coffee into a travel mug, needing every last drop to become the fun-loving Dr. Alex my patients, and their parents, expected.

"You have to be honest," she said, ignoring my question. "I can't imagine wanting details, but if I ask…"

"I'm always honest."

She gave a rueful laugh.

"Why are you acting like this?"

"Like what?"

"Distant." My temple throbbed. Headaches came daily now. Too much stress, too little sleep. No sex.

"I think this arrangement requires a certain amount of distancing, don't you?"

A time machine. A genie. A half-assed witch. Anything with the power to change history would do.

"You want me to be honest?" I stepped towards her, tilted up her chin and kissed her. If she puckered at all, it was lost on me. "I need you."

She turned around, rinsing the breakfast dishes. "You have me. You always will."

Not like this, I almost said. But it was a dead-end conversation. She was content treading water, recycling what if scenarios, ignoring all my suggestions on how to move forward.

I grabbed my briefcase and yelled goodbye. My resolve hardened as I reversed my aged, but reliable Rav 4 out of the garage. How long were we supposed to live in this purgatory? The rest of our lives?

Twenty-eight weeks and four days. That's all we had with Milo. We heard the heartbeat. Had the ultrasound. Everything looked perfect. I surprised Lila with a weekend in Kohler. Spa treatments. Extra sleep. Delicious food. A babymoon to celebrate the start of the third trimester.

Three days later, Lila called me during a lunch meeting: the baby wasn't moving. I met her at the hospital, where they rushed to hook her up to the monitor. But it didn't matter. The baby had no heartbeat. The sound that came out of Lila's mouth was a low keening. Animalistic. Chilling. It awoke my protective instinct. Lila became my priority.

By the time they wheeled her into the birthing room, Lila fell silent. Her pale face whitewashed of emotion. She didn't make a sound, not even a grunt, as she delivered the baby. A full year passed since Milo's death, but in some ways, she never emerged from the shock. Sure, she rallied for the kids, shuffling them to practices and playdates, making goofy voices while reading, doling out middle-of-the-night cuddles if either presented with a stomachache or a nightmare. But me? I wasn't a priority. If she put a tenth of the effort she gave the kids into our marriage, we wouldn't be having this discussion.

As I backed into the street, she sprinted out of the house. I lowered my window. Her cheeks glowed a rosy pink, erasing a decade and a dozen disappointments from her face. She looked like the Lila I met at the drinking fountain.

"I need to know when it starts." Lila raised her hand in greeting, acknowledging our neighbor Shannon as she drove past. A pair of sunglasses disguised Shannon's prying eyes. "You'll tell me, right?"

Rules. Security. Trust. Maybe my proposal did serve as a wakeup call. This was the most we talked without the kids present in months. And crafting rules. Well, that was vintage Lila.

"I promise."

She nodded and walked back inside, while I idled in the driveway. It was an odd sensation to watch your own house like a stranger, wondering what secrets it held. No one would suspect that we were anything other than happy. Everything from the bikes laying against the front porch to the freshly cut lawn to the new coat of pigeon blue paint on the front door suggested middle-class domestic harmony.

But the façade masked a growing despair, a sense of hopelessness that filled our lives as we became more like roommates than husband and wife. I lit a match last night, one that had the potential to inject life back into our marriage. As I remembered the flatness in Lila's voice, as if she was negotiating the kids' carpool instead of the terms of our open marriage, my doubts receded. I *had* to shake things up, shake Lila out of her stupor. We couldn't go on this way.

CHAPTER THREE
GENEVA

Geneva walked up the glass stairs, wearing fuchsia skinny jeans, an Alice + Olivia black and white striped blazer, and Rag & Bone suede ankle boots—her outfit providing a sliver of joy in her otherwise depressing life. Betsy Abrams, the chair of the English Department, looked at her shoes earlier today and laughed. *You'll have to invest in a pair of rubber boots,* she said. Winter in Wisconsin. After growing up on the Upper West side of Manhattan, and spending her last five years earning her Ph.D. at Berkeley, Geneva nearly declined the position based on location. She was a diehard city girl. But common sense prevailed—a top fifty university wasn't something to shade because of boredom and a lot of snow.

Six weeks after moving to Madison, she regretted that decision. She felt feral—in mind and body. New cities, new people usually energized her, but from the moment she landed here, she felt deflated. Homesick, if she was honest. Madison was a cute city to visit—the farmer's market, the serene lakes—but living here was another matter. Especially for a young, single, lesbian woman of color. Madison billed itself as progressive, diverse, a haven for the LBGTQ community. And while that may be true, it was a microcosm of New York. Berkeley. Emphasis on the "micro." The lack of urgency, the repetition, left her feeling like she had a perpetual hangover. The bottles of wine piling up in her recyclable bin probably contributed, but how else to pass her nights? At the deluge of fratastic bars lining State Street? No, thank you.

Wanting nothing more than to turn around, go back to her apartment, luxuriate with a bath bomb and wine, she summoned Maya Angelou for inspiration: *My mission in life is not merely to survive, but to thrive.*

Wisconsin was the right choice for her end game. A tenured track position, as opposed to an associate gig. Research opportunities. Speaking engagements. Exposure. She'd work her ass off, write a dozen original papers, polish that resume. All while working her connections, scouring Columbia's job board, making monthly visits to her collegiate alma mater to ensure no one forgot her face or name. Three years max. New York would be home once again.

At the top of the steps, Geneva took stock of the bar, pleasantly surprised. A long rectangular quartz bar lit up underneath with white LED lights, open shelving with jeweled bottles and hand-blown glasses, minimalist furniture. The bar was called Home, and the name fit. The décor almost felt like New York. Almost.

The reception was for Louis Weiner, winner of the Man Booker Prize a few years back. As the newest and youngest member of the English faculty, Geneva had to make a showing. Despite having not spoken to her parents in months, their advice came across loud and clear—*Attend everything! Each day's an opportunity! Make yourself heard! Indispensable!* Did they know she was in Wisconsin? Were they tracking her career? Or had they divested themselves of her permanently?

She pushed away these thoughts, making her way to the bar where she ordered the special: a grapefruit gimlet. The sweetness coated her tongue, relaxing her muscles, readying her for a night of feigned enthusiasm.

Flashing her megawatt smile, she mingled with her colleagues. From boarding school to grad school, her smiling face always found its way into the campus brochure. *You're a prop,* Lexi Hamilton informed her during their sophomore year at Chapman. She paged through the brochure, her long blonde hair tickling Geneva's forearm, her blue eyes ignorant of the pain she was bestowing. *There's, what, four of you guys here and yet you're in almost every picture?* Geneva's smile was her ticket in. It worked like the sun, drawing people into her orbit, taming their prejudices, softening her edges.

"And what's the feeling out west?" Professor MacGregor asked. He was a wiry man with bushy eyebrows and oversized glasses. "Are they calling for impeachment?"

Geneva laughed. "I can hardly speak on behalf of the entire state of California."

Professor MacGregor pushed the brim of his glasses up his nose. "I'm trying to gauge the temperature. We're isolated in our liberal bubble..."

You mean in your white cis-hetero-normative faux liberal bubble of privilege that has never felt marginalized or faced any real discrimination? Much as that zing appealed, she pasted *that* smile on her face, savvy enough not to directly insult a tenured professor.

"Students are always exercising their civil rights at Berkeley. Police shootings. The removal of eucalyptus trees. Impeachment," Geneva said. "They take all injustice seriously."

The other professors nodded along—squinted eyes, lips slightly parted, pointer fingers at the ready—all waiting for the chance to exercise their overeducated and underappreciated brains. That was the problem with academia. No one just talked. Chilled. Enjoyed a drink without debate. Everyone regressed to kindergarten, playing a game of show-and-tell, except knowledge was the currency and no one, under any circumstances, ever oohed and aahed at your display.

Geneva felt drained, suddenly missing her friends, her life back in Berkeley, desperately. *More liquor, now!* her brain screamed. She excused herself for a top-up, ordering a shot of tequila along with her gimlet. A shot she immediately threw back.

"An IV might be more efficient."

Geneva turned, taking in the man next to her. He was tall with a full head of dark hair, a slim-cut suit that emphasized his chiseled shoulders and narrow waist, and a...batman tie? It had a pattern of miniature grey Batman insignia on a bed of black silk. Real silk, not some starchy, scratchy knockoff. Add one point for quality, deduct two for taste.

"But less enjoyable," she said, pointing to his tie. "Headed to a costume party?"

He fingered his tie, grinning boyishly as if pleased to find it there. "I'm a pediatrician. The kids love it when I wear these ties."

Geneva laughed. "It's all for the kids, huh?"

His artic blue eyes sparkled with humor as he accepted a beer and a water from the bartender. "It's the cross I have to bear."

He waved at a woman across the room. She walked over, her matchstick legs swimming in a short, blush shift dress. Her hair was pulled into a low ponytail. Nude flats and a hint of lipstick finished the look. Geneva preferred the gloss of an Instagram model, but this woman was striking—high cheekbones; heavy, dark eyebrows; Elizabethan skin; strawberry lips begging to be tasted.

"Babe, this is—" He handed the woman the water and turned back to Geneva. "I'm sorry, I didn't catch your name?"

"Geneva."

"Alex." He shook her hand. Firm. Confident, but not finger-crushing cocky. "And this is my wife, Lila. Geneva was complimenting my tie."

It amazed Geneva how often men mistook observations for compliments.

"You've made his day," Lila said, giving him an indulgent closed mouth smile. She looked familiar. Uncannily so. Especially her eyes. They reminded Geneva of a melting Hershey bar. The most luxurious shade of brown. The Louis Vuitton of eyes. "He's obsessed with superheroes. Particularly Batman."

"Obsessed? No. Deep admiration? Absolutely. Think about it, he's human." He paused to drink his beer. "No magic powers. No mutations. He uses sheer will and intellect to fight evil. I like to think he and I have something in common."

"He does know Batman's not real, right?" Geneva mock-whispered to Lila. She walked a tightrope with her sense of humor—not everyone got it. *You're not funny,* one of her exes said. *You're just a bitch.* Geneva preferred to think of herself as an acquired taste, a fine wine, thick skin required. Yet, the words stayed with her, a warning.

Lila smiled at Geneva. "I haven't found the right time to break the news."

A warm glow spread across Geneva's chest. She wanted to ascribe it to the alcohol, but the instantaneous response, like a switch flipping, made her believe otherwise. No one made her breath hitch like this since moving here.

"You'll never convince me," Alex said, grinning. "Hell, I named my practice Superhero Pediatrics because I believe."

"I admire your passion," Geneva said.

Lila studied her husband's face like a *Jeopardy* clue. "He's a little too passionate."

Silence followed. Geneva felt every awkward second acutely as Lila and Alex communicated with their eyes, something Geneva witnessed only between married couples and siblings—neither of which Geneva could relate. She had no intention of third wheeling it, but before she could say goodbye, Alex set down his drink.

"Excuse me, ladies. I have to take this call," he said, head bent over his phone as he retreated down the stairs.

Lila watched him leave, lips pressed together. Geneva felt an immediate need to cheer Lila up. Fruitless as it may be, a little flirtation never hurt. Nor did basking in the glow of one of Lila's smiles.

"Pretty ring." Geneva pointed to the rose-colored jewel on Lila's ring finger. It wasn't a traditional engagement ring, which Geneva admired. "How long have you been married?"

"Fourteen years."

"Impressive. I have a hard time committing to a second date."

Lila laughed to acknowledge the joke, but her eyes remained fixed on her ring. "And here I married my first boyfriend..."

"Did you guys meet when you were fifteen?" Geneva said.

A subtle blush tinted her cheeks. "In grad school."

"Waiting for someone worthy. I like it. Tell me, how did you know Alex was the one?" Geneva had a string of exes longer than Fifth Avenue, but since Cristina, an ex she avoided thinking about at all costs, it was a point of pride that no one broke through. "Give me a little advice on what I should be looking for."

Lila's eyes inched back towards the stairs. "I guess, with Alex, no wasn't an option. It felt like destiny when we met." Lila blinked, holding her eyes closed a second too long. When she opened them, that forced closed-mouth smile returned. It reminded Geneva of one of those vintage dolls where a string controlled the movements. Tug, smile. Tug, smile. "Sorry, that sounds contrived."

"No, it sounds...romantic," Geneva said, surprising herself. She didn't believe in romance, experience leaving her jaded, but she had to admit the appeal of a serendipitous meeting.

Lila yawned, covering her mouth with her hand. "Sorry, it's been a long couple of days."

"Something stronger might help." Geneva tipped the rim of her gimlet against Lila's water cup. "What's that Bukowski quote? 'Almost everyone needs a drink, they just don't know it?'"

"I'm kind of working."

"Right now?" Geneva stepped closer to Lila to be heard over the noise in the bar. Close enough that their shoulders touched. She inhaled Lila's perfume—Clinique Happy. A revealing choice. Lila was busy. Pragmatic. No frills allowed.

Stuck.

The simple dress, the strained smile, the generic perfume. It might have fooled most, but Geneva had x-ray vision when it came to recognizing a haunted soul. Lila's marriage might have had a fairytale beginning, but from the way she patrolled the stairs like a secret service agent to the defeated look in her eyes, Geneva knew all was not right in paradise.

"I'm the associate director of university relations and campus outreach," Lila said. "Which is a fancy way of saying I coordinate campus speakers, like Mr. Weiner. Technically, I'm here to support him, but—"

"It doesn't look like he needs you." The bar was standing room only now. Louis Weiner was to lit junkies as Taylor Swift was to broken-hearted teenagers: a cultural demigod.

"They never do," Lila said. "And yet I always have to come."

"Hey, it's not all bad. You got to meet me." Geneva fluttered her eyelashes in a way she hoped was both comical and endearing. "Which makes you the first official non-work friend I've made since moving to Wisconsin. Congrats."

"I'm...flattered." Lila blushed again, a quirk Geneva found cute. It reminded her of Cristina, how she would blush at the smallest compliment thrown her way.

Jesus. Two thoughts of Cristina—a warning to slow down on the liquor.

"What drew you to Wisconsin?" Lila asked.

"Other than the microbreweries and the frigid temperatures?" Here, she got an actual laugh out of Lila. She had to strain her ears to hear it above the din of conversation, but she felt certain it was an auditory expression of enjoyment. "You're looking at the newest professor in the English department."

"Congratulations. How do you like it so far?"

"Difficult. I'm from New York, so..."

"It's quite a culture shock, isn't it?" Lila stole the words from Geneva's brain. Moving to Wisconsin felt like visiting a foreign country—without the historical buildings, language barrier, or currency exchange. But, somehow, hearing it from Lila, felt much more ominous. A predictor of an arduous few years.

"I'm afraid I might never acclimate," Geneva said.

Their eyes met, a moment of understanding before Lila looked away. "I felt the same way. We moved from Chicago. Alex loved it on sight, but I had a hard time. Madison's quite—" Lila frowned. There was beauty in sadness, a trait Geneva found alluring in women, a trait Lila had in spades. A trait which probably explained why Geneva would forever be single. She'd read enough literature to know that two haunted souls didn't typically equal bliss. "Insular. It's a college town—"

29

Before Lila could finish, Alex materialized.

"Mind if I steal my wife?" Alex flashed a smile and led Lila away, his hand pressed against the small of her back. Geneva finished her drink and ordered another shot, annoyed that her chat with Lila was cut short. She finally found someone she was attracted to, enjoyed talking to, and, of course, she had to be straight. And married! The love Gods were assuredly not on her side. Nor were the sex Gods.

As the night progressed, Geneva hobnobbed with her colleagues, determined to present herself as both intelligent and witty. Despite her best efforts to focus, her eyes kept seeking out Lila. The raw attraction left her flustered. Aching. Imbibing more alcohol only enhanced her fixation. When Alex kissed Lila, Geneva felt sucker-punched. She reached out for the bar, stumbling, noting, too late, that she was drunk. Past buzzed and on the precipice of a blackout. She needed to leave. Now. Before she committed career suicide. While she was out and proud, she also didn't need to give her colleagues a front row seat to her love life.

As she made her way towards the stairs, tottering on heels that felt like stilts, Geneva took one last look at Lila. Ridiculous. They just met! Why was Geneva acting crazy? She never let women wind her up like this. Somewhere in the recesses of her brain, Geneva knew something else was at play; every time she looked at Lila she felt overcome with déjà vu, but she couldn't connect the dots. Couldn't figure out why Lila, a stranger, felt so familiar, elicited such strong feelings. Perhaps it was the six weeks of celibacy—no sex, no flirting, *nada*—since moving here. No wonder she came out of the gates hot.

Lila caught her staring and walked over. Geneva smiled, betraying no sign of nerves despite her heart slamming against her ribs, ricocheting off her organs, like her own personal pinball game.

"Sorry about what I said before," Lila said. "Madison's great. Just give it a chance."

Geneva held on to the railing, as much for stability as a reminder to keep her distance. Normal rules were not at play. This wasn't some hookup she wouldn't see again. Lila was special, although she couldn't say why. All the same, she trusted her gut.

"Don't apologize. Women apologize far too much."

Lila's eyes drifted back to Alex. "I'll work on that."

She yearned to ask Lila for her number, but the single percent of sobriety cautioned against it. Instead, Geneva smiled and dared to lightly squeeze Lila's arm. "Hopefully, I'll see you around."

With that, she floated downstairs and out into the cool fall night. Geneva repeated her name—*Lila, Lila.* The alcohol, isolation, and desire combined to make it sound like a love poem.

She was so fucking fucked.

CHAPTER FOUR
LILA

A week passed since Alex blew apart my carefully constructed world by asking for an open marriage. The waiting was the worst part. I felt like I was walking a gangplank, Alex pressing the knife against my back, pushing me towards the night where he would sleep with another woman. A tremor ran through my fingers, my toes tapped to an imaginary beat, random muscles twitched. My body was waking up—a terrifying prospect.

I couldn't have it both ways. Keep Alex to myself, but not give myself to him. Rationally, I knew this, but intellectually, my mind kept searching for a solution. I tried to resurrect the emotion of happier times—how he left his baseball game mid-play as I ran by, scaling the fence, finally catching up with me at the water fountain, breathlessly introducing himself; laughing so hard, I cried after he gave me my first orgasm, realizing that sex wasn't something to endure, but enjoy; accepting his proposal at "our" water fountain; camping in our furniture-less house the night we moved in; the love with which he first held Levi and Charlotte, the delicacy with which he held me through each miscarriage. But those memories inevitably led me down a rabbit hole, one that started with Milo and spiraled to today.

Unable to muster any enthusiasm to persuade members of the intellectual and cultural elite to visit our campus, I stood up and walked to my office window. I used to enjoy my job. But ever since my post-Milo leave of absence, what would have been my maternity leave, I found it hard to care. Perhaps I should quit. But what would I do? The kids were in school and busy with activities afterwards. Alex worked long hours. No one needed me.

I stared at the midnight blue of Lake Mendota. Storm clouds hovered, ready to cleanse the campus. A rumble of thunder erupted, drawing the normally docile water into angry shards. Waves broke over the rocks like an exhale, before the pressure, the need of the water, drew it back into its belly. Inhale. Exhale. So fundamental. And yet Milo never got the pleasure of a single breath.

I pressed my head against the glass, wishing, as I had thousands of times, that I called my doctor upon waking that morning. Confided in Alex when he kissed me goodbye. Drove myself to the hospital. Done anything except lying around waiting, pleading with Milo to wake up, move. Praying to God to intervene. Convincing myself I was overreacting. Freezing in denial. Anything to suggest I was a capable mother.

My cell phone buzzed. Alex.

"What's wrong?" I asked. He rarely called during the day. His singular focus remained on his patients. While Alex's intellect and work ethic laid the foundation for his success, it was his ability to make people feel understood, to ease their fears, empathize with everything from the trivial to the fatal, that made him an excellent pediatrician. He was a "doctor, cheerleader, friend, and advocate, wrapped in a McDreamy package." Direct quote from a review of *Ask Dr. Alex* in the *Madison Times*.

What lucky patients. To have him listen to their feelings. Not act without permission. Be amenable to compromise.

"Nothing." He paused. Pounding snaked through the telephone. The building next to his office was renovating—the bane of Alex's existence. Actually, a sexless marriage, a wife that was no more emotive than a mannequin, was probably the bane of his existence. But construction noise pulled a close second. "I'm going out tonight."

When he got the vasectomy, he excised a chunk of my heart. Without anesthesia. A betrayal so swift and cutting, I didn't think there were any nerve endings left to feel pain. But I was wrong. Like a sore throat issuing its first tickle, I felt the hum of fresh betrayal.

"You asked me to tell you before I started," he said.

An alarm sounded on Alex's end, a beeping that signaled a construction vehicle reversing, but maybe it was inside my head, a final warning to either speak up or accept the consequences. But what would I say? I'm not ready to be with you, I don't know whether I'll ever be ready, but I don't want you to be with anyone else either. I doubted he would want to stick around to see how that played out.

"Lila, talk to me. I can't read your mind. Not anymore. Are you having second thoughts?"

I hated him for putting me in this position. For coming up with such an asinine solution. For taking away the one pleasure I had—numbing myself to the pain. I didn't want to be angry. Sad. Frustrated. I wanted to feel nothing. Beautiful, exquisite nothingness.

I took a yoga breath, envisioning the cells of my brain shutting down, one by one, a power outage leaving me in a veil of darkness.

"It's fine," I said. "This is what we agreed."

"We didn't sign in blood. Say the word, tell me you don't want this, and I'll cancel."

I turned the framed photo of Alex and me—grinning, holding hands, airborne, atop a mountain in the Berkshires on our honeymoon—face down. "It's fine."

Silence. Things would never be fine again.

"All right." He sighed. "I'll see you at dinner."

"Just go from work."

"But then I won't see the kids."

"Yeah, well." What did he expect? That I'd send him off with a kiss, waving goodbye from the driveway like a wartime bride?

"I'll pick up the kids," he said, always Mr. Fix-It. "Take them over to Nick's for dinner and then drop them off when we're done."

How seamlessly we transitioned into separate lives. A de facto divorced couple. Did he realize it? Did he see how easily we could lose everything? How an open marriage would become a break and ultimately a divorce?

Did he care? Was this step one in a plan to ultimately leave me? "Fine."

"Fine." He didn't say goodbye.

My phone switched back to the lock screen, a picture of Levi and Charlotte smiling with chocolate ice cream on their faces, holding the cones up like souvenirs. I couldn't have it both ways. I had to agree. For them.

CHAPTER FIVE
ALEX

I walked inside Ghostbar twenty minutes late, having spent those minutes inside my parked car, deciding whether I was going to go through with this. Whether I had the balls to sleep with another woman. I held my phone, waiting, hoping, that Lila would call. Say she changed her mind. But both she and the phone stayed obstinately silent.

Ghostbar was trendy—a millennial's wet dream. Florescent LED lighting, open seating to ensure everyone can see and be seen, tight tuxedo dresses on the cocktail servers, and loud music with an insufferable beat. Not my scene. I preferred a sports bar with Bud Lite on tap, TVs as wallpaper, comfy leather chairs. If there's a jukebox playing John Mellencamp, all the better.

But, as I learned in college, you go where the girls go.

And the term girl applied to the blonde waiting for me in the corner of the bar. Izzy could be no more than twenty-five, a recent nursing school grad. I met her at the hospital a few months ago when I walked in on her singing *Wheels on the Bus* to one of my patients. Hand gestures and all. Her beauty—wide blue eyes, Rapunzel hair in a loose braid, not a trace of makeup on her flawless skin—combined with her kindness, caught my attention. When I joined in the horn verse, her smile grew three sizes, as if I volunteered to be the Sonny to her Cher.

After that, she finagled her way onto my service most days. She was sweet, easy to work with, and, best of all, genuinely cared about the kids. Her crush, while obvious, didn't hurt anyone. I kept things professional even as she stood a touch too close when looking at a chart, invited me along for happy hour drinks, and admitted to recording *Ask Dr. Alex*.

Until today. Izzy mentioned she was craving a pomegranate martini from Ghostbar. It was a two-foot putt, a chump with the yips could hole it, but the question was whether I wanted to. I thought about Lila, how she didn't fight me on the open marriage. If she was ready to let our sex life go without a farewell tour, then why shouldn't I?

"Sorry I'm late," I said now, sitting next to Izzy at the bar.

When Izzy turned to me, I flinched. Gone was the fresh-faced beauty whose scrubs hinted at curves. A seductress with pouty lips and kohl-rimmed eyes took her place. Her long hair cascaded and dipped beneath the deep V of her tight black dress. I was a sucker for long hair. Loved running my hands through Lila's—

Nope. Not going there. Not after Lila acted comatose when I told her about tonight.

Izzy smiled. Her lips were a glossy pink, like the inside of a watermelon. "I was beginning to wonder if you would show."

"I thought about cancelling," I admitted, before ordering a Yuengling from the bartender.

"We don't have to talk about it." Her words came short and fast. "I mean, I know you're married."

I loosened my tie. "We're...we're going through a rough patch. It's not something I'm broadcasting."

She held up her hands. "Your secret's safe with me."

"Christ." I ran my palm over the stubble on my chin. "I feel like such a jerk—"

"You're not." Her eyes looked like two sun-sparkled pools, begging me to dive right in. What a change, to see kindness instead of emptiness. "Trust me, I've dated plenty. You're smart, caring—"

"Izzy..." I sighed. Coming here was a mistake. I couldn't change my feelings. I loved Lila. Even if she had given up, I had to keep trying. How? I had no idea. "You should go. Honestly. I can't promise you anything."

"I like being with you, okay?" She reached over and set her hand atop mine, her thumb casting soothing circles. It was a gesture I'd seen

37

her make countless times with patients, but this time, I was the one in need of reassurance. "Isn't that enough? For tonight?"

Staying wouldn't be fair to her. Or Lila. But it also wasn't fair being stuck in a sexless marriage, sharing my life with a robot.

I exhaled, avoiding my eyes in the bar mirror. I had Lila's permission. Sex. Nothing more.

"So, tell me," I said, drinking my beer, relishing the way each sip made my worries about staying here with Izzy appear fuzzy and distant. Twelve ounces of liquid valium. "What do you like to do when you're not moonlighting as a singer in the peds unit?"

She covered her mouth with her hand. "Don't laugh, okay?"

I crossed my heart. "Promise."

"I'm trying to become a wellness influencer."

I suppressed a groan, feeling both disappointed and geriatric. Social media was a virus infecting our culture. Facebook, Twitter, Instagram, Snapchat—what was the point? Look up old girlfriends? Post pictures of food? Rant about politics? Needless time sucks. I'd rather be watching a game. Even the IFL.

She, however, saw it as a viable career option, whipping out her phone to show me her "work." She played a video of herself in microscopic spandex, working her glutes, hips, abs. The camera angles, the suggestive way she moved her body, the whimpers of "effort," made the video look like soft-core porn.

My cock twitched in response. I'd take her sweaty over this Malibu Barbie act she was trying on for size tonight. That's where her youth showed. She was pretending, playing dress-up like Charlotte with her plastic high-heels, fake pearls, and elaborate ball gowns. Beauty was the only asset she learned to leverage. She hadn't learned that authenticity opened doors.

Out of the corner of my eye, I saw her watching me watch her on the screen. The charade became obvious: she wanted me to see her as sexy, provocative. Change the dynamics of our working relationship.

"Wellness is where the real money's at," Izzy said, setting her phone on the bar. "Although nowhere near the coin doctors make."

"You've been deceived."

"Come on. You're an attending with your own practice. Oh, and let's not forget your TV show." She leaned forward, exposing a sliver of cleavage. In med school, we dubbed this reaction "the panty destroyer." Once you dropped the MD bomb, a woman became blind to all other deficiencies. Izzy, however, got off on my minor celebrity as the host of a medical talk show. *Minor* being the key word. Think *The Doctors*—with a hundredth of the budget, a fiftieth of the market, and exploring a single area of medicine: pediatrics. "You're practically famous."

My siblings would have a field day if they could hear her. Our close relationship thrived on being each other's ego checks. My dad and brother David, both esteemed cardiothoracic surgeons, acted like any doctor who worked outside the OR should have an asterisk next to their degree. *Did they teach you how to make incisions in nursing school?* David quipped while I carved the turkey each Thanksgiving. My younger brother Paddy, a ski bum who spent his six years of college exploring the hallucinogenic effects of mushrooms, nicknamed me Hollywood. While my youngest sibling, Angela, a casting agent in New York, spliced together footage of *Ask Dr. Alex* to make me look like a bumbling idiot and sent it out on a sibling group chat. My mom shared Izzy's awe regarding my career trajectory, but her enthusiasm meant little—she exhibited the same pride when Paddy made it through a summer without filing for unemployment.

Having Izzy look at me like I shit gold made me hard. No one looked at me like that anymore, certainly not Lila, who I doubted watched my show.

"I'd do anything to be on TV," Izzy continued, subtly massaging my thigh. "Maybe you could drop my name at the station. For, like, an exercise segment."

"Why nursing?" I asked. "Wouldn't you have been better off in broadcasting?"

"The truth?"

"Always."

She closed her eyes, her shoulders relaxing from their clothes hanger position. "My brother was born at thirty weeks."

The beer lodged in my throat and I started to cough. Unattractively. I strained for air like an emphysema patient on a ventilator. Izzy flagged down the bartender and asked for a glass a water.

Did she know about Milo? When I went back to work, I accepted the condolences, the pitying looks, the whispered conversations that abruptly ended when I approached. While I appreciated their concern, my short answers made it clear I wasn't up for talking. Ben and Nick, my partners at Superhero Pediatrics, knew enough to buy me a beer and leave it at that. An invitation to talk or escape. Whatever I needed.

"You okay?" she asked when I drained the entire glass.

I cleared my throat. "Sorry. Please, continue."

She polished off her martini, grimacing as she swallowed. "I was only six, but I remember how tiny he was. Like, barely three pounds. He looked like a doll—except he had all these machines hooked up to him."

Just like that, I was back in the hospital room, holding Milo in the interwoven palms of my hands. Lips as blue as a stormy sky. Fingers like matchsticks. Hair as dark as the night's sky. I wished we would have taken a picture. But pictures are for celebrating. Commemorating. Still. I only have my memory of his face, a fading jigsaw puzzle, and most days, not even that.

"I would visit him after school, sing songs while my parents argued in the corner. Anyways." She ordered another drink. "I wanted to help kids like that."

"Is he okay now?"

"Oh, God, yeah," she laughed. "Annoying as hell."

Listening to her sibling stories provided a hit of nostalgia, and I shared a few memorable turf battles of my own. Except her battles sounded recent. As in, this morning. I had a feeling they still lived under the same roof. "How old are you?"

"Twenty-three," she said.

I whistled. Practically jailbait. "Izzy. Izzy. Izzy. What are you doing here with me?"

She leaned in, her eyes a magnet that pulled me closer. Neither of us spoke.

"I want you." She ran her tongue across her upper lip, slowly, before biting her lower lip. A choreographed move for my enjoyment—probably straight from her ex-boyfriend's porn collection. But it worked. Hell yeah, it worked. "I've wanted you from the moment I saw you on TV."

Her response was as straightforward as a street sign: Dangerous Curve Ahead. Turn around. She may have claimed to be cool with tonight, that she could handle a casual one-off, but her calculated pursuit, months of pining, the adoration in her eyes, suggested differently.

My head and cock battled it out, neither part surprised with the outcome. "Let's get out of here," I said.

Out on the street, she took my hand, swinging it, nearly skipping during her victory lap. I didn't share her enthusiasm; the cool breeze having slapped some common sense into me.

I tried to imagine Lila at home, but the picture wouldn't download. On a normal night, she'd put the kids to bed, fix herself a snack, read a book. But tonight? Would she wait up? Sleep in the guest room? Act like nothing changed? I wanted her to be standing at the door, demanding answers. Then I would know she had a pulse, that my Lila still lived.

"Follow me," Izzy said, steering us down an alleyway between two brick buildings. Behind some scaffolding, she kissed me. She tasted like raspberries fresh off the vine—sweet with a hint of bitter.

I tried to get lost in the kiss, but my mind retreated to Lila. Our first kiss. We stood on a street corner outside Wrigley after a Cubs loss, waiting for the light to turn. I bent down to kiss her and kept kissing her as fans walked around us. The more disgruntled and drunken ones nudged us out of the way. But my mouth never left hers. Slow. Sweet. We were just starting our lives together. And we knew it.

Izzy, on the other hand, worked like she had an arousal checklist, whizzing from one erogenous zone to the next. She bent down, unzipped my fly, taking me into her mouth. My knees nearly buckled in surprise. I glanced around, ensuring we were alone. The last thing I needed was to be arrested for public indecency. Or caught on someone's iPhone camera. But the city buzzed—sirens, a dog barking, the squeal of car brakes—oblivious, uninterested.

I looked down at Izzy, her hair spun gold in the blinding white spotlight of the capital building, eagerly servicing me. This was too fast. Too much. I wasn't this guy. I was a father. A husband. A respected doctor. Everything about this felt seedy and wrong.

But that didn't stop my body from responding. Heat coursed through my veins, awakening urges I forced into hibernation. The thrill of sex. Of being wanted. Touched. So elementary and yet so vital. I closed my eyes and let go, my brain turning to quicksand, banishing all introspective thoughts.

CHAPTER SIX
GENEVA

Geneva sat on her grey Modloft sofa, wine glass in one hand, scrolling her iPad with the other. It took a matter of seconds for Geneva to locate Lila's contact information. That should have been it. Mission accomplished. But she didn't stop there. Nope. Geneva had a habit of getting obsessed when crushin' on someone new; a habit that verged on mania when consuming alcohol. She glanced at the empty wine bottle on the table, ignoring the whisper of common sense that said to call it a night. Instead, she friended Lila on Facebook, devouring her page as she would a Meg Wolitzer novel.

Unlike Wolitzer's writing, Lila's Facebook page left her quite unsatisfied. It was anemic with neglect. Under the "about" section, she listed herself as married to Alex Cole, mother to Levi and Charlotte. Occupation: Associate Director of University Relations. Nothing else was listed. No hobbies. No groups. No favorite movies or songs or books. She posted a dozen photos. Most of her children. A dark-haired boy with Alex's steely blue eyes. A miniature Lila with long inky hair, almond eyes, and the same smattering of freckles beneath her left eye. Except her daughter's smiles bounced off the screen. Geneva remembered Lila's strained smiles, as if her cheeks were being pulled up by puppet strings.

Only one photo captured Lila. She snuggled against Alex's chest on a wooden porch swing, smiling up at him with sun-kissed cheeks. Alex's neck tipped back, his laughter revealing a mouthful of expensive orthodontic work. Lila posted it at the start of last summer, nearly sixteen months ago. No caption. Natch.

Lila looked like a different woman. It wasn't the navy-blue maxi dress, the bare feet, or subtle makeup, all which showcased the simple elegance on display when they met. No. Lila looked alive. Her spirit free. *What happened to you?* Geneva wondered.

Alex. It was always the husband, right? They looked picture-perfect here, but Geneva witnessed cracks the other night. Unlike Lila, when Geneva Googled Alex, dozens of articles, pictures, and videos followed. Research papers. Speeches. A five-star Healthgrades rating. She assumed women were behind the rating based on the abundance of adjectives and exclamation points used nearly wetting themselves with praise. *Smart! Attentive! Worth the long waitlist!* Flattering articles on his volunteer work at a women's shelter. *Dr. Alex Lends a Helping Hand.* He even had a weekly TV show called *Ask Dr. Alex.* The man was stalking Dr. Oz's career.

Having hit a roadblock, Geneva decided to open another bottle of wine. She looked around her pristine kitchen, ready to defend herself. Was two too many bottles for a weeknight? She laughed. What did it matter? There was no one here to judge her. She had no one.

Bottle in hand, Geneva returned to the couch, debating whether she should contact Lila. She glanced out the window where the Capitol stood, strong and imposing, like a king on a chess board. Fact: she felt an insane attraction to Lila. An all-consuming *need* she only felt once before. But, and this was a huge but, Lila was married. To Mr. Perfect. And they had children. Did she want to get involved in that? She had enough family drama of her own, thank you.

On the other hand, Geneva needed to make new friends. Needed to get out. Find activities to keep her from drinking herself silly each night. She could offer Lila friendship and wait...see if they clicked. See if this attraction was some alcohol-exhaustion-depression induced psychosis. At worst, they would both get a new friend. At best, Geneva could finally vanquish Cristina—

No, she wasn't going there.

She poured the last bit of wine, squinting inside the bottle. Should she wait and do this sober? Nah. Carpe diem, baby!

Hungry and bored, Geneva captioned the email. *Care to meet for lunch? Show me one of Madison's hotspots?* Cute. Casual. Friendly.

After sending the message, Geneva hopped on Instagram. Unlike Lila, Geneva's exes used social media to spark envy, posting pictures of glamorous nights out, angling their ass to look like two ripe peaches in the gym mirror, and showcasing their toned legs on white sand beaches. Writing a thesis on YOLO.

They were all beautiful, fun, worthy of a night, a week, or, in rare cases, months. But saying goodbye never tore her up. Not in the way Cristina tore her apart, where she couldn't eat, sleep, or move without a Herculean effort. As if she contracted some sort of bacterial infection, one that feasted on her organs. Losing Cristina gutted her heart, transformed her brain into a skipping cd: *Cristina. Cristina. Cristina.*

Geneva vowed to never let that happen again. She told women up front that she wasn't looking for love; that monogamy felt like a toothache, dull, but constant pain. They took her warning as a challenge. Convinced themselves they could change Geneva. Inevitably, Geneva would bail and they would accuse her of being selfish, impulsive, afraid of love. Amnesiacs. Every single one.

No. She didn't miss these women, but she missed her life. Sitting outside a café on Fourth Street, laughing with friends, and watching the beautiful women walk by. Beautiful women that were in all likelihood sexually fluid. Boost's happy hour specials. Ah, the pink Cadillac margarita! Eating in Chinatown. Indie bookstore crawls. Weekends in wine country. Reading in the bay window of her apartment, the sun kissing her face.

Lila's reply popped up on her screen, snapping her back to reality. *Friday around one? Za-Za café is a favorite of mine.* Direct. An underrated feature in the dating world. Not that this was a date, Geneva reminded herself.

Geneva clicked back on Lila's picture. She studied her eyes, two burnt pennies. A sudden wave of dizziness engulfed Geneva, that déjà vu feeling, the one that took hold of her at Home. She felt as if she already knew Lila. As if she could see the way Lila would tear her apart. She gripped the arm of the couch, swallowing a heavy dose of saliva.

Sweat dotted her eyebrows. She sprinted to the bathroom, her head darting over the toilet as a surge of sour wine spirited out of her mouth.

It was the wine. Playing tricks with her head. Unlocking memories. Memories, she knew from experience, that were best kept under lock and key.

CHAPTER SEVEN
LILA

I crossed the street, walking towards Za-Za Café, a single-story red brick building with rooftop seating and live music during the summer. Za-Za's vibe was chill, yet cozy with bright colors—aqua, lime, coral—befitting a Caribbean bar instead of a midwestern college town. A hidden gem; one of those restaurants you'd walk right by if you didn't know it was there.

I spotted Geneva through the window. She waved, a gigantic smile lighting up her face. I smiled in return, my face muscles protesting the sudden exercise.

A bee hive of nerves swarmed my stomach as I opened the door. I hadn't had a close friend since freshman year of college. Friendship required trust, a leap of faith that they wouldn't turn on me, use my own words against me. Women excluded other women for sport. Long ago, I decided the risks outweighed the benefits.

Which begged the question, why did I agree to meet Geneva today?

A distraction, for one. I needed to get out of my head. Ever since Alex's phone call alerting me to his "date," my brain funneled from one question to the next. Who? What? Where? I made a mistake, asking him to tell me when he started. To remain sane, I had to be clueless to his extracurricular activities.

And there was something that drew me to Geneva. She had the unquantifiable *it* factor, a golden touch that lit up everyone around her. Normally, I capped small talk at a minute, two tops, but when I met her at the Louis Weiner event, I found myself smiling. Laughing, even. The agony of my marriage, the new rift Alex introduced, didn't pierce quite as acutely. When I got her email, I immediately said yes. Anything to blunt this onslaught of feelings.

"I *love* your hair!" Geneva said, bouncing up from her seat. I froze as she enveloped me in a quick, but tight embrace. I wasn't big on unsolicited touching, but, surprisingly, I found myself missing the comfort of her touch when she pulled away.

God, how pathetic. "Thanks."

"I used to have long hair as a teenager," Geneva said, rolling her eyes so hard that her entire head did a circle. She had short curly hair, dark as black licorice, that spiraled away from her head like corkscrew pasta. "I spent hours at the salon, suffering like hell to get the perfect weave. Blond, if you can imagine! All to fit in. By college, I got sick of having half my scalp yanked out and went natural. But, damn, do I love your hair."

I blushed, thankful for the interruption of the server. Her praise felt unearned, considering I didn't wash it this morning. But then I remembered her complimenting my ring at the bar. She was effusive by nature, wanting others to feel as good as she did.

"Don't. Ever. Cut. It," she said after we ordered.

"That's what my dad used to say."

One of the few memories I had of my dad was him brushing my hair after the bath. Unlike my mom, who wielded the comb like a rake, he gently untangled the knots, making me promise to keep it long. I was six when he left. The afternoon he said goodbye, I grabbed a scissors and lopped off my ponytail. I chased after his car, my ponytail as thick as a horse's tail in my hand. He didn't stop. I chucked the hair at his taillights. It stayed in the street for a week, like a dead squirrel everyone drove over, waiting for it to decompose.

"You're lucky. My dad's a professor in linguistics at Columbia. He's married to my mom, but his true love is words. The origin of language," Geneva said, using jazz hands. "Needless to say, he wouldn't notice my hair if it was on fire."

I shrugged. "Men."

The server delivered our drinks. I inhaled the ice-cold sweetness of my Coke Zero. For most of the last decade, I boycotted soda. Along with gluten, dairy, and sugar. I was all about living clean. Removing toxins. Making my womb hospitable. Now I put back sodas, one after another, like an alcoholic that fell off the wagon, making up for the dry years.

"What about your mom?" Geneva asked.

"Hmm?"

She strummed her blush nails against her cappuccino mug. "Your mom. You guys close?"

Was it a New York thing? The assumed right to pick my family scabs? But she did it with a smile, making these get-to-know-you questions seem natural. And maybe they were. I was the one out of practice, semi-retired from this friendship business. "She did her best."

Geneva laughed. "That bad, huh?"

I thought about my mom's crippling depression after my dad left. The drinking. The pills. The men. To her credit, she recovered. Got in AA. Remarried. Only to have him cheat on her. Shower. Rinse. Repeat.

"I'm a lot more forgiving, now that I have kids," I said.

"How old are your kids?"

"Charlotte's four and Levi's eight." This foray into my family tree made me more determined than ever to power down my brain and survive the open marriage. My children's first experience with heartbreak would come from a disinterested lover or friend, not their parents' divorce. "Do you have any?"

"Me?" Geneva raised her eyebrows. "No. That's one lesson I learned from my parents: don't have children unless you're ready to put in the time."

"They didn't make time for you?"

"No-o-o-o," Geneva said. "My dad, 'the professor—'" She used air quotes. "—and my mom, the esteemed violinist—" She spoke with an English accent that could cut glass. "—barely had time for each other, let alone me. I grew up in a gilded cage, raised by a series of nannies and homeschooled by tutors, seeing my parents for dinner, if I was lucky. Then, for high school, they sent me off to boarding school."

"I'm an only child too."

"My mother told me they stopped after one, having achieved perfection," Geneva said wryly, before sipping her cappuccino. "It took me until I was ten to understand the real reason; children interfered with their careers."

I felt an unexpected kinship, both of us neglected and lonely as children. Whereas her parents were never home, my mom stumbled around like a sad puppy, waiting for someone to notice her. Hug her. Listen to her. It made me angry. *I wouldn't have stayed either,* I said one morning when I caught her pouring vodka into her coffee. *And the first chance I get, I'm leaving too.* At the time, I felt vindicated. Who wanted to live with a drunk?

Now, those words haunted me. Made my stomach cramp with guilt. It didn't occur to me until the miscarriages started that maybe she drank because my dad cheated. The old chicken and the egg conundrum. I understood now how the threat of losing what you desired most could slowly drive a person mad. Grief legitimized all sorts of abhorrent behaviors.

"Being an only child wasn't all bad," Geneva continued. "I fell in love with reading, which gave me a career, but more importantly, inspired me to get out. Explore the world. New cities. New people. New experiences." She nodded along. "That's the food for my soul."

"Just think of Madison as your next adventure," I said, feeling guilty for the way I bad-mouthed it. "Have you been to the art museum? They have this great rooftop restaurant called Fresco. And on Saturday mornings, at the Capital—"

"Yeah, not gonna lie, Madison—it's not for me." Geneva rested her chin in the palm of her hand, holding my gaze. Her black eyes sparkled, like the surface of a moon-lit lake. "But making new friends helps. You're the first person I've felt connected to. We can talk—not just surface level." She tilted her head, smiling. "It's...refreshing."

She was right. We had an ease that reminded me of being a child, when you could meet someone and become best friends by the end of the day. That rarely happened as an adult. But it was happening now.

Then again, I'd intuit friendship from a scarecrow—that's how alone I felt—so it helped to hear she felt the same.

"I'm glad we met for lunch," I said. "With the kids, I don't get a lot of 'me' time, to cultivate—" I was about to say "friendships" when the server dropped off our food. The word sat on my tongue, sending me headfirst into another cyclone of questions. Was Alex's "date" a friend? But he didn't have any female friends—that I knew. Was he harboring secrets?

"Hey." Geneva wagged her soup spoon at me. "You okay?"

"Sorry." I shook my head, the bags under my eyes hanging like five-pound weights. A souvenir of the last three nights—sleepless ever since Alex's date. "Tired."

"Something keeping you up?"

I traced the pad of my thumb against the line that bracketed my mouth, deep as the Grand Canyon, the only visible scar of my grief. "Too many things to count."

But one in particular. My husband was having sex. With another woman. Not that we talked about it. When he returned from his date, I pretended to be asleep. He showered before coming to bed, but the sex still wafted off of his skin like a cheap prostitute's perfume. *I got laid,* his pores screamed. The next morning, he glided through our house, the rush of endorphins having erased the tension and stress from his muscles.

Alex cornered me in the laundry room last night, asking how I felt, like he was Dr. Phil. I drew upon the lengthy history of scorned women in crafting my response: *Fine.* Every audacious question received this equally uninspired answer. As I folded the clothes, determined to keep my face expressionless even as his words burned my skin like acid, I reminded myself that I agreed to this arrangement. Drove him to it, in fact. Except he was the one that forced us in the car.

Geneva squeezed my hand, imbuing me with her warmth. "You'll talk when you're ready."

I smiled my thanks, meeting Geneva's attentive eyes. While I didn't have words now, I liked the possibility that someday, if I chose, I would have a friend to confide in. Alex wasn't leaving, but he wasn't with me either. Not in the all-consuming, attentive, unbreakable way that made up our bond for the first fifteen years. He chose to let someone else into our tightly knitted circle.

I wanted to let someone in too.

CHAPTER EIGHT
ALEX

"I don't get it," Lila said. We sat on lawn chairs strategically placed midway between the soccer field and the playground, warmed by the sun on this balmy late-fall afternoon. She kept an eye on Charlotte, who was impossible to miss in her sparkly purple leotard and rainbow tutu, while I watched Levi sulk on the sidelines with his marinara-hued hair. "Why would they prank him? They're friends."

Levi scared us this morning, locking himself in the bathroom and refusing to leave. I picked the lock, walking into what looked like a Jackson Pollock painting. Red liquid splattered across the countertop, mirror, and sink. I grabbed a towel, ready to use it as a tourniquet, when I realized Levi wasn't hurt. Sure, his face looked like Hannibal Lector after a tasty meal, but it wasn't blood. Turns out, Cameron and Tyler gave Levi red hair dye and told him the entire team was doing it.

Cameron and Tyler, surfer blond locks untouched, laughed uproariously when they saw Levi. They claimed their moms wouldn't let them dye it, but I recognized future Biffs in the making.

"Kids are mean." I rummaged through the cooler. Fresh fruit. Sandwiches in saran wrap, tiny works of art with a rainbow of meats, cheeses, and veggies. The kids wouldn't go hungry on Lila's watch.

"Where did they get the dye?"

I took a bite of a kale and ham sandwich on whole-grain. "Cameron knows Shannon's Amazon password."

She narrowed her eyes at Shannon, holding court among the moms at the playground. Brett and Shannon lived next door with their kids, Cameron and Audrey, one of three houses on our cul-de-sac. Proximity begot closeness, ensuring fast friendships between the children.

The same could not be said of the adults. Brett was a banker with an ego the size of Lake Michigan, while Shannon devoted herself to

53

maintaining her beauty. And she was beautiful. She had smooth, honeyed skin; glacial eyes that could bite or bless you; and an ass firm enough to double as a tennis wall. But it was the type of mid-thirties beauty that took hard work and a fat bank account in addition to a genetic blessing. Both enjoyed the finer things in life and made no apologies for it.

Outside of functions for the kids, we avoided them.

Lila frowned. "Maybe we should leave. He looks miserable."

Levi stood outside the huddle, arms crossed, doing what looked like a two-step, evidently confused about *how* to join the huddle. While gifted intellectually—he skipped first grade—interpersonal relationships baffled him. His utter uneasiness in his skin made my skull throb.

Sex was supposed to help with the headaches. Lower my stress. Allow me to relax. Be a better dad. Husband. Doctor. But my hookup with Izzy a few nights ago came with a side of guilt, intensifying the pounding. It started after my morning run, stalking me the entire day, reminding me with each pulsation that I was moving further away from Lila. That this plan to shake up our marriage was causing me *more* stress, while leaving her as unaffected as ever.

"Levi has to adapt," I said, shoving the rest of the sandwich in my mouth. "We can't always rescue him."

"He's only eight."

She looked beautiful in a wide-brim straw hat, denim button-down, and rolled-up jeans. "You look like a cowgirl." I tugged the brim of her hat. "I like it."

"Huh?"

"The hat. The denim. I could get into that."

Before Milo, she would've promised to wear the hat in the bedroom. Now? She glared at me as if I was sexually harassing her before retreating to the playground. I rolled the saran wrap into a ball and chucked it in the bag. Why bother trying?

Turning my attention back to Levi, I found him sitting at the end of the bench, head down, kicking dirt with his cleats, looking like he didn't want the coach to put him in. He was upset. Embarrassed. All understandable. But if he laughed it off, the other kids would too. He was like Lila, ruminating on a problem until it was impossible to see anything else.

Much as I hated to admit it, the kids weren't oblivious to the problems in our marriage. While Lila put on a good face, they saw the way she interacted with me—dismissive, short, impervious to my touch. When I mentioned this, as yet another reason to seek help, she scoffed, *I'm not my mother.* But she had a blind spot—she assumed that because she wasn't drunk or high, she wasn't hurting the kids. That they wouldn't take her mood personally or emulate it.

"Boys look good today," Brett said as he planted his folding chair in the grass next to mine. "Energetic."

Was that a dig on Levi? My all-star benchwarmer. "They're getting better."

"Take the shot!" Brett yelled. He slapped his hands against his thighs. "Shit. You know what's going to keep Cameron from being elite? He needs..."

Brett was one of those hyperactive dads that would push their kid to the breaking point to accomplish their own unfulfilled dreams. He'd watch Cameron's practices, review game footage, but wouldn't notice if his kid was mainlining heroin. Or bullying other kids.

Tuning Brett out, I glanced at Lila. She stood apart from the other moms, praising Charlotte as she soared on the swings. Lila loathed playground chatter. She called it the "mommy toll," where moms alternatively bemoaned, exploited, and competed over their children's achievements.

It wasn't hard to see where Levi's social anxiety came from.

"That bar, on Doty. What's the name?" Brett snapped his fingers. "Tally's? Ta-ta's? Hell, that's a sweet name if you ask me."

Brett was a relic of a bygone era, one where "boys will be boys" suited everything from drunk driving to date-rape. He may have shucked his Pi Kappa Phi shirt for a suit, but Brett wore his MAGA hat proudly and would argue that "All Lives Mattered" until he was blue in the face.

"Never heard of it."

"I saw you there last night, man." Brett laughed, his smile so wide that his incisors glowed like vampire fangs. "Standing outside the bar with a tasty little redhead."

"Wasn't me," I said instinctively as thousands of nails slammed, millimeter by millimeter, into my cranium.

Last night, Nick, Ben, and I met downtown at Taylor's to discuss hiring another doctor. Business was booming, thanks to *Ask Dr. Alex*, but my schedule—two mornings a week at the hospital, another at the studio, nights volunteering—meant they worked overtime at the clinic.

After crafting a job posting, the guys split, but I stuck around to watch the Cubs game. It was the playoffs; I wasn't moving. A group of women approached me, professing to be huge *Ask Dr. Alex* fans. I chatted, took a few selfies, then left once the game ended. An attractive woman in the bunch—merlot hair and grassy green eyes—followed me outside.

We talked for a few minutes before she lit a cigarette. The chemical smell of nicotine razed my libido. I called it a night. Apparently not fast enough.

"I get it." Brett snorted, watching Lila walk towards us. "You don't want wifey to find out."

Was he blackmailing me? I refused to be beholden to anyone, especially him. "Brett thinks he saw me at a bar downtown last night," I said as Lila joined us, assuming she'd have my back. We were a team. Ride or die. But when I looked up, I saw hesitation—dare I say hurt?— in Lila's eyes. And I knew the open marriage shifted her allegiance. My stomach lurched. Would she choose now to take a stand?

"You're right, Brett. It was us," Lila said, sitting next to me. "Between *House Hunters* and laundry, we jetted downtown for a martini."

I exhaled. God bless my beautiful, smart, *private* wife. Quiet in most social situations, Lila was an alpha wolf when it came to her family— she'd do anything to protect the pack. She let the hair dye incident pass, but there was no way she'd leave Brett unscathed after two attacks.

Brett shouted to Shannon, a dog refusing to let go of his bone. She sauntered over, wearing navy leggings, a lightweight, curve-hugging tank, and a full face of makeup. Dressing down and yet up. I didn't get it.

"We saw Alex downtown last night, right?" He jutted his thumb towards me. "He says it wasn't him."

Shannon appraised me. "It was dark...and you were tipsy." Our eyes locked and she winked. Which was worse? Being indebted to her Neanderthal husband or Shannon, who leveraged gossip with the finesse of a Wall Street trader?

Brett's face turned fire-engine red. "You're one to talk, sweetheart. You haven't been sober since Audrey—" Brett jumped up. "Block him!"

By now, I regretted lying. I talked to the woman—no harm there. A fan. An easy explanation. But, knowing Brett, he would've intuited a baser desire. And he'd be right. This open marriage was turning me into the type of man I detested—a liar and a cheat.

"New rule, Alex," Lila whispered. "Don't get caught." Her eyes darkened, turning a shade of black probably only found in the depths of a lake in Antarctica. The rest of her face remained impassive, a horrible mask of nothingness that greeted me each morning. She pressed her cheek against mine, her lips vibrating against my ear. "You wanted this, not me. And the moment anyone finds out, I'm done."

I didn't want this! I wanted to shout as she walked away. *I want you. My Lila. The one I married.* But that woman was gone. Little more than a memory. Instead of adapting, learning to love what was left, I grew angrier each day. Resentful. I had as much right to grieve, but did I give up? Fall silent? Refuse help? Nope. I got on with it. It's called being an adult.

"Don't worry," Shannon said, taking Lila's empty seat. She gazed at me with the smile of a nymph. Dangerous, yet alluring. "Your secret's safe with me."

"Excuse me." I stood up, striding towards Levi. That was one problem I could solve.

CHAPTER NINE
GENEVA

Geneva liked to start relationships in fifth gear. She wanted to spend every possible moment together, analyzing each strand of their personalities with the diligence of a geneticist until she could compile a set of data to predict their future. Hookup or girlfriend? Flight risk or clinger? This method ensured she left each relationship unscathed.

But Lila was making research difficult. Since their lunch last week, they met for coffee and exchanged a series of texts—always initiated by Geneva. Their conversations operated like a traffic jam, arbitrarily gaining speed, giving Geneva a sense of the real Lila, before Lila slammed on the brakes.

Geneva, impatient by nature, would normally call it quits. Next, please. But something visceral, deeper drew Geneva towards Lila. She felt herself starting to fall, wondering what it would be like to let go. The intensity of these feelings left her shaky, hyperalert, as if she snorted Ritalin. What was her deal? They hardly spent any time together.

That's what tonight was about. Geneva called Lila an hour ago, inviting her out for a post-work drink, needing to feed her frenetic mind. Was their connection real? Or was Geneva idealizing her? Mistaking boredom for interest?

She weaved through the student traffic, spotting Lila outside *La Cortina*. Dressed in tailored grey pants, a black sweater, and ballet flats, Lila exuded understated beauty. Upon seeing Geneva, she smiled. Geneva beamed. Nerves tickled her skin like a light breeze.

She hugged Lila, inhaling the scent of lavender, a scent that shot her back to boarding school. Cristina would emerge from the shower, sit on her bed, and lather her freshly shaven legs with lavender-scented lotion. Geneva slyly watched, confused as to why it stirred her.

"I'm so happy you came," Geneva said, determined not to succumb to her memory. Cristina was the past. Lila was her present.

"Me too." Cars zoomed past like it was the Indy 500, despite the narrow street clogged with mopeds, bikes, and people. The traffic made it difficult to hear.

"Come on, let's go inside." Geneva led the way through the brightly lit restaurant to the intimate back garden. Six circular metal tables filled the stone patio, half-occupied with guests. Tall, leafy trees strung with fairy lights shone above. Perfect for a balmy October evening.

"This is cool," Lila said, sitting down.

It was nice. But Geneva had already been here twice. Madison's nightlife options spanned a half square mile, most geared towards the students. Familiarity, not variety, was the spice of life in this cozy college town.

Geneva ordered a pitcher of margaritas, but Lila declined to share, ordering a Coke Zero. "Come on. I bet there's a part of you dying to recapture those wild prebaby days."

Lila smiled sadly. "I was never wild."

"Never?" Geneva remembered Lila drinking water the night they met. Was she an alcoholic? She didn't strike Geneva as one. Then again, the best addicts are expert concealers.

"Big crowds, drunken idiots..." Lila's foot tapped the leg of the table, reminding Geneva that an invisible ticking clock hovered over their evening. Lila had children, a husband—she didn't have endless hours to frolic away. "I was always happier at home."

Geneva saw Lila's attention drift towards the couple making out in the corner. Slow kisses. First date kisses. A prelude. Lila's fingers brushed her lips, but Geneva couldn't read the expression in her eyes. They looked like two caves, dark and forbidding.

"Alex didn't mind sparing you tonight?"

Lila pressed her lips together. "He owed me a night out." She paused, seemingly catching herself. "And he's leaving for Boston tomorrow so I'm sure the kids enjoy having him all to themselves."

Lila's words slid down Geneva's back like an ice cube, awakening her senses. Warning her to tread lightly. Lila wanted to talk, but on her terms. Geneva had to go slow. But maybe this was for the best. Maybe these incremental steps, the awareness of the risks each one held, would protect Geneva, too.

"So, I must ask," Geneva said. "Without the benefit of alcohol, how do you relax at the end of a day?"

"Movies. Books. Yoga." Lila pressed her hands against her cheeks and frowned. "Does that make me sound completely boring?"

While books were the love of her life, Geneva could barely touch her toes, loathed almost everything produced by Hollywood, and couldn't go a day without wine. These lifestyle differences should have set Geneva running, but Lila's sweetness drew Geneva closer. She was so damn likeable. Geneva felt a need to protect her, although she couldn't say from what. "Maybe I'll join you for yoga—"

Lila's phone vibrated. She stared at it, nostrils flaring, before apologizing and retreating to the corner to answer it.

Wanting to look busy, Geneva scanned her emails. Her heart thumped when she saw a message from her father, but it was a forwarded announcement of his guest lecture at the University of Chicago. For a man who studied language, he used words sparingly. No personal invite. No note asking about her new job. No apology. Geneva squeezed her eyes shut, trying to erase the thought that he was disappointed in her. Or worse, indifferent to her life.

Yes, she flipped out Memorial Day weekend when her parents suggested that Dani, now an ex-girlfriend, sleep on the couch. She issued threats. Told them not to call until they accepted her—all of her. But they were her parents. And they were wrong. They should cave first.

She inhaled her drink, relishing the sweet burst of tequila as it hit her taste buds. Alcohol would tame her annoyance that, at thirty, she felt neglected by her parents. That her father would send such a passive aggressive email. That her mother would remain stubbornly silent.

Lila returned to the table. "Everything okay?" Geneva asked, fearing the night might end.

A cold breeze blew through. "Have you ever felt like you disappointed someone, just by being you?"

Geneva laughed. "Yes. Pretty much every day."

Lila shivered. "Maybe I'm not explaining myself well."

"Try." Geneva stood to flick on the heat lamp.

"It's like I lived in one world, where I felt loved and supported—" She shook her head. "—and me. But someone shook it and...now everyone looks at me differently. Like I'm...damaged. But it's them. They're the ones that changed."

"I'm familiar."

Lila squinted at her. "Really?"

"Yes, *really*." Geneva leaned back. Here it was, Lila's first flaw. Lila thought she alone tasted the unfairness of the world, couldn't imagine that others battled similar demons. "My parents are quite disappointed in me, in fact."

"That's hard to believe."

"Believe it, baby," Geneva said, finishing the remainder of her drink. Shame and anger rose in her throat like heartburn. If only she could take a pill to fix it. Medication to cut the cord, make you immune to your parents' criticism, the feeling that you would never measure up. "I came out during my freshman year. And you know what they said? *Life is hard enough being Black. Don't do this to yourself.* As if it was a choice."

Lila froze, her lips parting. "Wait. You're gay?"

Geneva laughed. "Is Trump a narcissist?"

She joked when she was nervous. A way to downplay, minimize, her loss of control. Because Lila held the power now. If she pulled away, Geneva would be sentenced to the friend zone. But if she came closer, tried to understand Geneva's pain? Well, an entire world would open up.

CHAPTER TEN
LILA

Geneva was gay. My brain scrambled to unpack this information. How had I missed something as important as her sexual orientation? Was I that self-involved? Geneva hadn't mentioned a significant other, woman or man. Then again, I avoided talking about Alex. It was this lovely friendship bubble all about us.

"Most people are surprised. Good ol' heteronormative bias." Geneva rolled her eyes. "The pervasive thinking that lesbians are butch doesn't help either. Any beautiful woman *naturally* wants a man."

Geneva was beautiful—full lips; cheekbones like four-carat diamonds; flawless skin. But this lapse was due to my distracted mental state. "True, but it's more—"

"It's because I'm Black," Geneva finished, using her finger to flick sugar off the rim of her glass. "That doesn't fit the stereotype either."

"No!" I raked my nails across my thighs. "God, no. Listen, I'm—" *dead inside, a horrible mother, wife, friend.* "—distracted, too distracted, evidently, by my own problems." I needed to make this right. Her friendship helped. She was a flicker of light in this dark time of my marriage. "But that's what I love about hanging out with you. I can leave it all behind. Just...detox from my life."

The silence felt oppressive. I held my breath, fearing she might leave.

"I need to be less confrontational," Geneva finally said. "Too often, I assume the worst. But you? You've been nothing but kind."

"Inattentive, but kind." I smiled. "Have your parents adjusted?"

"My parents refuse to acknowledge it." She refilled her margarita glass. "They choose to believe my girlfriends are friends and that I'm too career-focused to prioritize relationships."

"That must be hard."

"Harder when I see them. Which isn't often. I'm more frustrated with myself for hoping they'll change. I'm an adult; why do I need their approval?"

It was strange seeing Geneva at a loss. Stranger having to dispense advice.

"I doubt that ever goes away," I said. "I've come to recognize that while my mom loves me, she rarely knows what's best for me." She didn't know what was best for herself. "I let her talk and then move on. But I can see how frustrating it would be if she disapproved of Alex. If she ignored him altogether."

"It's horrible." Geneva spoke softly, directing her thoughts to her drink. "So, yes." She looked up. "I know what it's like to disappoint someone. What's your story?"

I want another baby. But that topic would crack me open like an egg, my heart the vulnerable yolk, bleeding feelings no one could put back together. Our family's survival depended on me locking those feelings away. Not breathing new life into them.

Nor was I capable of discussing the open marriage. How could I explain why I agreed without unearthing my history of miscarriages? Milo? The vasectomy? It was like a string of dominos—one event toppling the next. I let my frustration with Alex escape earlier, a careless stream of consciousness provoked by the couple kissing in the corner.

And yet, I ached to talk. It had been years since I had a close girlfriend. But I remembered how we shared secrets as easily as a tube of lipstick. Geneva's willingness to be vulnerable, trust me tonight, made me miss that connection.

I took a deep breath. "On Halloween, during my freshman year of college, I was raped," I said, as always, shocked those words applied to me. That this was my history. But my voice remained steady. Hopefully, after hearing this, she'd understand my reluctance to open up. "Wade Mills was a junior. An NFL-bound all-conference wide receiver. Everyone thought I was trying to ruin his career."

Geneva's drink appeared frozen to her lips. Then, carefully, she set it down. "How did they know it was you?"

"The complaint was supposed to be anonymous, but Wade and his teammates talked. Branded me a liar, a slut, a stalker. Everyone ganged up on me. No one considered that I might be telling the truth." I closed my eyes, remembering those wintery walks to class when both the wind chill and insults slapped me in the face. "Overnight, my life imploded. My roommate ignored me. Friends ditched me. I was treated like a zoo animal whenever I went out."

"Kids are vicious. Girls especially. I've journeyed through that hell." Geneva looked down, her thick eyelashes spanning the length of a penny, before shaking her head. "But this is about you. Tell me what happened."

I looked around, observing five objects—Coke Zero, stringing lights, space heater, purse, phone—reminding myself that I was here, safe, not stuck in that nightmare. "I was at a party and couldn't find my friends so I, *stupidly*, walked back alone. I was dressed up as a bunny—leotard, tail, tights, a tiara. Sexy was my intention." I twisted my hair into a bun, instinctively trying to desexualize myself. Back then, I was experimenting, learning how to be sexy, but having sex wasn't my intention. Hundreds of miles lay between those two points, but some people blurred this distinction. "Flirting, partying—it was all new."

"I get it."

"Everyone on the street was in costumes; shouting, groping, stumbling. It was crazy. Very *Night of the Living Dead*. Some guys started harassing me and Wade stepped in. Offered to walk me home. And yes, before you ask, I recognized him."

She shrugged. "So?"

"Fuel for the stalking rumor."

The couple in the corner got up to leave, his fingers skimming her back pocket. They'd probably have sex against the entry door, quick and furious, before retreating to bed for round two. Alex and I used to do that. A quick one, to release the sexual tension, and then a second round to savor the experience.

What's wrong with me? Before the open marriage, I never thought about sex. But now, random sexual thoughts skirted through my brain unbidden. I chewed a chunk of ice, enjoying the zap of the nerve. I didn't miss sex. I wouldn't *allow* myself to miss it.

"Anyway, he invited me over. We kissed in his room. In my deluded, drunken mind, I thought he liked me." I paused, remembering how I imagined our future in that two-second blip. But when we brainwash girls with fairy tales about handsome princes and happily-ever-afters, how can we blame them for not being suspicious? "But it switched so fast. *He* moved so fast. He ripped my tights, shoved my leotard to the side and pushed inside me with all his weight. I told him to stop, tried to squirm away, but he told me he was almost there. He heard me. That's what I never understood. How he could keep going."

"I would've killed him," Geneva said, the hard line of her mouth leaving no doubt.

I couldn't help but contrast her fierceness with Alex's response. *You're so strong,* he said when I told him everything a few months into dating—my alcoholic mother, cheating father, the rape. *Now we need you to believe it.* Four years had passed since the assault. Four years of whittling down my world. I studied. Ran. Practiced yoga. Never partied. Never drank. Never walked home alone. Rules designed to keep me safe.

Alex broke through my barriers. He made the ordinary extraordinary—holding hands; grocery shopping; Cubs' games—jumpstarting not only my heart, but my life. He introduced me to the magic of sex, the way it can transcend your body, your mind, the moment; the intimacy of knowing someone inside and out. With Alex, it was love, lust, and friendship; a combination I never knew existed outside of the movies.

"I don't remember much, afterwards. An officer stopped me walking home—she knew, somehow—and convinced me to come to the station." I shook my head. "Not that it mattered. The police declined to file charges. I ended up transferring."

"It's not your fault. You're a victim," she said, her voice steely. "Not only of the rape, but of rape culture, which is especially toxic surrounding athletes..."

She didn't get it. Blaming myself *saved* me. Allowed me to move forward. There is comfort in believing you had control all along when someone violently rips away your power.

And playing the blame game was second-nature. I started the day my dad left. Solidified my participation when my mom decided drinking superseded raising me. Earned VIP status with each miscarriage. Became president with Milo. Anger directed inwards was safe. It could never retaliate.

"I'm telling you this because the experience made me cautious," I said. "Not only with men, but with friends. It's difficult for me to open up."

"I understand."

"I know I come off reserved—" My phone buzzed. Alex. *Home soon?*

Kids okay? I texted back.

Yes. ETA?

I glanced up. Normally, when someone pulls out a phone, everyone follows suit. But Geneva rested her chin in the palm of her hand, pinning me with her gaze. "Sorry. I'm being rude."

"Little bit."

I flinched. She was fire and ice, but she had a point. *If you were on a date, I wouldn't bug you,* I texted, inspired by Geneva's unapologetic honesty. I found a friend, someone to talk to, escape the chaos he brought into our lives, and he couldn't give me that for one night.

I thought you were at an event, he wrote.

I lied earlier, telling him I had a work function, not wanting him to join us. As childish as it sounded, I didn't want to share. And Geneva was right: I needed a night off. Particularly from him.

Another text, *Are you on a date?*

Should I lie? He proposed the open marriage. Open implied two-ways, but I knew Alex. He needed to be needed. My cooling off drove him to an open marriage. And if I warmed to someone else? He'd flip out. Even though I gave him permission to pass Go. Classic Alex, not thinking through the details, only seeing the benefit and stopping the analysis.

No, I texted back. Much as I'd like to make him wonder, that would create questions. Require conversation. And, right now, he topped my list of people I wanted to avoid.

I turned off my phone and apologized to Geneva. I wanted to enjoy my night with her—without further interruption. Alex monopolized enough of my time.

CHAPTER ELEVEN
ALEX

I needed to leave. I felt dizzy. Claustrophobic. Three hundred feet swirled around me, my brain a kaleidoscope of images. I hadn't noticed how cramped and stifling the space was on the way in. Sex-induced tunnel vision. But now, after, I saw everything through a magnifying glass.

A studio apartment. Queen-sized bed in the corner. Piles of clothes sprouted from the ground like baby camels. A tower of cardboard boxes blocked the window. Stacks of hardcover books served as nightstands. Coffee mugs littered like dust mites. The granite peninsula and stainless-steel appliances were the only signs that, when clean, this place wouldn't be a hovel.

Ynez lit a joint, inhaling deeply, exposing the piano keys of her ribs. The brown eyes that sparkled this afternoon when she introduced me as part of the panel discussing vaccine hesitancy at Harvard Medical School now appeared sad, as if she couldn't figure out how she got here.

I felt the same. When I flew into Boston this morning, I was still reeling from Lila's late night, the infuriating text she sent. *If you were on a date, I wouldn't bug you.* She downplayed it, saying she was trying to make a point about respecting her time. But what if she was lying? What if she was seeing someone? Some guy at yoga? Or maybe another parent? In my gut, I knew it couldn't be true—she lived like a nun, shunning any touch that wasn't platonic. Nor did she have a duplicitous bone in her body. Yet, the thought lurked, leaving a bad taste in my mouth. A hook-up was the last thing on my mind.

And Ynez wasn't my type, short black hair, a cross tattoo on the inside of her left wrist, and enough eye makeup to make Mick Jagger envious. But she was funny and self-deprecating. At the conference reception, she launched a litany of complaints—her cheating ex-husband kicked her out to live with his mistress, she took a second job as an Uber driver to pay attorneys' fees, her dad was a diabetic with a Krispy Kreme addiction—with the finesse of a standup comedian, massaging the material until it sounded like she was lucky to have these problems.

When the reception ended, she asked me if I wanted to grab dinner. I had envisioned a quiet night at my hotel—Facetiming the kids, updating patient charts, uninterrupted sleep—before catching an early flight home. But she was funny. And I had to eat.

We went to The Painted Cow, a sports bar with graffitied tables, leather seats, and messy burgers. Nothing about the atmosphere or her behavior suggested this was a date. No flirting. No meaningful eye contact. We talked sports and Hollywood, argued about politics, laughed about her ex. It was as we were walking out that she said, "You know the old adage that to get over an ex, you have to get under someone new?" She raised her thick eyebrows. "Care to volunteer?"

My cock, the shameless opportunist, hardened. Sure enough, my brain hopped on the bandwagon. Being in Boston made it the perfect hookup. I'd never see her again. Shannon and Brett wouldn't accidently spot me on the street.

Now, lying next to Ynez, I wish I would've trusted my gut. The physical chemistry between us was flatter than day old soda. Sure, my body responded, but it felt like taking a shit when constipated. Relief at the end, but the process was taxing.

"Do you think your wife suspects what you get up to on business trips?" Ynez asked, blowing smoke rings towards the ceiling.

I sat up. Sweat glistened my forehead. My penis stood at half-mast. But Ynez's decision to bring up Lila served as an alarm clock—time to go. "I have no idea."

Lila's warning rang in my ears: *If anyone finds out, I'm done.* Done? With what? The open marriage? Me? I pulled on my boxers, not wanting to find out.

"Come on, *Dr. Alex.*" She hit the consonants of my name hard, her good humor having vanished. "You're like the love child of Tom

Cruise and Dr. Oz. Charisma. Intelligence. A smile that has the stay-at-home moms reaching for the shower nozzle. She must have an inkling."

I continued to dress, while she grabbed an oversized Red Sox's t-shirt from a clothes pile. She threw it on and stood before me, hands on her hips. "Don't you feel guilty?"

Marijuana was supposed to mellow you out, but Ynez appeared invigorated. Was it sexual frustration? Maybe I should have endured it and gone down on her. But the sex was bad enough without extending it.

"Yeah," I said. "I do." Ynez's willingness to wear what I presumed to be her ex's shirt was further proof of her fragile mental state. By having sex with her when the ink was still wet on her divorce papers, I unwittingly became the fall guy, required to answer for the sins of her ex-husband. Why didn't I understand that an hour ago? See through her jokes to her broken heart?

"Not guilty enough to stop." She looked two seconds away from chucking a shoe at my head, but thought better of it, plopping back down on the bed. "I don't get it. Why is it so hard to stay faithful?"

I never wanted to cheat. But Lila refused to touch me. Talk about anything other than the kids. Her brain skipped like a CD, stuck on that moment of horrific silence in the hospital where Milo's heartbeat should've filled the room. She couldn't remember the happiness from before or see the promise of tomorrow.

How much rejection was I supposed to endure? How many years should I have waited? Passion fueled our relationship from the moment we met. Sure, we had hardships, gutting losses, but we always found comfort in each other. How did she think I would react when the intimacy died? Did she think? Did she care?

"We have an open marriage," I said, lacing up my shoes. "She knows what I'm up to. And she doesn't care."

Her eyebrows crisscrossed, softening her face. "Do you love her?"

I rubbed my eyes. It was all this smoke, blurring my vision, messing with my emotions. "Yes." I cleared my throat. "It's just sex. I would never leave her."

"Just sex?" She nearly spit her disdain. "Open marriage. Hall pass. Freebie list. Whatever you want to call it. You're cheating. If you loved your wife, you wouldn't be screwing around." She squeezed her eyes shut. "You should go. Now."

"Hold on." All I did was accept her offer. An *unprompted* offer. "If you're against cheating, why proposition me? You knew I was married."

Smoke swirled around her face like a tangled vine. "I thought it might feel good to screw over another woman. Even the cosmic score." She laughed harshly. "Turns out, I only want to hurt Jared and Kara."

"Give it time—"

She mimed shooting herself in the head. "Spare me the motivational speech."

I gathered my jacket. "Do I have to worry about this getting out?"

She scowled. "I have bigger problems than ruining your golden boy image."

Could I trust Ynez? And what about Izzy? Shannon thought she had dirt on me too. I never considered how I'd be beholden to these women. How I was asking for their complicity in staying silent. How this open marriage might hurt my career, as well as Lila, if someone talked. For some reason, I thought it would be like it was in college—casual, fun, easy—expectations checked at the door.

Back at my hotel, I showered, eager to wash away Ynez's scent, her sweat, the marijuana smoke. But the grime clung to my skin like curdled cheese.

I couldn't wash away these feelings. Frustration. Guilt. Shame. The thought that I turned into the guy that cheats on business trips. That I could lose everything if I continued down this path. And then, as always, the feeling that I could've done more to revive my marriage. But what? *What?*

Dripping wet, I jumped out of the shower to call Lila, tell her I loved her, that she was the only one for me. But as the phone clicked over to voicemail, the monotone pitch of her recorded voice reminded me that she wouldn't care. Professing my love, begging her to get help hadn't worked in the past and it wouldn't work now. She needed to tell me to stop. Show me she was ready to be my wife instead of my co-parent.

As Marvin Gaye sang, it takes two. Until she was ready to try, I wouldn't call off the open marriage. It was just sex, I reminded myself. A release. The only thing more miserable than nights like tonight would be accepting a life sentence in my sexless, depressing marriage.

CHAPTER TWELVE
LILA

"Her name is Fable," my mom said, her voice crackling over the Bluetooth speaker with the same amount of scorn one reserved for introducing children to heroin. "She's twenty-six."

"That's a short story, not a person," I said, unbuckling my seatbelt and reclining the seat, content to watch Levi's soccer practice from the car. Relax for the twenty minutes before I had to pick up Charlotte from gymnastics.

Across the field, Shannon held court with her mom-squad. She probably assumed I resented her beauty. She was an Abercrombie model, *didn't you know?* But I steered clear because of her duplicitous personality. Her feigned concern and fake laugh epitomized every girl that befriended me after Wade, only to twist my words as they held vigils for his damaged reputation. Being neighbors for the past decade hadn't changed my opinion.

"He's a walking cliché. New car, new girlfriend, what's next?"

"A tattoo?" My role was to make pithy comments so that she didn't plunge into the deep levels of despair. The ones only a bottle could fix.

"I'm lonely." She paused. Did I hear a sip? "Maybe if you ever came to visit."

My mom played my guilt like a bow to a fiddle. It wasn't my job to take care of her. It never should've been. But the images of my mom passed out on the bathroom floor in a puddle of piss and puke were not easily left behind. This recent breakup had her on edge, going to daily meetings. Or so she said. She wielded her sobriety like a sword, using it to her advantage at every turn.

"I'd love to." *I wouldn't.* "But the kids are busy and Alex's practice is insane."

"You always say that..." And off she went, listing the numerous ways I failed her.

I watched Levi sprint across the soccer field, chasing the ball. Long and lean, like Alex. I missed his chubby thighs, velvety cheeks, candy apple lips. My baby. One minute, he was cooing in my arms, and the next, he was slapping high-fives on the field, aching to be one of the guys. Soon, there would be high school. Then college. Then he would be gone.

One more child. That's all I wanted.

I gripped the steering wheel, wondering whether Milo would've grown up to look like Levi. Act like him. Or, would he have been gregarious like Charlotte? Perhaps an identity of his own: wild child, peacemaker, artist. I turned around, imagining Milo in the car seat, babbling nonsense, a stream of consciousness speckled with the few words he'd know by now. *I'm sorry*, I thought as the poisonous regret threatened to suffocate me. A fitting end. *I'm so sorry.*

Another baby won't replace Milo, Alex said when I told him shortly after Milo's death that I wanted to try again. This was about love, family, purpose; not supplanting Milo. Never. But how to explain this ache to Alex? On good days, it felt like a dark cloud following me, one I could outrun by focusing on Levi and Charlotte; but most days, I felt listless, like I was floating in space, unable to connect, feel, be myself. An avatar impersonating the old Lila. These elucidations fell on deaf ears. Alex decided I was depressed, and nothing, surely not my half-baked explanations, could convince him otherwise.

In fact, I think explaining myself drove him to get the vasectomy. Maybe, if I stayed silent, let nature take its course, we wouldn't be here. But I never thought he'd use my words against me, value his desires over mine. Not on something this important.

"How is the famous Dr. Cole?" Mom asked now.

"Busy." *Busy screwing around.* But I kept that thought to myself. My mom thought Alex was the second coming. Handsome, successful, loyal. She marveled at his ability to work all day and still have energy to play with the kids. Only a spoiled brat would refuse him sex.

"I bet one of the networks will scoop him up soon. With that face and expertise." She sighed. "You don't know how lucky you are, Lila."

Lucky. Getting through each day was like trying to breathe with splinters in my lungs. Not that I could tell her. My mom cornered the market on loss and betrayal, refusing to share airtime. When I told her about the rape, she relayed a "similar story" where she got drunk and had sex with a stranger. From that point on, she was privy to the highlights of my life. We were better off, closer and yet further apart, because of my reluctance to share.

"I do, Mom."

Levi hurriedly packed up his gear, calling for his friends to wait. They didn't turn around. He might have looked like Alex, but he didn't inherit his easygoing demeanor. There was something cloying and desperate about Levi's desire to fit in, a reminder of my childhood.

"But you need to keep an eye on him." My mom was an expert on cheating men, doling out advice to everyone from Khloe Kardashian to the grocery clerk. But she was too late. "His show is opening a world of opportunities—"

"Gotta go," I interrupted, as Levi got into the backseat. "Babe." I turned around, a fake grin plastered to my face, a clown in need of a facelift. "How was school? Soccer?"

He looked out the window, scowling as he watched Cameron and Tyler pile inside Shannon's Porsche. I wanted to hug him, tell him that one day, he would find his people, but I knew this promised day may never come. And if it did, there was no guarantee they would stay.

* * *

Later that night, I stood in front of the mirror, my reflection that of a stranger. Skinny jeans, a cropped cashmere sweater, ankle booties. All purchased yesterday during a lunch hour shopping trip with Geneva. There were moments yesterday when I caught her looking at me and I wondered whether she found me attractive. Then I felt dumb. The smile on her face didn't emote desire, but rather pleasure at having successfully rescued me from my boring wardrobe.

"You look cute," Alex said as I walked into the kitchen.

"Thanks." He looked adorably comfy in an old blue Notre Dame Cross-Country shirt and a pair of grey sweatpants that rode up one of his calves. I loved his calves. Sinewy bits of muscle that popped from his legs like two ripe pears. I wanted to run my lips across them, inhale the sweet aroma of home. The thought both surprised and confused me—since when did I start craving him again?

I rummaged through my purse until the gravitational pull he had on my heart subsided.

"Wait," he said. "Are you going out?"

"Yeah. Why?"

"I thought we could make dinner. Catch up." He rubbed my shoulders from behind. His voice sounded raspy and drawn, a sign he talked too much today. "Come on. The kids are asleep. Stay home."

"I can't."

"Why not?"

I stepped away. "I have plans."

"Cancel 'em." His words were clipped. A gun shot in a deserted field. The tone he used when the kids whined.

Pent-up rage boiled inside me, erasing any desire I felt for him. I spent the last year feeling sad, regretful, impotent. Anger was like a rain cloud in the distance. I could see it, but stopped short of experiencing it. Anger wouldn't change the past, but it would harm the kids to grow up in a toxic environment. His decision to have an open marriage, however, freed something within me. I wanted to drive through the storm. I wanted to feel it rain down upon us.

How dare you? I wanted to shout as I pounded my fists against his chest. Why was it always about what he needed? Why didn't what I want matter? Fury wormed its way to my tongue, threatening to emerge. "I've never asked you to cancel."

"I would if you did." His voice was reasonable, as if talking to a parent that didn't want to vaccinate their child. In time, they would see the wisdom of his ways.

And he was right. He would cancel his plans if I asked. But I didn't want to. I had fun with Geneva. What started as a way to detox from the open marriage had become a renaissance. I was rediscovering me. The woman I was before Milo. Perhaps the woman I would've become if not for the rape. It was liberating.

"Who are you meeting?" he asked, not quite suspicious but nearly there. "What are these important plans of yours?"

My subtle dig last week about not bothering him on dates must have rattled him. He wasn't used to being the one left behind, waiting on me for answers. And now, I was going out again. Refusing to stay home. Ultimately, rejecting him. But what could he say? He was up to far worse.

"My friend Geneva." I heard a trace of pride in my voice, as if I was twelve again and Lisa McIntosh invited me to her birthday party.

"Geneva." He sounded surprised. Perhaps relieved it wasn't a man. "Why do I know that name?"

"You met her at Home."

"And now you're—" He squinted his eyes. "Friends?"

His confusion wasn't without merit. I didn't have many friends. But still. It stung. I dreamed of this life: loving husband, adorable kids, financial stability. It never occurred to me that I might need more. My friendship with Geneva was more.

"Is that so hard to believe?"

"'Corse not." He grinned. "I'm proud of you, kid," he said, using the infantilizing endearment he knew I hated. He held his hand up for a high five, which, much to my own disgust, I met with a limp hand. "Making friends. Getting out. This is good. This is progress."

He preheated the oven, before retreating to the couch. As I watched him scanning through the DVR, I debated cancelling. I was too angry to enjoy myself. He made me feel like a charity case. It preyed on all my insecurities as to why someone as dynamic as Geneva wanted to be friends with me.

But perhaps Geneva was exactly what I needed. Somehow, whenever I was around her, Alex, Milo, my desire for another baby, receded an inch or so. Somehow, she made life a bit more bearable.

CHAPTER THIRTEEN
GENEVA

Geneva opened her apartment door to find Lila simmering, her cheeks flushed with angry red butterfly blotches. Lila muttered a hello and brushed past Geneva, leaving behind a faint trace of leaves.

"Don't take this the wrong way, but you look like you need a drink," Geneva said, following her to the kitchen. Or maybe a Xanax.

"I don't—" Lila stood rigid, her hands curled in two tight fists, ready to explode like a shaken can of soda pop. "Actually, I could use a drink."

Geneva grabbed tequila, triple sec, and sour mix, wondering what prompted this abrupt shift in Lila's mood. When Geneva invited her over, Lila seemed excited. Geneva was too. She spent her afternoon discussing the Bronte sisters, but her mind was far from 19th Century England. She was daydreaming about the possibilities of being alone with Lila in her apartment.

This scenario, Lila livid and unhinged, was not one of them.

"Give it to me straight," Lila said, watching as Geneva mixed the ingredients.

Geneva hoped it wasn't an omen. She splashed a generous amount of tequila in a rocks glass and handed it to Lila, saving the margarita for herself. Lila's mouth became an angry frown as the liquid met her taste buds, but, to her credit, she didn't complain.

"What'd he do?" Geneva asked.

"Hmm...?"

"Alex." Geneva pried open Lila's free hand. She had nail marks, half-moons, embedded into the palm of her hand. "You have that feral, don't-fuck-with-me, look in your eyes of a woman scorned."

Lila pulled her hand away and walked towards the couch. "I don't want to talk about it."

"I'm a good listener." Geneva infused lightness into her words, trying to ignore the voice in her head, saying, *Choose me! Tell me I'm special!*

She remembered a conversation with her father, she couldn't have been more than five, when she asked him if he loved her. To this day, she didn't know what prompted this question. TV? A book? Human nature? Instead of answering, he lectured her on the origins of the word love, and how each generation eroded, abused, and sanitized the word of all meaning. She never asked again, and he never offered up the sentiment.

But why was Lila setting off this insecurity?

"Come on." Geneva sat down next to Lila. "You'll feel better if you let it out."

Lila looked at Geneva, her dark eyes beckoning, intoxicating. A siren, straight out of Homer's *Odyssey*. Geneva felt a rush of excitement. She longed to run her hands through Lila's hair, pull off her new cashmere sweater, feel the warmth of her breasts...

Geneva looked away, questioning the wisdom of inviting Lila over. Public settings kept Geneva restrained. Stopped her from doing something stupid. Something that'd scare Lila off.

Society hardwired the normalcy, the desirability, the *benefits*, of heterosexuality into the minds of babes from their first breath. The hyper-sexualization of the lesbian relationship didn't erode this power. *It's okay at a bar, under the lustful gaze of overgrown frat boys, or in a porn to fulfill a fantasy, but not as a lifestyle.* Women listened. Buried their baser desires. Even if something felt good, natural, they would put up a Stalin-like resistance to avoid being kicked further down the societal totem pole.

"I'm sorry. I should've cancelled," Lila said, plowing through her drink like a rookie, all determination, no experience. "Ahh! I need to let this go."

"No. You. Need. To. Talk. To. Me." Geneva clapped between each word to emphasize her point. Geneva's motives weren't one-hundred percent altruistic. Yes, she wanted to give Lila space to vent, cheer her up, be a good friend. But she was also curious. What had Alex done to upset her? How unhappy was she in her marriage? Unhappy enough to seek comfort elsewhere?

Lila shuddered as she finished her drink. "Can you promise—"

"Done."

"How do you know what I'm going to ask?"

"Because I know you," Geneva said, realizing it was true. Becoming friends with Lila instead of jumping into bed led to something deeper. It wasn't only the content of the conversations, but the trust, the emotional leaps they were taking with one another. This was foreign territory for Geneva, too. "You want me to promise that I won't tell anyone. That I won't judge you. That we'll still be friends. Done, done, and done."

"Alex and I," Lila started. "I need another drink for this."

Lila jumped up and fetched the tequila from the kitchen, swinging the bottle by its neck. She slammed it down on the coffee table, oblivious to the loud bang, before falling onto the couch in one liquid movement. Her shoulder pressed up against Geneva's, erasing the cushion of space that previously sat between them.

Geneva knew it was the alcohol, the slow disembodiment of Lila's spatial functions, but she hoped it was something more. Alcohol unleashed your true self, right? Lila was drawn to her, even if on a subconscious level. A couple shots couldn't completely alter your desires. The connection had to have been there all along.

"We've had a rough year," Lila continued. "It's tested us. Tested our marriage. And he wants to gloss over it, like it's nothing. But I can't move on."

Geneva leaned in, eager for the details. "What happened?"

Lila bit her lip. "I can't...I'm sorry. It's still too raw. I thought, maybe with a drink—" She frowned at her glass. "—but I'm...I'm not ready to talk."

Disappointed, Geneva took a large gulp of her margarita. Much as she wanted, she knew she couldn't push Lila on this. Trust was the way in. Lila *would* let her guard down...in time. But patience was not Geneva's strong suit.

"If I've learned anything," Geneva said, "it's that the past should stay in the past. Bury it. Don't resurrect it." Over the past decade, Geneva became an avid devotee of this philosophy. "You guys need new adventures, new *friendships*—" She nudged Lila's shoulder. "—to move forward."

Lila sighed. "That's what he says."

"You can't change what happened, so, why not try it his way? Forgive and forget?"

Lila clutched her drink tighter. "That'd be easier if he ever apologized."

Apologize for what? Geneva wanted to yell. "I feel you, but..."

"But what?"

Geneva hesitated, not wanting to come off disloyal. "That's why I'm not a relationship person. The constant rehashing, the grudges, the keeping score of who apologized. At the first sign of a rut, I'm out of there."

Lila turned and looked at Geneva, frowning in a pitying way that was both familiar and bothersome. "That's one way to never get hurt."

Geneva rolled her eyes, having defended this claim numerous times with numerous exes. "It's not about that. You can get hurt in any relationship, regardless of the length. Besides, humans were never intended to be monogamous."

"That's not true." Lila wasn't slurring, but enunciating took an obvious effort. "Not for me."

"To be fair, you got married young. Maybe, if you hadn't met Alex, you would've found happiness in spurts, instead of trying to mold one person to meet your every need." A voice inside Geneva's head warned her to tread lightly. But Geneva ignored it. She wanted to broaden Lila's perspective, tease her with the possibility that more than one person could make her happy. Conversation innocent enough to be innocuous, ambiguous enough to spark curiosity. "Maybe, and I know this sounds insane, you'd be sitting here, unable to imagine being married with kids."

"That sounds...horrible." Lila raised her glass to her mouth, swallowing air. "A world without Levi and Charlotte isn't one I'd want to live in." She grabbed the bottle, pouring a couple inches into her glass, and letting another slop onto the table, before throwing it back.

Geneva rested her hand on Lila's wrist. "Maybe you should slow down."

"Please don't tell me what to do." Lila wiped her mouth with her sleeve. "I'm sick of people making decisions for me, as if I'm too naïve, or stupid, to know what's best."

Her complaint set off alarms inside Geneva. "You remind me of someone."

"Who's that?"

"Cristina," Geneva whispered, too surprised to censor herself.

"Who?" Lila leaned closer, her forehead knocking Geneva's.

"My ex."

Geneva hadn't made the connection until she spoke the words. The thought took her breath away. The resemblance was uncanny. True, Cristina was Latina and Lila was white, but they both had long, rich hair, almost ebony in color, with matching brown eyes so deep that the iris was indistinguishable from the pupil. The same strawberry-lipped half-smile, as if they were afraid to commit to a feeling. Slim bodies. Shy dispositions, a reluctance to share, trust you had to earn by showing up each day.

The intense familiarity, the bond, she felt with Lila suddenly made sense. How had Geneva failed to see it until now? Was it a black hole in her brain? Here she was, spouting off about keeping the past in the past, yet Geneva's past was haunting her present.

She rarely let herself remember the last time she saw Cristina. It was too painful. But when she did, a series of images came to mind. A yellow pillow stained black from Geneva's mascara-filled tears. Cristina's lacrosse uniform on the floor, spread out like a chalk outline of a body, commemorating their aborted sex. The door half-opened. Girls peeking inside, whispering.

The memory left her cold, but she took it as a warning: she couldn't continue concealing her feelings for Lila, risk razing her heart, only to have Lila reject her after falling in love. Because that's where this was headed. The more time she spent with Lila, the further she fell.

No one tempted her since Cristina. Thirteen years. Thirteen years of hookups, dates, girlfriends, but never once did she feel herself falling. Until Lila. She wasn't lying when she told Lila that she preferred relationships short. But it wasn't whole truth either. She had eight months, two weeks, and three days with Cristina, yet she would've stayed forever, if given the chance. A small part of her, a part she battled like hell to keep stifled, craved love.

She had to know how Lila felt. Whether she was interested in more than a friendship. And she had to know *now*.

Geneva turned towards Lila. They were close, mouths inches apart. Too close for friends. But Lila stayed put. Geneva could smell the spicy tequila on Lila's breath. Before she could second-guess herself, she leaned over and kissed Lila, momentarily winded by the desire that whirled inside her lungs.

One kiss. A moment. A taste. That's all she would allow herself.

She pulled herself back from the brink. Opened her eyes. And waited.

CHAPTER FOURTEEN
LILA

My lips tingled, whether from alcohol or the kiss, I couldn't tell. It happened fast. One moment we were talking, the next we were kissing. Kissing! Me and Geneva, sitting in a tree, K-I-S-S-I-N-G! First comes love...

I giggled. I never giggle. "You kissed me."

"I've been wanting to do that since we met." Geneva flashed in and out of focus, smiling that enigmatic smile of hers. Like one of those old flip projectors. Darkness, followed by her beautiful face. Then, complete darkness as my eyes closed, heavy and spent. I longed for my bed, but it felt impossibly far away, more a memory than an actual destination. And it was—at least, the bed I wanted. The one where Alex buried his face in the back of my neck, his breath a heated vent, his fingertips skirting the lining of my underwear. These days, we kept to our sides, immoveable blocks of granite.

"Lila? Lila?" The call was faint, an echo that bounced off trees as it travelled through the forest. I opened my eyes, watching, but not necessarily feeling, as Geneva tucked my hair behind my ear. Her face was close, her eyes kind. Are you going to kiss me again?

"Only if you want me to," she said.

It took a second to realize I asked the question out loud. But before I could decide whether I wanted to kiss her, the room started to spin, as if I hopped on a Tilt-A-Whirl.

"You okay?" Geneva held my wrist, steadying me.

I looked down, focusing on a single plank of hardwood. "I think I'm drunk."

"Do you want to stay here? Sleep it off? I could make up the couch—"

"No! No," I repeated, softer. "I can't. The kids, work. I have oblig—" My tongue twisted, unable to form the word. "—obligations."

"I'll drive you home," Geneva said. "You can get your car in the morning."

Home. Alex. How would I explain this to him?

Using Geneva's arm as my walking stick, we made it to the parking garage and into her Mini Cooper. She plugged my address into her GPS and started driving, while I concentrated on not puking. Beads of sweat formed along my hairline, warning me that time was of the essence. By the time she pulled into my driveway, I was down to seconds.

I stumbled out of the car, falling to the ground, the floodlight spotlighting my shame. The freezing cement felt like a balm to my fever. But the relief didn't last long. I gripped the sides of a flowerpot for leverage and puked. Puked like it was my life's passion.

Out of the corner of my eye, I saw a warm, buttery glow. If I was religious, maybe I would've thought it was an apparition. A reminder that I strayed from my path.

Instead, I saw Shannon's curvy silhouette in the frame of her bedroom window. I wouldn't be surprised if she was taping me on her phone. She was *that* cunning.

Alex appeared at my side. "You're okay, babe." One hand pulled my hair out of my face, while his other one lightly massaged my back. "Let it out."

I didn't know whether it was his gentle touch, the concern melting his voice, the countless hours spent imagining him with other women, or that Geneva kissed me, but I started crying. I wasn't okay. In too many ways to count.

"What happened?" Alex asked, still holding my hair.

"She drank too much," Geneva said.

"Drank? Like alcohol?" Silence. "Lila doesn't drink."

Geneva laughed. "She wanted to tonight."

"How much did she have?"

"Hard to say," Geneva said. "She was drinking tequila straight."

"Tequila?" He stood up, letting go of my hair, strands of which became glued to my lips with puke-filled saliva. While I couldn't see them, I knew an argument was brewing.

"Stop," I muttered.

"If she's this drunk," Alex said, "don't you think you should've cut her off?"

"She was upset and needed to let loose. I was trying to be a good friend."

"Next time, try harder." Alex scooped me up in his arms, carrying me up the front steps and through the door like the bride I once was.

"Wait," Geneva called.

"She needs to rest." Alex kicked the door closed.

Alex set me down on our bed, grunting as he pulled off my skinny jeans. Gravity had its way with me, and my head crashed into the mattress. The sudden movement proved too much for my delicate stomach. I raced towards the bathroom, stubbing my big toe against the corner of the wall. Tomorrow would hold some nasty bruises, not all of which would be visible.

A gush of liquid shot from my mouth, the suddenness I could only compare to having my water break with Charlotte. The sensation of being beholden to my body was similar, although nowhere near as fulfilling. Nothing good would come from this ordeal.

"I did something bad," I mumbled, resting my head against the toilet seat. Disgusting? Absolutely. Comfortable? Like a bed in the Ritz, with a thousand thread count sheets and a pillow made from clouds. "Bad. Bad. Bad."

Alex squatted next to me, combing my hair into a ponytail. "Cut yourself a break. If you want a drink, great. But you can't go from zero to sixty."

I wiped saliva from my chin. "I will never drink again."

He laughed. "First line in the drinkers' bible, babe."

I looked at him. He was gorgeous, even with bed-tousled hair and dark circles under his slate blue eyes. I reached out, running my fingers across the stubble on his chin. Stubble I loved. Stubble he would shave in the morning. Was there a deeper meaning at play? Had he always put his needs first? Regardless of what I wanted?

Or was I just drunk?

"I'm sorry," I said, unsure what I was apologizing for. Getting drunk? Kissing Geneva? Ignoring him for months on end?

"No need to apologize." He pulled off my new cashmere sweater, likely spackled with puke, never to be worn again. "I'll get you some pajamas."

"Don't." I unclipped my bra, sighing in relief as the cool air ran its hands over my breasts. "I'm sleeping naked. Right here."

Through heavy eyelids, I saw Alex appraising my body, chewing his lower lip, a sure sign he was lusting after my hardened nipples. It was a look I came to detest this past year. But instead of my usual emptiness, or a spike of anger, I felt something new: guilt. I cheated. It was only a kiss, but the specific act was inconsequential.

"You sure?" he asked. "I'll put a garbage can next to the bed."

"Go. Please." Tears pricked my eyes. I couldn't look at him. Such sweetness. The opposite of the jerk that bid me goodbye tonight with a high five. It would've been easier if he was angry, if he gave me a reason to justify my treasonous actions. But no. Of course not. Alex was never better than when in the caretaker role. Each miscarriage was a testament to that.

Reluctantly, he went, but not before fetching my pillow, a blanket, water, and a couple ibuprofen.

I spent the night hugging the toilet bowl, but I couldn't expel the guilt. It felt like a tumor pressing against my organs, metastasizing with each passing hour.

If it was a one-off, a misunderstanding, I could forgive myself. The knowledge that it would never happen again would be enough to move on. But this was worse. Because with sobriety came truth. The inability to lie to myself. And the truth was, I wanted to kiss Geneva again. When I was sober. Just to see if I really liked it.

CHAPTER FIFTEEN
ALEX

Something was off with Lila. More than the undertow of sadness that threatened to sweep her away each day. She covered that up with a mask, one that focused on keeping our lives scheduled, orderly, and efficient. But ever since she came home drunk two nights ago, she acted flaky. Distracted. Yesterday, I assumed she was hungover. She stared off into space, her eyebrows knitted together, her fingers like windshield wipers brushing against her lips. We had to repeat ourselves several times before she responded. But today wasn't any better. She forgot we were leaving for Chicago when the kids got home from school. *Forgot.* Not a loaf of bread or to gas up the car. Nope. Nothing so trivial.

With the delay, we'd be lucky to make it to my parents' house by the kids' bedtime. The Cole siblings were flocking back to the nest—David from L.A., Paddy from Denver, Angela from New York—to celebrate an award my dad was receiving for his work on 3-D mapping of the human heart. We lived the closest and would be the last to arrive. I hated being last.

"Are you okay?" I asked Lila once the traffic thinned out. The kids were installed in the backseat, both with an iPad and headphones that ensured a tornado wouldn't disturb their listening pleasure.

"Mm-hmm." She gazed out the window, immobile except for her fingertips, which tapped her knee in rhythm with "Paint it Black."

I cleared my throat, frustrated with her silence. For fifteen years, I had an all-access pass to her thoughts. Witnessed her most vulnerable moments. But something hardened inside her since Milo died. A resolve I didn't understand. Privacy, not communication, became the hottest commodity in our marriage, as she retreated to the corner of her mind like a boxer in the ring.

"Is the open marriage stressing you out?" It was a softball question. Clearly, the open marriage was taking its toll. Exhibit A: Coming home drunk; stumbling, crying, and puking. You didn't need a psychology degree to understand she was acting out because her world was out of control.

She glanced back at the kids. "Not now."

"They can't hear. Watch." I turned up the music and belted the lyrics, doing my best Mick Jagger impression. Neither child flinched, but Lila laughed. She tilted her neck back as the sound rose from her belly, her face lighting up like a Christmas tree. Moments like this made me believe. A few simple changes. We'd be back. "Admit it. My talents are wasted on medicine."

A second's hesitation before her smile widened. "You missed your calling."

During my residency, Lila used to meet me at a karaoke bar near the hospital. After a back-breaking thirty-six hour shift, I, along with the other residents, wanted nothing more than liquor, music, and sex before passing out. My memories of that time softened over the years. It felt majestic. Gilded. Because I survived. More than that. I thrived, rising to the top. There's no high like that after school. Once you're married, with kids, a career, there's always a stressor to bring you back to earth.

"Maybe we should swing by Avenue B after the awards dinner."

"I doubt it's there," Lila said. "Everything cool in Chicago closed when we left."

I smiled. It was our inside joke when we moved to Madison for my fellowship. While I fell in love with the small-town goodness of Madison—the lakes, the running trails, the tight-knit community—Lila missed the energy of Chicago. Not that we ever considered leaving once Levi came. City life made everything more stressful, expensive, and time-consuming. Until last year, I thought we discovered a slice of paradise.

"Do you still miss it?"

"Feels like a different life," she said.

I reached across the shifter, lightly massaging her thigh, encouraging her to move closer, embrace the intimacy. But she remained still, a frozen street performer, unwilling to break character.

"Lila, I'm worried. You're more distant than ever. I know it's the open marriage. It's been hard on me too. I just wish we could talk about it."

She pressed her lips together, a subtle, but telling sign that my words reached her. She was always controlled, careful. Even during our happiest moments, I could see a flicker in her eyes, the fear of what was lurking. She had good reasons. But when I proposed, I promised to protect her. And I've tried my hardest to live up to that promise.

"It's easier to pretend," Lila said.

"Pretend what, exactly?"

"That you're working late."

Hope blossomed. She was talking. Cracking open the door to her feelings. "And this works?"

"Sometimes." She checked on the kids again, and whispered, "If I think about what you're doing, I feel ill. So, I try not to think."

"This was only intended to be a short-term solution," I said, wondering why she didn't tell me to stop if it made her ill. Was she lying to me? Or herself? "More of a stopgap."

Wasn't that what we both wanted? To go back to the way things were? For this godawful celibate period to end? Having sex with other women was a poor substitute for Lila's love. I needed intimacy. Openness. My goddamn marriage back. I'd never met a woman like Lila and it was insane to think I ever would. But I'd done everything to resurrect that woman and still, she refused to emerge. The prospect of this open marriage continuing indefinitely, of continuing to have sex with strangers, exhausted me.

"A stopgap?" she asked.

"Well, yeah. Until you're feeling more like yourself."

"Myself." Her lips tugged downward like taffy. "Meaning wanting to have sex?" She paused. "With you?"

With you. Why would she say that? "Who else would you have sex with?"

"Never mind," she muttered.

Mick Jagger droned on about not always getting what you want. As if I needed another reminder. "Answer the question: have you met someone? Yes or no?"

"Does it matter?"

I gripped the steering wheel, my knuckles turning white. "Are you kidding? You're the one that preached about transparency. It was one of your rules, remember?"

"And you said this was an *open* marriage." Her voice low, but fierce, the first crack in her plastic mask. "Meaning we could both...participate. Or did I get that wrong? I know how you love to make decisions without me."

Decisions without her? She agreed to the open marriage. We talked about it—at length! I practically begged her to tell me no. "If you wanted to have sex, there'd be no reason for an open marriage."

She closed her eyes, letting out the smallest of sighs. "I don't. I'm just..."

"*What?*" Pulling details out of her was as tough as interrogating a terror suspect.

"Thinking about it."

I tasted blood. Hot. Metallic. Bitter. I assumed it was a figment of my imagination, the rage burning so strong, I could taste it. It wasn't until I wiped my mouth with the back of my hand and came back with a trail of bloody saliva that I realized I bit my cheek.

"You let me know when you're done thinking," I said through gritted teeth.

Cars raced past me, exaggerating the feeling that everything was moving too fast, spinning out of control. What started as a simple plan, a way to wake up Lila, save our marriage, had taken on a life of its own. The scariest part? I had no idea how to get us back on track.

CHAPTER SIXTEEN
LILA

Alex and I sat on the loveseat in his parents' great room, his hand resting on my thigh. It was the most we've touched in months. All to play happy couple in front of his family. Not that it mattered. Alex's parents, Roger and Clara, had already retired to bed, worn out by tonight's awards banquet. The kids were all asleep. And Alex's siblings were far too tipsy to notice.

I watched Alex as he threw his head back and laughed as Paddy detailed his lucrative business selling pot brownies in high school. Alex was at ease here—kind, attentive, funny. Nothing like the smug man that suggested this open marriage was a "stop-gap" until *I* changed. Not him. Never him. He ran around, treating this open marriage like a visit to the Playboy mansion, never once considering why I wasn't keen to hop back into bed with him. His cavalier manner enraged me, railroaded my usual restraint. I let the truth slip. I was thinking about someone, Geneva; but he didn't have to know that.

That kiss. I couldn't get it out of my head. The softness. The delicacy of her tongue. The sweetness of her breath. Even now, after running the scene through my head dozens of times, I couldn't believe it. If she pulled out a gun and coldcocked me, I'd have been just as surprised.

I blamed myself. For showing up angry at her apartment, vulnerable enough to talk about Alex. For getting drunk. For leading her on. Because, I'll admit, I enjoyed her attention. The way she fawned over me. Hung on my every word. Held my gaze as if she wanted nothing more than to climb inside my head and bathe in my thoughts.

Geneva texted me yesterday. *I like you. Let me know what you decide.* Decide? Decide what? Whether we would remain friends?

Could we? Did the *When Harry Met Sally* logic apply here? Or could we be more? Was I capable of cheating? Being with a woman?

You liked kissing her, my brain insisted. *I'm curious*, I retorted. I'd never kissed a woman before. Never wanted to. And yet, kissing Geneva, from what I remembered, felt...natural.

Still. I had too many questions, too many thoughts circulating, to answer her.

"One more drink," Paddy said, brandishing a bottle of whiskey from the bar. "A toast, really, to myself." Everyone groaned, but no one stopped him from pouring. Except for me. Paddy winked at me, his eyes bloodshot, as I shielded my cup of water.

"Are you finally off probation?" David joked, chucking a pillow at Paddy. As the oldest, he was swift with his judgments, quick to make Paddy feel like a second-class citizen for not having a career beyond snowboarding or Alex inferior for choosing pediatrics over cardiology.

"Have Mom and Dad finally stopped paying your bills?" Alex's sister, Angela said. She wasn't tactful, either. None of Alex's siblings were. Competitive. Cocky. Passionate. There was a frat house quality to their relationship: festive teasing and cultish loyalty.

"Nope," Alex said. "I think he's met someone."

"No. No. Yes," Paddy said, pointing at Alex. Alex celebrated with a fist pump. "Natalie. She's from Michigan, so good Midwest stock. Teaches snowboarding. Knows more ariel tricks than me. Matches me drink-for-drink. And gives two fucks about me showing up on time or calling at a certain hour." He grinned, an adorable man-child. "It's promising, guys."

Having heard some version of this soliloquy for the past ten years, no one took him seriously. Paddy would never settle down.

"Should we set an extra plate at Thanksgiving?" David's wife, Cassandra, asked.

"That's three weeks from now," David answered while Paddy theatrically shuddered.

"Since we're making announcements, I have some news..." Angela held her hand up, waiting for silence. With every eye on her, she licked her lips and said, "I'm pregnant."

I froze, imagining her words as an arrow, shot straight from her mouth and landing dead center in my heart. Angela could be crass—growing up with three older brothers fueled her locker room sense of humor—but this joke felt heartless.

Everyone else laughed. Angela unabashedly dated a string of actresses and models, a "perk" of her job as a casting director. Some famous. Some not. Some long. Some not. But none with the ability to impregnate her.

"Alex, do you want to explain how you need a penis to conceive a child or should I?" David asked, egotistical, as always.

"I thought I'd give hetero sex a try. See what all the whispering is about. Oops," Angela said, covering her grin with her fingers.

"Pregnant your first time. You always were an overachiever," Paddy said. "But I thought it was just to make me look like an asshole."

Alex toasted Paddy. "You accomplished that all on your own."

I bit down on my tongue. Hard. Why was everyone humoring her? Yes, she was the baby of the family, an unplanned gift nearly eight years Paddy's junior. Spoiled and indulged for every whim. But she was an adult now. With a mildly functioning sensitivity chip. Wouldn't she understand that Alex and I might not find this funny?

Angela stomped to her feet, lifted her shirt, and pooched her stomach. "I'm. Pregnant."

"That's from the pizza you wolfed down after the ceremony," David said.

She narrowed her eyes, pausing to give each person the stink eye. Except for me. For me, she softened her eyes and pouted. A plea. The exact face Charlotte made when begging to finish her movie before bed. "I'm sorry. Do you hate me?"

Everyone quieted, knowing then that it was true. I twisted the blanket, wishing I could stuff it inside my mouth to stifle the screams inside my head. "Congratulations," I said softly.

Angela was pregnant? On accident? In what world was that justified? I started to get up, unable to endure a celebration, but Alex grabbed my hand, pulling me towards him.

"It's not about us," he whispered, his face inscrutable. No trace of sadness. Regret. Guilt. Did he have a conscience? For a smart man, his willful blindness as to his culpability in my unhappiness was maddening. "Let's try and be happy for her."

I sat back, wondering whether this was part of my punishment. Having to listen to Angela gush about accidently getting pregnant, as if she caught a cold instead of creating a human life, while my tampon soaked with blood, my uterus mourning another month passing without child.

Much as I wanted to pin this all on Alex, it started with me. My decision to wait instead of rushing to the hospital. I deserved this torture. I deserved so much worse.

"A new member of the Cole clan," Cassandra said. "How are you feeling?"

A smile as liquid as cream washed over her face. "Amazing. I've always wanted a baby."

Worlds lived between being pregnant and having a baby. Complications and battles she could not foresee. But I let her bathe in her delusions. Not only because saying otherwise would be needlessly mean, but because most of it was out of her hands.

Alex stood up. "First piece of advice—"

His siblings cut him off, hollering and jeering. "Yes, let's hear what the famous *Dr. Alex* has to say," Angela said.

Alex took her glass. "Stop drinking whiskey."

Paddy promptly relieved Alex of the glass, draining the contents. "Ah, to be a man."

"Spare me," Angela said. "I've been dumping it in the sink."

Responsibility and Angela didn't always go hand-in-hand, so this was a relief.

"I'm confused. Are you still gay?" David asked impatiently.

"You can't ask her that," Cassandra muttered, covering her eyes with her hand.

"Why not?"

"You're trying to label her."

"And?"

Their confusion wasn't without merit. Angela celebrated coming out long before Facebook made it trendy. She ordered a sheet cake for her sixteenth birthday party with the words, "Surprise! I'm GAY!" scrawled in hot pink. It was quite a surprise, one which she often reminisced about, like an athlete reliving a peak performance. I thought of Geneva, how her parents still refused to accept her. Angela joked because it never occurred to her that her family might reject her. After all, they put her every accomplishment, from being born a girl to getting her masters at the famous Tisch School of the Arts, on a pedestal.

"As long as I'm happy," Angela said, "who cares who I'm fucking?"

There were no rules anymore. In marriage, dating or otherwise. Everyone slept with everyone. Life was one big sex-fest. Had the rules ever existed? Maybe they were a figment of my imagination, roadblocks my mind constructed after the rape to keep me safe. But safety, when mixed with time, became a fluid concept. Where I once felt safe in my marriage, I no longer did. Where I once assumed Alex would be my one and only, I was no longer sure.

Angela's blasé attitude unlocked something in my mind, and I realized if the rules were mine, I no longer had to play by them. I could change them. Throw them out. Alex asked permission to break his vows, but I never gave myself permission to do the same. Growing up without a dad, I promised myself I would never cheat. But that was a girl's promise, one made from fear and abandonment.

A world of opportunity opened before me.

And with this realization, came another: I didn't care. I didn't want to cheat, to have kinky sex. All I wanted was to reverse time. Let it be my face that glowed with the beautiful cocktail of elevated progesterone and estrogen. My nose that inhaled the powdery scent of a new baby. My lips that kissed their silky cheek. My eyes that gazed into their milk drunk eyes as they fluttered closed, wondering what adventures they would get up to in this amazing, complicated, and heartbreaking world.

"Hey," Alex said, crawling over to Angela and wrapping his arm around her. "The only thing we care about is that you're happy. You just caught us off guard."

I watched him, noting his empathy, his patience, his desire to take care of his loved ones—all reasons why I fell in love with him. But I didn't feel that love. How could I? Angela's announcement taunted me with the life I could be living right now.

"Yeah," Paddy said. "You go off if I don't immediately ask about your girlfriend."

"Well, now I expect you to immediately ask about my baby."

"Who gets pregnant from a one-night stand?" David asked, shaking his head.

Angela grinned, enjoying the chaos. "Perhaps I wasn't as careful as I should've been."

This was too much. Maybe Alex could pull this off, considering he spent his days with new parents and babies. But I couldn't. I stood up, pleading exhaustion, certain that if I stayed a minute longer, I'd start screaming, throwing pillows, basically lose my tenuous grip on sanity.

After washing up, I lay in bed, too agitated to sleep. Angela was pregnant. Alex was having sex with random women. Geneva kissed me. It was as if we were living inside a snow globe and someone gave it a vigorous shake. Our brains scrambled and scattered, the outcome of this experiment yet to be decided. I started to drift off, wondering how things would settle. Wondering whether the changes would be permanent.

CHAPTER SEVENTEEN
ALEX

I stumbled into my childhood bedroom, drunk, but smiling. Unlike most people, I liked my family. Sure, David acted like he was the sun and the rest of us were planets orbiting his world, Patrick couldn't commit to anything beyond the moment, and Angela was a snob that thought leaving New York qualified as visiting a third world country. But they were my assholes. Hanging with them reminded me of a time when life was far less complicated.

Lila lay sleeping on her back, one hand thrown over her forehead like a damsel in distress. She looked beautiful in the slatted moonlight, dark hair and pale skin, utterly at peace. I stripped down and snuck inside the crisp, cold sheets. Lila's body radiated heat, drawing me in. I inched closer, inhaling the sweet smell of lavender in her hair, before trailing a series of butterfly kisses along her neck.

I used to greet her this way during my residency. We'd have sex, her half-asleep, me nearly there. No words necessary. Only soft moans of appreciation.

Lila stirred, giving me access to the tender spot above her clavicle that drove her mad. Instantly, I got hard. It had been months. Long, lonely—

Her eyes snapped open, wide and alert. "I was sleeping."

"Remember when this was a nightly occurrence?" I kissed her cheeks, the freckles beneath her eye. One time. That's all it would take. Her neurons would fire, reconnecting the familiar pattern of arousal, reminding her that while she was hurting, she wasn't dead. Sex could be part of the healing process. "You'd sleep naked, waiting for me."

"Alex."

"Please, you're enjoying it. Just give your body a chance to remember."

She wiggled away from me, sitting up. "My body's not the problem."

I collapsed back onto my pillow, once again thwarted by the great wall of Lila. "Enlighten me. What is the problem? What can I do?"

Silence coated the air like jelly, thick and sticky.

"You can start by saying you're sorry." Everything about her diminished after Milo, including her voice. But she found it now, loud and clear.

"I am sorry," I said, truly meaning it. I propped up on one elbow. "I never wanted this. These other women—"

"The vasectomy, Alex. You explained. You rationalized. But you never apologized."

"Apologize?" The alcohol made my brain sluggish. What did the vasectomy have to do with the open marriage? "For getting the vasectomy?"

She leaned close to my face, her breath coming in short, hot, angry bursts. "You knew I wanted more kids. We agreed on three—"

"Agreed? That was before we had any idea how difficult it would be." After all the times I tried talking to her, she chose tonight, in my parents' house, when I was halfway up the flagpole, to discuss it? "How many more times did you want to put yourself through that? Me? The kids? They're old enough to understand."

Her silence said enough. She would've tried until she succeeded or died. It was the only way she knew how to operate.

She might not agree, but Lila forced my hand. When we returned home from the hospital, she spent her days in bed, sobbing, making inarticulate apologies, refusing to eat, shower, move. We met with her doctor a month later. After explaining there was a blood clot in the placenta, preventing oxygen and nutrients from reaching Milo, the doctor suggested several tests, including testing for APS, an autoimmune disorder that can cause reoccurring miscarriage due to the clotting of blood in the veins and arteries. Lila asked about treatment options, infusing hope into the doctor's cautionary words. He said that daily aspirin, plus possible injections of heparin, could lead to a higher rate of live birth. I, however, knew that APS was an evolving area of medicine. Dozens of factors could've contributed to the stillbirth. The complications of pregnancy were high—miscarriage; pre-eclampsia; pre-term birth; thrombosis. Too high, in my opinion, for a mother. A wife.

After the appointment, Lila started getting up. Cooking meals. Helping with homework. Still emotional, but functional. Then, she straddled me in bed, looking down at me with heavy, dark moons under her eyes. We made love, each kiss, a promise to protect her, to never let her feel this pain again. Our bodies fused together, as we grasped what little comfort we could take in each other. But after a few nights of this, she stopped me as I grabbed a condom. *Let's make a baby*, she whispered. I froze, certain I heard her wrong.

Over the next couple weeks, we had circuitous arguments, her desperate for another baby. Me, treating her like a patient, one that needed to hear the truth, slow and steady. She was thirty-seven; suffered five miscarriages, one stillbirth. APS only increased those odds. I talked about the dangers to her, the potential complications for the baby, the way caring for a special needs child would alter our lives. She batted away my concerns like Rodger Federer at the net.

I put her stubbornness down to grief, anger, exhaustion. Each baby was a lost dream. I felt it too. Every time I passed what would have been Milo's room, I turned away, the emptiness too much to bear. Instead, I focused on our two amazing kids. It wasn't the big family we envisioned, but they were spectacular. Yet she refused to listen. Appreciate our blessings.

I had to act. Protect not only my family, but Lila from herself. From making a decision that could have catastrophic effects, effects she either refused or was unable to comprehend.

Should I have told her I made the vasectomy appointment? Absolutely. But every time I tried, she flipped out. I feared if she knew about the appointment, she might pinprick our condoms. Freeze my sperm. She was *that* gone.

It needed to be done. And so, I did it.

Needless to say, she was furious when she found out. Our worst fight to date. Lila, who never swore, rarely raised her voice, dealt a verbal lashing. Told me she'd never forgive me, that if not for the kids, she'd leave. Her words stung, but I also knew she was jacked up on hormones, shock, adrenaline. She left to visit her mom. When she came home, all the fight was gone. I explained my reasoning, that day and in the weeks after, but each time I brought it up, she shut down. I put the decision behind me and focused on helping Lila, distracting the kids from her grief.

The vasectomy slotted into place like a puzzle piece. I blamed Milo's death for her depression because that was the most obvious loss, but I realized now that didn't quite fit. After Milo died, she let me hold her. If I looked closer, I would've realized that Lila's infuriating mask of nothingness appeared when she returned from her mother's. That was when I first felt like I was talking to a shell, when she erected an impenetrable wall to keep me out, when the Lila I knew vanished.

It seemed obvious now, but the whirlwind of events—I got the vasectomy a couple months after Milo died—caused my mind to conflate the two. Compared with Milo's death, the vasectomy felt insignificant, an unfortunate consequence. Her unwillingness to discuss the vasectomy was further proof that, while initially upset, she understood I did the right thing, no, the *only* thing, given the horrific circumstances. Otherwise, wouldn't she have said something?

Judging by the fact that she leveraged her demand for an apology like an atomic bomb, I was wrong. Catastrophically wrong.

"Why can't you be happy with what we have?" I asked now. "Two healthy kids. A husband that loves you—"

"A husband that betrayed me."

"I saved your life."

She rolled her eyes. "Don't be sanctimonious. You're a doctor, not God."

"You don't have to be God to realize that another pregnancy could've spelled the end." I didn't specify the nature of the ending. Her life. The baby. My heart. It wasn't a risk I was willing to take. Nor should she.

"That wasn't for you to decide!"

"Why are you bringing this up now? It happened months ago."

She scraped her nails across her naked thighs. "I think about this every day, Alex. Every. Single. Day." With each word, her nails dug deeper. "Wondering whether I'd be pregnant by now. Whether—" I held Lila's hands, stopping her before she drew blood, but she snatched them away. "Seeing Angela tonight, listening to how excited she is—which she should be! But I deserve to be happy too. If you hadn't—"

"But I did." I took a deep breath, reminding myself to be patient. Let her vent. But that was a difficult mandate to follow. I was a solutions guy. Now was the time to find some common ground, a launching pad towards the future. Not dredge up the past. "Tell me how to fix this. How can we move forward?"

"An open marriage, apparently."

"That's not what I meant," I muttered, closing my eyes. My head spun, reminding me that I was drunk. That I should table this conversation. But by tomorrow morning, Lila might shut down again. "It's like you've given up. You won't even try to be happy."

"I've tried, Alex. Harder than you know."

I spread my palms against the cool sheets. "Sure fooled me."

"Sex." She spat the word. "Don't you get it, Alex? I can barely look at you, let alone want to have sex with you."

"A few minutes ago, you wanted it."

"Not from you."

The alcohol in my stomach sloshed menacingly as I remembered her cryptic words in the car ride here. How she was "thinking" about partaking in the open marriage. But what use would Lila have of the open marriage? She never enjoyed sex before me. "If not me, then who?"

"No one. It just—" She held her hands parallel, stretching each finger apart, as if she wanted to strangle me. "—frustrates me how oblivious you are. How selfish. It's always about what you want, what you need."

"You think this is what I want?" I sprang up on my knees, kneeling before her. "I want you. But you won't let me touch you. Hell, most days, you don't speak to me unless it's about the kids. So, what should I have done? Taken a vow of celibacy? Found a new best friend? Tell me."

"You shouldn't have gotten the vasectomy."

"Jesus."

"Part of me fell out of love with you that day," she whispered, staring up at the moon. "And I'm terrified I can't get it back."

"You can." I cupped her chin so our eyes met, refusing to let her words take root. This wasn't Lila talking. Depression changed her brain chemistry. Made her fixate, *obsess*, over the vasectomy; an endless loop of catastrophizing thoughts. A cycle she needed professional help to break. "But not by pushing me away."

Her brown eyes looked glassy, reflecting unshed tears. "Is any part of you sorry?"

A lie could end this. Provide the momentum we needed to find our way back. But I couldn't do it. Love drove me to get the vasectomy. She wouldn't survive another loss. Each miscarriage left a scar, Milo the most devastating. And I couldn't survive without her. Say nothing for the kids. Or my grief, as I said goodbye to each baby.

"I'm sorry I had to get the vasectomy. I'm sorry it still upsets you. I wish you would've talked to me. Jesus, we could've avoided—"

"You didn't *have* to get it done." She narrowed her eyes, the coldness sobering me up instantly. "You're not innocent here. You *made* this happen."

"Lila—"

"Save it." She turned away from me, laying back down. Her body buzzed like a nuclear waste site. Danger. Do not approach. I knew better than to push the conversation.

As I lay awake, I thought about the last year. How I believed that Milo's death wedged a brick of silence between us, destroyed our intimacy, forced us to cope separately. But now I knew that Milo wasn't the reason for our estrangement. It wasn't that our pain was too raw or deep to overcome. Milo's death was a spark, one that time would have extinguished. The vasectomy, on the other hand, set our marriage ablaze.

CHAPTER EIGHTEEN
LILA

I watched as Alex bent over in a sprinter's crouch in our front yard, craning his neck to the side to glance at the kids. He wiped underneath the brim of his hat, pretending to remove beads of sweat, which sent Charlotte into a fit of giggles. Levi shouted go and Alex set off, running and diving into an enormous pile of leaves. The leaves flew up, decorating the air like confetti, before falling back atop him. The kids followed his lead, using his flattened body as a target.

Usually, watching Alex play with the kids flooded my body with endorphins. He was a natural at fatherhood. The way he would come home from a twenty-four hour shift and scoop up baby Levi, cradling him in the nook of his shoulder, while he whispered about his day. Or how he signed up for a hair braiding class with Charlotte to learn the intricate designs she craved. He cherished them. Knowing from my own deprivation what a gift he was bestowing upon them, only made me fall more in love. Made me stay, despite our problems.

But watching them play now brought back my rage from last night. A rage I unleashed on Alex when he drunkenly woke me up with kisses. My demand for an apology erupted through my lungs and spilled out of my mouth like lava. I would never be pregnant again. Because of him.

And yet, he wouldn't apologize. He didn't lose sleep, wondering whether he made the wrong choice by getting the vasectomy. Whether I'd be pregnant now if he showed some patience, some understanding, forethought. Nope, he skipped the whole reflection and apology portion, wanting to know how he could fix the situation, fix us, now. I scoffed at the sentiment. Nothing could make us whole again.

The solution knocked me sideways around four this morning. A vasectomy reversal. I researched it on my phone until Charlotte came begging for breakfast. It might be messy, painful, an ego check, but it was only fair, given what he put me through.

I took a deep breath as a fist of excitement twisted in my stomach. After a long car ride back from Chicago, lunch and laundry, I couldn't wait another second to talk to him. With the kids distracted by the leaves, I seized the moment. "Alex!"

He jogged towards me, his rugged good looks on display. The wiry muscles, the wind-blown hair, the heartthrob smile. This was my husband. He loved me. Despite his decisions, I still believed he wanted us to be happy.

"We're making a mess," he said, laughing.

I thought of Geneva. The way she faced every situation head on, not afraid to court controversy if it meant getting what she wanted. I remembered Alex's words many moons ago. *You're so strong. Now we need you to realize it.* I could do this. Fight for what I wanted. Alex argued I wasn't in the right head space to decide whether to get the vasectomy, but neither was he. Milo's death was too fresh. Fear made Alex impetuous. But time brought perspective. I was ready to wrestle with his fears.

I tucked my hands inside my pockets to hide the shaking. "I want you to reverse the vasectomy."

His smile faded. "I'm not going to do that."

Mentally, I prepared for an initial no. "Why not?"

He stepped towards me, closing the gap. "Lila, we've been over this. You've had five miscarriages. One stillbirth—"

"And?" I pointed at Levi and Charlotte, both doing cartwheels into a pile of leaves. "We've also had two healthy kids."

He sighed. "Babe, it's not worth it. I'm saying this not just as your husband, but as a doctor. With APS, you're not only putting the baby at risk, but your own health."

"I'll take that chance." I knew he wouldn't change his mind easily, but I was hoping it would be a different conversation than we had last winter. It wasn't about statistics or risks, but love. Completing our family. This was once his dream too. "Dr. Rodriguez said there's medication to help prevent the blood clots. That sixty percent of women with APS don't have complications." I grabbed his hand. "I'll be one of those women, Alex. I can feel it. It won't happen again."

Truth is, I *hoped* it wouldn't happen. But I knew all too well the randomness and unfairness of tragedy in life's lottery. Alex, however, didn't need my fears to stockpile as ammunition.

"And if you're in the other forty percent?" His grey eyes conveyed as much warmth as the dreary sky. "If, God forbid, something happens to you? Tell me, how should I explain that to Levi and Charlotte?"

I pulled my hand away. "You always envision the worst-case scenario. Can't you try to think positive?"

"Fine. Let's assume the medication works. No blood clots. You and the baby both make it through the pregnancy. Great." He gave a little golf clap. "At forty, your risk of Down syndrome skyrockets. Not to mention genetic abnormalities, preterm birth, autism, schizophrenia. The list goes on. How does a special needs child fit into your fantasy?"

I dug my fingernails into my thighs. He always did this. Talked circles around me, intimidated me with his logic, his medical expertise, his certainty, until I agreed with him. But not this time. He couldn't know that the pregnancy would fail just as I didn't know if it would succeed. Only God did. And doctors were not Gods.

"I'd love the baby—" I cleared my throat, willing away the tremor. But his words needled. Was I selfish? Should I let this go? Trust his judgment? "—no matter what."

"Who's that?" Alex asked as a Mini Cooper pulled into the driveway. He started walking towards it, but I stayed put, knowing exactly who it was. Geneva.

Did she come here for an answer? Yesterday, I fixated on our kiss, wondering whether I had feelings for her, whether I was capable of cheating, capable of being intimate with a woman. Now those thoughts felt like they belonged to a stranger. Someone lost and lonely, in need of a distraction. Someone like my mother. But I no longer felt lost. I felt renewed with purpose.

Alex leaned inside Geneva's passenger window. What were they talking about? I saw my two worlds colliding like tectonic plates, an earthquake imminent, and jogged over.

I squeezed in next to Alex, nudging him to the side. "Do you want to come in?" I interrupted, too frantic to even say hello to Geneva. I needed to separate them. Immediately. "I was going to make hot chocolate."

"Absolutely." Geneva smiled at me. "I love hot chocolate."

Despite my thoughts a moment ago, my heart flipped. Guilt flushed my cheeks. My lips buzzed and I pressed my fingers against them, trying to silence the desire. Man. Woman. Labels didn't matter. Angela was right; it was the person. And standing before Geneva, I knew. *She* sparked these inexplicable feelings.

Did Alex sense the tension? Could he intuit that a kiss passed between us? But as we walked back towards the kids, joking about saving some hot chocolate for him, I realized, he was oblivious. Not only to my relationship with Geneva, but to how much I wanted another child. How he single-handedly destroyed the trust in our marriage by getting that vasectomy.

He thought this discussion was over. That I would cede to his wisdom, as I did countless times before. But this time, I believed in me. In my wisdom. As a mother. As the agent of my body. If this was any other scenario—a salary issue, dragging my mom back to rehab, the removal of art class from the school curriculum—he'd encourage me to fight. He'd be my biggest cheerleader. In a weird way, I think he might be proud of my persistence. I am becoming the woman he always thought I could be.

CHAPTER NINETEEN
GENEVA

Four days passed since Geneva kissed Lila. Four days without any texts, emails, or phone calls. Although, if Lila texted as if nothing happened that would've infuriated Geneva more, the idea that they could go back to normal. No. It would've been like rereading *Wuthering Heights* for the thousandth time. Unfulfilling and unsurprising. Geneva had friends. What she didn't have was Lila.

And, oh, how Geneva wanted her. After that kiss, how could she not? Soft, supple, the slightest flicker of tongue. It was only a tease, but the tentativeness made it hot. The promise of what she could experience with Lila.

Geneva felt certain the attraction was mutual. Otherwise, why did Lila kiss her back? Why wouldn't she text Geneva and say she was happily married, straight, not feeling it, or any number of excuses? Because she liked it. Unfortunately, that realization could fry a straight person's brain. Geneva feared the longer she waited, the likelier it was that Lila would convince herself it was the alcohol. Refusing to let that happen, Geneva hopped in her Mini Cooper.

As Geneva turned onto Lila's street, she saw Alex, Lila, and the kids playing in the front yard. They looked straight out of a J. Crew catalog with their rosy cheeks, flannel shirts, and mud-splattered jeans, surrounded by a tableau of burnt colored leaves. A pocket of sadness opened inside Geneva, as she struggled to remember a single weekend, a single leisurely *afternoon*, she spent with her parents. Time spent together was always pragmatic, geared towards polishing Geneva's resume. Enjoying the moment, enjoying each other, didn't factor highly.

While the attention would've been nice, the way she was raised—tutors, violin lessons, readings at the 92nd Street Y—gave her the best start in life. She resented many things about her childhood, but couldn't blame her parents for showing her that as a Black woman, she'd have to work twice as hard to get half as much. The fact that Alex and Lila had time to play with their kids, she understood now, was another form of privilege. One her parents couldn't afford.

Geneva felt a pang of longing. As dysfunctional as their relationship was, she missed her parents. Missed her father's measured approval, her mother's astute advice. But if she gave in, called them, nothing would change. They would never accept her.

Banishing these thoughts, she pulled into the Cole's driveway. Alex walked over, staring down her car as if she was a pedophile staking out a school. A tinge of apprehension rose in her throat. Did Lila tell him about the kiss?

"Hey there," Alex said when Geneva put down the passenger window. He rested his elbows on the window ledge, his chiseled shoulders and photogenic smile filling the frame.

"I feel like I'm interrupting a Hallmark moment."

"Nah. It's always fun when Lila's friends stop by." Alex's smile nearly twinkled as he lit on the word "friends." Was he making amends for inferring she was a bad friend for letting Lila get drunk? Or did it penetrate deeper? A subtle reference to the kiss? She hated being behind the eight-ball. "Besides, we could use an extra pair of hands."

"I'm a city girl." Geneva held up her pearly nails. "Manual labor's not my jam."

"And what is your *jam*?" he asked, drawing out the syllables, teasing her.

"Rooftop bars. Sunday brunch—"

Lila popped her head into the window, nudging Alex out of the way. "Do you want to come inside?" Lila said. "I was going to make hot chocolate."

"Absolutely." Geneva smiled, playing it cool despite her nerves. After four agonizing days, she would finally hear what Lila was thinking. "I love hot chocolate."

Lila led her through the garage, past a small pile of shoes inside the door, and into the kitchen. Immediately, Geneva heard Beyoncé's

"Irreplaceable" being played on their Alexa. Cristina loved Beyoncé. Geneva closed her eyes, remembering how Cristina belted the lyrics into her highlighter, using her bed as a mock stage. While random, the evidence linking Cristina and Lila continued to mount. She'd been able to control the impulse to think about Cristina, avoid flashbacks, intuit meaning from coincidences, for years. Why was Geneva suddenly vulnerable? Could a simple resemblance between the two resurrect Cristina's ghost? Put her back in the trenches?

Apparently.

"I was going to call you," Lila said as she grabbed a pan from the pot rack that hung above the island. Then, she collected the ingredients. Sugar. Cocoa. Chocolate Chips. Salt. Milk. "We just got back from Chicago and, well, things are...complicated."

Geneva joined her by the stove, mesmerized by her swift movements. "You're making hot chocolate...from scratch? Bless, you are full of surprises."

"I had this vision of the type of mom I wanted to be. Basically, everything my mom wasn't." Lila shrugged. "Homecooked meals made the list."

"My mother wasn't exactly Julia Child either," Geneva said, remembering how holidays were catered. "I haven't had a homecooked meal in, like, ever."

"You should come around more. I always make too much."

Geneva smiled, a warm, gooey feeling washing over her. Damn! One kiss and she was acting like a teen on a CW drama. "Do you mean that?"

Lila's cheeks flashed scarlet. "You have to understand, I've never—"

Geneva tucked a stray hair behind Lila's ear. "Kissed a girl?"

"Shh!" Lila turned to look out the window. "Obviously. But I was going to say that I've never cheated on Alex."

Geneva didn't want to admit it, tried to ignore it, but Lila's marriage tripped her up too. It complicated matters, brought in the potential of hurting innocent people. Geneva found love complicated enough without adding a hit of guilt. But it was still workable. Plenty of successful relationships grew from affairs. Anything was workable if, *if* Lila wanted to be with her.

"But you want to." Geneva struggled to contain the hope in her voice. How lovely would it be if someone she was falling in love with, loved her in return? "You've thought about it. Us together. What it would be like."

Lila twisted her engagement ring. "Alex and I have problems. But we've chosen this life. I owe it to him to make it work."

Geneva gulped for air. How had she misjudged things? Again?

Much as she yearned to retreat, she pushed herself to be honest. Pushed herself to say words that would likely lead to a humiliating rejection. Her one solace, no witnesses. Unlike her breakup with Cristina. Geneva would never forget the way the girls crowded outside her dorm room, metaphorically munching on popcorn, finding her heartbreak so damn tasty.

Stop it! Stop thinking about Cristina! Stop putting that negative juju on Lila.

"If I could forget our kiss, forget you, I wouldn't be here." Geneva rested her chin on Lila's shoulder.

Lila's breath hitched. "I'm married."

"And you're miserable." Geneva pulled away. "Don't think I haven't noticed."

"My dad cheated on my mom. Left her for another woman. I was only six, a little younger than Levi—" Lila shook her head, her teeth munching on her lower lip.

"This doesn't have to be dramatic. Let's see where this goes," Geneva said, underplaying her hand. But appealing to Lila's need, for whatever reason, to break free from the constraints of her life, was her only option. "Have some fun."

"Fun."

"Yeah." Geneva laughed, as the ingredients simmered. A whirlpool of deliciousness. "You look like you could use some fun."

"You are fun," Lila said with a small smile.

Geneva spread out her arms. "One-hundred percent satisfaction guaranteed."

Instead of laughing, Lila busied herself grabbing mugs, pouring the hot chocolate, sprinkling marshmallows, before carrying everything to the table. "I've become everything I feared: a bad mom, a bad wife."

Geneva looked around the kitchen. Love poured from every nook and cranny. Art work dangled from the windowpanes by fish wire; shelves were crammed with books, games, and puzzles; a collage of candid family shots decorated the fridge; a color-coordinated calendar boasted today, as every Sunday, as "Family Day." Lila was either delusional or had crippling self-esteem, because her house suggested the kids and Alex were both adored and loved.

Geneva sat down next to Lila. "You're too hard on yourself."

"I'm healthy, I have two beautiful children, a successful husband. That should be enough, right? But instead of enjoying it, I obsess about a baby I'll never have." The sun dipped behind a cloud, shadowing Lila's face. "I'm going to ruin everything. Maybe I already have. And yet I still can't let it go."

Geneva blew on her hot chocolate, thoroughly confused. Baby? What baby? What exactly were the "problems" she had with Alex? And why, if miserable, did she insist on working through them? Lila spoke like she was writing a whodunit novel, dropping clues only the most sophisticated detective could piece together. "You lost me."

"Alex doesn't get it, either."

"Give me a chance." Geneva squeezed Lila's hand. "Alex might not want to listen, but I do."

Lila looked up. "You do?"

"Yes. Day, night, whenever. Call me." Geneva swallowed her fear, encouraged by new life in Lila's eyes. "You do something to me. And I think, if you're honest, you feel it too."

"It's all so...unexpected." Lila shook her head. "I mean, look at you. You're beautiful. Smart. Sophisticated. You could have anyone."

Geneva leaned forward, her lips inches from Lila's. She could smell both fear and desire wafting from Lila's pheromones. "But you're the one I want."

The kids rushed in through the garage door. Lila sprang away from Geneva as if burned. Fumes of sweat, leaves, and smoke filled the air. Charlotte jumped up and down, screaming for hot chocolate, while Levi covered his ears, taking the seat across from Geneva.

Lila glowed, their presence draining the fatigue. Alex stood behind Lila, both of them smiling at the kids as if they figured out how to supply a steady stream of clean water to Africa instead of drinking cocoa without scorching their tongues.

Geneva's stomach hurt, witnessing how disposable she was in Lila's life. She was falling in love and Lila was, what? Confused? Guilt-ridden? Curious, if Geneva took a positive spin. Geneva felt confident with more time together, Lila's feelings would grow. But it was a risk to give Lila all the power. One she refused to take after Cristina.

The abrupt end of her relationship with Cristina didn't just devastate her, it left scars, emotional coils branded into her mind, reminding her to run at the first sign of unrequited love. That once you made yourself vulnerable, gave away parts of yourself without receiving the same in return, you wouldn't leave with a flesh wound. You would lose everything.

But then Lila smiled at her. *That* smile. One look. My God. It made Geneva's doubts and fears nebulous. Yes, she was terrified that Lila would break her heart, but she hadn't felt this magical spark since Cristina. Didn't she owe it to herself to find out whether this spark could become an explosion? To honor this feeling after spending a decade plus without?

If Lila was happy with Alex, Geneva would've walked away. But she wasn't! She said as much. Practically invited Geneva to show her an alternative way of living, one where she put herself—her wants, dreams, happiness—first. One where she felt cherished. Being together wouldn't be easy. But as every writer, artist, and philosopher concluded, love isn't supposed to be easy.

Geneva made her excuses and left. She couldn't watch them play happy family, knowing that if Lila wanted to be with her, she would say yes. A decision that would hurt Alex, possibly the kids, if they weren't careful. But as she drove home—the smell of lavender tickling her nose from Lila's goodbye hug—her guilt morphed to excitement. Alex had his chance. Sixteen years to make Lila happy. And he failed. It was her turn to fall in love. To feel loved.

CHAPTER TWENTY
ALEX

A cold breeze greeted me as I exited the hospital and walked into the parking garage, a good two hours past when I hoped to be home for dinner. I texted Lila earlier, letting her know I was staying late with a patient. Her response was curt, one word, a sign that she was still angry with me for torpedoing her vasectomy reversal plan. Whereas she usually created a happy façade between us for the kids, the past few days, she either ignored me or snapped at me over nothing.

"Alex! Hey! Wait up!" I turned to see Izzy jogging towards me, having changed out of her scrubs into jeans and a leather jacket. She'd been on my service a few times since our hookup, but the patient always served as a buffer. Now, we stood, face to face, in the empty parking garage. The rich scent of her perfume reminded me what happened last time we were this close.

She smiled coyly. "Can I buy you a drink?"

"I..." I rummaged my brain for an excuse, knowing I shouldn't encourage her. Definitely shouldn't hook up with her again. But I needed a drink. Three or four, actually. And with the kids in bed, Lila likely following in their wake, there was no reason to go right home. "A drink sounds good."

Izzy gave me a 1000-watt smile, reminding me how easy she was to please. To be around. A stark contrast to Lila, whose moods cast a permanent storm cloud over our lives.

But when Izzy hopped in the passenger seat of my car instead of driving hers, I felt a tingle of unease. She switched off my classic rock with a theatrical shudder, while suggesting various popular bars around the capital. It took a mile to pinpoint my anxiety; this felt like a date. Her flirty tone. The light touches. The invasion of my space, as if she belonged here. In my car. In Lila's seat. With me. This wasn't just a drink, a harmless encore. Izzy was hoping for more.

Hoping *I* was wrong, I drove to Pop's, a hole-in-the-wall on the East Side where I was certain no one—friends, colleagues, patients, a bored reporter—would recognize us. If she was disappointed when we pulled in the parking lot, she didn't let on. We got out of the car and started walking towards the bar, but Izzy grabbed my hand, pulling me back.

"I've missed you." She stood on her tip-toes and kissed me, wrapping her hands around the back of my neck, her tongue a flame. Burning. Smothering. Dangerous.

The fight or flight response kicked in and I staggered backwards. This didn't feel right. It wasn't the fear of exposure. The idiocy of kissing another woman in public. I didn't want to be here. With her. Cheating. It took my body physically recoiling from this beautiful woman to understand that I was a dog chasing its tail, looking for a replacement for Lila when there was none. Why was this so hard to accept? Why did I keep putting myself in precarious positions?

"What's wrong?" she asked, her eyebrows knotted in confusion. "Last time, you couldn't get enough."

That was before. When I thought I was blameless in the breakdown of my marriage. Patient, kind, supportive—a model husband. The husband that tried everything to reignite the spark, accepted every rejection with a silent sigh, cared for the kids while his wife grieved. Back then, I felt ignored and desperate, justified in finding a release elsewhere.

But the story I sold myself wasn't the truth. At least, not the whole truth. Not Lila's truth. And while I disagreed with her actions, or *inaction*, it still mattered—if I wanted to save my marriage.

"I'm trying to work things out with my wife," I said, running a hand over my face.

Seconds passed. A group of people exited the bar, thankfully, not giving us more than a passing glance.

"You said you were going through a rough patch. I thought—" She worked her tongue over her top teeth, giving them a glossy spit finish. "I thought you were leaving."

She agreed to keep this casual, but it was my fault for believing her. For believing that sex could come without a side of complications. For entertaining her crush. "I'm sorry, Izzy."

"You're sorry." She crossed her arms, leveling me with her stare.

What else could I say? Yes, I was an asshole for starting this, but it was one hookup. Did she need a paint-by-numbers explanation? "Can I take you back to your car?"

She flinched, muttering something incomprehensible as she marched to my car. As we drove back to the hospital in silence, I wondered whether she would stay on my rotation or leave, unleash some nasty rumors. I spent the last decade building my reputation and I doubted one woman could torch it.

But I was arrogant to risk it. Arrogant to think I could get away with it. To not foresee this outcome. And for what? A blow job? After all my hard work, to have even the hint of something unsavory following me— regret made me furious. At myself. Lila. Izzy. God for taking away Milo, sending us down this treacherous path.

I pulled next to the parking garage. "I never should've involved you in this."

"I really liked you, you know?" She sighed and opened the door. "It's disappointing to find out who you really are."

"I agree," I whispered to the empty car.

I leaned back, trying to breathe through the lingering scent of Izzy's perfume, trying to forget all the ways she could complicate my life, but my blood pressure continued to rise.

All the times I tried to console Lila, draw out her feelings, tempt her, had been in vain. Grief hadn't rendered her asexual. No. She made a choice. A choice to refuse me. To stay silent. Deceive me. She stockpiled her anger, watching as the distance between us grew, as her choices pushed us to the brink. Where was the virtue in hiding your feelings? In playing the victim?

She villainized me, all because she couldn't accept that it wasn't safe for her to have another child. And now she wanted me to reverse the vasectomy? Ignore years of medical training and instinct? Forgive her silence as easily as a harsh word?

Months! Months, we wasted. Vows broken. Trust tarnished. All unnecessarily. Christ, sometimes it felt like she welcomed misery into our lives. Gave it a homecoming parade.

I looked in the rearview mirror, taking in my dark stubble, rigid jaw, and bloodshot eyes. I looked fierce, ready for a fight. And I realized that's exactly what I needed. To stop being Mr. Nice Guy. Let my anger boil over. Listen to her half-baked arguments and pulverize them one by one. Get everything out in the open, until we were both raw and spent, until we had no option left but to start from scratch.

CHAPTER TWENTY-ONE
LILA

I sat on the couch, snuggled beneath a blanket, shrouded in darkness except for the moonlight peering through the second story windows. Waiting for Alex to come home. I felt calm until I heard the garage door open. The back door shut. Now, my heart jumped into my throat, making it difficult to breathe.

"I want to forgive you," I whispered as he walked past me.

"Jesus!" Alex stopped up short, clutching his chest. "You scared me." He flipped on a lamp, his loosened Spiderman tie dangling from his neck like a noose.

"I want to forgive you," I said again.

He collapsed on the couch and rubbed his eyes, a warning that he was too tired for this conversation. "But you can't."

I spent all night summoning my courage, reciting my words. I couldn't chicken out now. "You once told me that you felt like you were born to be a doctor, that you couldn't imagine doing anything else. That's how I feel about being a mom—"

"You are a mom."

"Can you listen? Please?"

Alex's jaw twitched. "Sure."

I forgot my words, thrown off track by his interruption, the impatience of his tone. "The moment you handed me Levi, I felt—" I shook my head. "—euphoric. I burst into tears. Remember? And then Charlotte came, and it felt like doing heroin. Or so I imagine." My nervous laughter abruptly stopped when I took in his humorless face. "But I wasn't done. I'd hold her each night, dreaming about giving her a little brother or sister, dreaming about the big family we always wanted."

His face softened. "Lila..."

"It feels like there's this gaping hole in my heart. This pocket of love waiting for another child. This empty space in our house. But you won't let me fill it and I'm, just, suffocating. Like I can't get enough oxygen, or my blood's not pumping correctly, or..."

"You're depressed, babe." He rubbed my leg, giving me a smile that was caring or condescending—depending on your perspective. "You need to talk to someone, go on a short-term anti-depressant. First Milo, and then the vasectomy. I get it, now. It was too much for you to handle."

I jerked my leg away. "You're unbelievable. You'd rather medicate me, hope that magically works, than take responsibility for what you did." I wasn't going to be like my mom, popping pills to smooth out the edges. I thought he understood my stance on this. Then again, I thought he understood my stance on having more children.

"I need a drink," he said, retreating to the kitchen. He grabbed a beer from the fridge. Next stop: the medicine cabinet for ibuprofen. A moment later, he returned, standing over me. "Please. Continue."

"The Alex I married listened to what I wanted, took my happiness into consideration when making decisions. And yet you did this deliberately, knowing it would hurt me, knowing I would never agree. That's not love."

He tossed the pills in his mouth, grinding them between his molars. "I listened to you Lila. And then I did what was best. For you. For our family. That's the definition of love."

Over the past sixteen years, Alex and I discussed every major decision—leaving Chicago, buying this house, raising the children Catholic—but he had the final word. I trusted him. Alex wouldn't buy a new TV without ensuring I was onboard, but had no problem unilaterally deciding we were done having children. What changed? Why did my opinion, my happiness, no longer matter? "You went behind my back, broke the trust between us."

"You can't trust me?" He laughed, a deep belt that echoed off the ceiling. "I told you I wanted a vasectomy. That it wasn't safe for us to try. That I couldn't go through another—"

121

I nearly jumped off the couch. "*You* couldn't go through another miscarriage?"

"Yeah, me, Lila. I'm in this too. For the past year, you've acted more like my roommate than my wife." He started pacing. "But did I cheat on you? Nope. I talked to you, asked what I could do, time and again. But instead of telling me what was wrong, giving us a chance to fix it, you stayed silent, let me think you were grieving." He drained his beer, pointing the empty bottle at me. "You used our dead son as an excuse not to have sex."

He made it sound diabolical. I didn't want to have sex. I couldn't even *think* about sex. Sex reminded me of babies. Babies which we could no longer have. How dare he twist this, act like I betrayed him. He betrayed me. "You're not listening!"

"And you're not listening to me," he shouted. "What is it you want me to hear? You're sad. You're angry. You want more kids. What about what I want?"

"What you want? Call me crazy, but I thought we *both* wanted another baby." This baby was for all of us. Levi and Charlotte were ecstatic when we told them I was pregnant. Levi jumped on the couch, while Charlotte started whispering rules to my stomach, delighted by having someone to boss around. Alex held me close, both of us intoxicated with joy. Relishing the rare moment when life slows down enough to let you enjoy your dreams coming true. "Why do you get to change the rules? Make decisions that affect both of us?"

"Change the rules? Jesus—" He puffed out his cheeks, then released his breath. "Do you remember what you were like after Milo? There was no reasoning with you. Sleeping all day. Barely eating. Either crying or spaced out. The kids were terrified."

"No." I shook my head, but a memory poked through. I was "resting," my eyelids leaden with sleep, my brain craving oblivion. Every muscle ached, down to the marrow, as if each bone shattered in a car crash. Charlotte tattled on Levi for using his iPad. I ignored her, but she kept pestering me. Whining. Stomping her feet. *Shut up!* I yelled. *I don't give a fuck what you do. But go away!* Her dark eyes widened as she backed away in terror. I felt nothing.

"And what about me?" Alex continued. "I didn't have the luxury of falling apart. Of grieving our son. I was too busy taking care of you. The kids. Working insane hours. You never once asked if I was okay. Do you realize that? My son died—" He turned away, clearing his throat. When he spoke again, his voice was strained. "You acted like he was yours. Like you had a monopoly on grief." He shook his head before walking back to the fridge for another beer.

Could he be right? Milo was a part of me. My flesh and blood. We spent twenty-eight marvelous weeks together. I treasured every minute— even those first sixteen weeks where I puked at three p.m. every day. I felt his kicks. Kept up a running dialogue. Gave in to his salty cravings. Sang him songs. Whispered prayers as we fell asleep.

And I was the reason Milo died. Not Alex. It wasn't Alex's blood that clotted, suffocating Milo. Alex's mind that rationalized waiting to call the doctor. Alex's body that froze. Alex that lied at the hospital, saying it had only been a couple hours since Milo moved. Alex's guilt that kept him captive. Alex's uterus that tripped up time and again when performing a basic biological function. Me. All me.

None of this excused my selfishness. Pain was pain. And I never acknowledged his.

"I'm sorry," I said when he came back. I wished I had the courage to stand up and hold him. But I couldn't make my legs move. What if he rejected me? Stiffened under my touch? A fresh wave of grief took hold. All these months, I felt righteous in my resentments and he had a list of his own. "I should've been there for you."

He took a pull from his beer. "Well, we're even then."

"Even?" One didn't cancel out the other. He acted intentionally, knowing the vasectomy would hurt me. My selfishness was an unfortunate byproduct of a tragedy. "How can I forgive you when you don't understand why you're wrong?"

"You don't want to forgive me. Forgiving me would require you to move on, try to enjoy your life. The kids. Me. No-o-o," he said, lifting both arms in the air, adding gravity to his sarcasm. "Far easier to keep shuffling blame my way. Dump it on Alex. He can handle it. As if I'm not already doing everything to keep this family together."

Am I asking too much? Communication. Trust. Support. These are the pillars of our marriage. At least they had been until the vasectomy, when he went from teammate to dictator. No. I wouldn't back down. "I want you to reverse the vasectomy."

"Lila, please listen to me." He squatted in front of me, holding my hands. Part of me expected his eyes to start swirling black and white, attempt to hypnotize me. "I'm not going to reverse it. Ever."

"Mommy," a voice quivered. Charlotte pressed her head against the slats of the stairs. "Mommy, I'm scared."

Alex stood up. "Come here, baby."

She ran towards us, her Cinderella nightgown billowing around her waist. A perverse sense of pleasure made my heart swell as she crawled on my lap, as if she knew her dad committed mortal sins against this family.

I inhaled the rich aroma of sleep. "What's wrong?"

"I heard you and Daddy," she whispered, her breath hot against my neck. "Fighting."

Alex and I locked eyes, his regret reflecting mine. The kids heard us bicker, but we saved arguments for when they were out of earshot. I thought our midnight conversation was safe.

"You know how you and Audrey argued yesterday about who got to wear your Elsa dress? Well, Mommy and Daddy sometimes argue too," I said.

Alex picked her up. "But we always apologize and stay friends."

They started towards the stairs, Charlotte's head resting against his shoulder, her thumb popped in her mouth. A habit abandoned long ago, but which reappeared when she needed instantaneous comfort.

I convinced myself that Levi and Charlotte were too self-involved to notice the distance between Alex and me. But kids could sniff out pain. It was only in the middle of the night, awakened by our shouting, that Charlotte felt vulnerable enough to seek comfort. I remembered that terror as a child. The walls rattled, as flimsy as cardboard, unable to mask my mother's tears, my father's insults. The stomachache that inevitably followed as I internalized that all was not right in my world.

"You need to let this go," Alex said later, when he joined me in bed. "If you don't want to permanently screw up the kids, if you want to save this marriage."

I lay still for several minutes, refusing to respond, enraged that he put this all on me. That after everything I said, he remained willfully blind to his culpability. That he wouldn't honor me with an apology. That he thought he had nothing to apologize for.

He turned over, slamming his pillow against the bedframe. "Fine, Lila. Don't say a word. Silence worked out well last time."

Eventually, his breath got heavy, giving me another reason to resent him.

Our argument cycled through my brain, his accusations about hurting Levi and Charlotte making sleep impossible. Around three a.m., I realized he was partly right. I needed to figure out how to be happy before I inflicted the scars of my childhood on the kids. The double whammy of Milo and the vasectomy gutted me. I focused more on the babies I lost, the babies I would never have, than my own kids. While I laughed at Levi and Charlotte's silliness, helped with homework, played games, I wasn't present, enjoying their company. I was a robot, phoning in my motherly duties.

I needed to talk to someone. A therapist. I'd resisted for months, certain talking couldn't assuage my pain. But this wasn't just about me anymore. It was about how my pain was hurting those I loved. It was about being a good mother. I couldn't bring Milo back, but I could learn from my mistakes. Put my children first.

Always.

CHAPTER TWENTY-TWO
ALEX

I finished my beer and ordered a second, glancing around O'Malley's on the off chance that I missed Nick or Ben walk through the door. Sitting next to the large front window put me in a prime position to catch the comings and goings, not only in the bar, but the pedestrian traffic on State Street.

Nick and Ben pushed for this meeting, eager to decide which candidates to interview as our new pediatrician. Unlike them, I wasn't willing to hire the first impressive resume. Intelligence, drive, proficiency—that's a given. But with a small practice, we needed the x-factor; someone to earn the trust of the parents, the awe of the kids, and our desire to grab a beer. Yet both were late. Nick made a detour to the hospital and Ben's babysitter was a no-show.

While I usually detested waiting, I was in no hurry to go home. Lila's accusations last night—that she couldn't trust me, that I didn't love her, didn't listen—still burned. Did she really feel that way? Or was she lashing out? How could two smart, logical people look at the same data—five miscarriages, one stillbirth, complications from APS—and come up with drastically different conclusions? I didn't know what to do. Talking to her when she was, frankly, delusional, proved futile, but accepting another bout of silence felt like a step backwards. The arguments of late, while upsetting, proved my Lila was in there. I didn't want her to retreat again.

A knock on the window interrupted my thoughts. Seconds later, Shannon McArthur joined me, saying she couldn't let a neighbor drink alone. She said this while laying a splayed hand against her chest, as if giving her breasts a high five.

"I'm meeting my partners," I said, hoping to dissuade her. "They should be here any minute."

"Perfect! I'm early to meet my girls for a drink. We can keep each other company."

"All right." What could I say? I was trapped, forced to wait for the guys. Next time, I'd avoid the window seat. Madison was too small to go without being recognized for long.

"Seeing you tonight is kismet, I swear..." Shannon gushed, off and running, intent on making this drink count.

Despite living next door to the McArthur's for a decade, I didn't know Shannon well. But I'd witnessed enough birthday parties, fundraisers, and soccer games to know she was quite the force. Shannon enjoyed the best of everything—a Porsche Cayenne, a blowout extension on their kitchen, a post-pregnancy breast augmentation. According to Lila, she got what she wanted, always, rules and decorum be damned. From the way she pressed her knee against my thigh while fluttering her eyelashes like a butterfly, it appeared I was the latest object of desire.

Pissed off as I was at Lila, and as hot as Shannon looked in her curve-hugging black jumpsuit, I wasn't going there. I was done with this open marriage. I convinced myself I had no choice, that Lila's refusal to have sex changed the terms of our marriage. Homing in on sex as the problem prevented me from looking deeper into the reasons behind our estrangement. And why would I? I thought I knew everything. Had already diagnosed her: grief equaled asexuality. Looking back, I'm not sure what was more toxic, my conceitedness or Lila's stubbornness. Together, we made the perfect cocktail for martial disfunction.

Nope. The open marriage was over. Done. Two women. Not many. But two more than Lila agreed when we married. Enough to screw us up permanently if I hadn't hit the brakes.

No way was I about to make it three. I wanted Lila—even as she acted crazy, demanding a vasectomy reversal. No one else compared. The open marriage confirmed as much. When I looked at Shannon, I didn't feel lust. I felt relief. Relief that I wasn't using a stranger for a momentary escape. Relief that I saw past her beauty and knew one night wasn't worth torpedoing my life. Because Shannon would definitely see to ruining me. The queen of gossip would trade my stepping out to the highest bidder while my cock was still wet.

"Where does Brett work again?" I asked, aiming to keep the drink platonic.

"He's still at Willow and Goodrich. The money's amazing. How can I complain, right? But he's always travelling." Shannon twisted her long, blonde hair atop her head, exposing her cleavage. "Two, three weeks a month. It gets lonely."

Jesus. Was everyone having an open marriage? Was it like the key parties of the 70s? Or the martial version of *Fight Club*? The first rule of Open Marriage Club: *You don't talk about Open Marriage Club!*

"Having the kids around must help," I said.

"True..."

"But?"

She licked her lips, whispering, "It's not enough, is it?"

I texted Nick and Ben— *Where are you guys??*—uncomfortable with the way she tapped into my thoughts. She couldn't know. And yet she did. It struck me then that the circumstances of my marriage differed, but the problem was universal. Sexless marriages. Deadly infections of what if. Chronic loneliness. We were all going down. Only those that fought for one another had a chance to survive.

"Life's funny," she said, inching closer, ass cheeks skimming the edge of her seat. "At twenty-five, I thought I married the perfect man. Sexy. Successful. Adventurous. But ten years later, it's watching you play outside with the kids—"

"Hey, Alex."

I turned. "Geneva!" I stood up, squeezing past Shannon to hug Geneva. It was like embracing a mannequin, all hard edges and no reciprocation. "How are you?"

She stepped back. "Fantastic."

Geneva's presence tonight was as unexpected and confusing as her friendship with Lila. Lila had various acquaintances through work, the kids' school, but no one she socialized with. Until Geneva. When I asked Lila about it, she shrugged, saying she needed a friend. Not that

Geneva was much of a friend, letting her get blackout drunk. But if Lila was going to give her a pass, I would do the same.

"Sit down." I grabbed another stool, settling it between Shannon and me, pleased with the turn of events. Not only would Geneva's presence work like a cold shower on Shannon's desire, it would give me a chance to know her. Possibly turn her into an ally. Maybe Geneva could be a whisper of logic in Lila's ear, help her see the past year as a speed bump, instead of a life-altering disaster. Accept that I acted in her best interests. That having only two children was not a crisis, but a blessing in disguise. "Let me buy you a drink. This is our neighbor, Shannon."

Geneva's gaze paused on Shannon, me, our drinks. "I'm not interrupting?"

"We're planning the class Christmas party," Shannon said at the same moment I said, "Absolutely not."

Shannon and I glanced at each other. "You see, I'm the kindergarten room parent..." Shannon started listing her responsibilities, which included planning holiday parties and corralling parent volunteers. Me, allegedly.

"Wow." Geneva smiled, each tooth sparkling like a diamond. She ordered a glass of wine from the bartender before saying, "That must keep you very busy."

"I take it you don't have kids," Shannon said, matching Geneva's condescending tone.

"No." Geneva took off her pea coat, revealing a sleeveless hunter green turtleneck sweater, fitted black pants, and black fuck-me heels. Now I knew who to thank for Lila's new wardrobe. "Nothing knocks you off the career ladder faster than kids."

"Come on," I said. "It doesn't have to be that way."

"Because you're a man." She accepted her wine, taking a healthy drink, all the while staring at me. The thick layer of mascara darkened her almond eyes. "I didn't get my PhD so that I could sit around singing nursery rhymes and teaching night classes at a community college."

I cleared my throat. Was she joking? Did I catch her in a bad mood? "Surely there's a compromise—"

"You would think so," she said. "But no."

"Having kids is the best thing I've done," Shannon said.

"Maybe you'll change your mind," I said. "Statistically, more educated women are waiting until their mid-to-late thirties to have kids."

Geneva rolled her eyes. "Thanks for mansplaining. I was struggling to understand why I didn't want to throw away my career."

I drank my beer, wondering what set her off. When she came over on Sunday, she was friendly. Now, she looked like she wanted to set me on fire and dance on the ashes.

"Where's Lila?" Geneva asked, her tone suspicious, as if I stashed her body in my trunk. "Why wasn't she invited to this...meeting?"

"Home." I glanced at my phone. No messages. Unlike Lila, I'd enjoy a call or text from her when out. Any sign she was thinking about me. That last night decimated her world too. "She's probably in the middle of bedtime hell. Bath, books, bed. Never an easy undertaking."

"Nice of you to help out." Geneva tapped my beer with her wine glass, a mock toast.

"I do my share." I laughed, but Geneva's eyes hardened into two bowling balls. I had one of those likeable, trusting faces. All-American, boy next door. Not model looks, nothing overtly intimidating, but worth a second glance. *Reality star hot*, my sister Angela phrased it. Women lit up when I flashed a smile their way; some men too. Geneva? Not so much. Her vibe remained distant and cool, a fish I couldn't reel in. "Trust me, helping with the kids is one thing she can't complain about."

Geneva leaned forward. "So, what is her big complaint?"

"If she's smart, she wouldn't be complaining," Shannon said, meeting my eyes, her eyebrows rising a quarter-inch higher than her dermatologist ever thought possible.

Geneva smiled. "I'm sure Lila could come up with something, if pressed."

The air was heavy with unshared knowledge. Geneva knew Lila and I had issues; her cagey smile made that clear. But how much did she know? Unless I was being paranoid, Geneva had an agenda. The defiance in her tone suggested she wanted me to own up to something. But I didn't owe Geneva anything. "I overcommit. Too many late nights. Volunteering, sitting on boards—"

"Late nights working. How cliché." Geneva polished off her wine and stood up, nearly tossing the glass on the bar. "Sorry to run, but I'm late. Thanks for the drink."

With a wave, she was gone. I watched Geneva through the window until she disappeared, mystified by our conversation, her abrupt exit.

"I should go too." Screw the guys. They were over an hour late. "Help with bedtime."

Shannon rested her hand on mine. "You don't always have to be perfect, Alex." I recognized the swell of longing and loneliness in her eyes. But I couldn't be that person for her.

I gently pulled away. "Have fun with your girlfriends."

My jaw ached the entire drive home, my teeth reflexively grinding against one another like accordion bellows as I replayed the conversation. It wasn't until I pulled into the driveway that I realized why I was rattled: Lila never brought up the vasectomy, hadn't even hinted it was a factor in her depression, our estrangement, until she starting spending time with Geneva. Could Geneva be baiting Lila? Encouraging her anger? Manipulating her pain?

But why would Geneva insert herself in our marriage? Why would she care? Was I crazy? Clearly, Geneva relished being Lila's confidant. Her eyes said she held a wealth of knowledge about Lila that I couldn't ever hope to regain. Her attitude suggested she had no use for me.

Avoiding Lila, enduring her silent treatment, while waiting for her to agree that a vasectomy reversal was insanity, was no longer a viable plan. If I was right, that Geneva was slowly polluting Lila's brain, time was of the essence.

I took a deep breath, steeling myself. I couldn't walk inside the house, tell Lila that I thought her friend was manipulative bunny-boiler.

Couldn't complain about Geneva at all. That would incense Lila further. I needed to shelf my anger, listen to her, subtly show her all the reasons I was her best friend. Her husband. Her everything.

CHAPTER TWENTY-THREE
GENEVA

Geneva called Lila as soon as she turned the corner from O'Malley's. She had to act now, before she second-guessed herself. Lila may not be able to see it, she was too entrenched in her marriage, but Alex didn't love her. Not the way she deserved to be loved. Not the all-encompassing way Geneva would love her.

Alex knew Lila's history. How her dad cheated on her mom, left them for someone else to pick up like pieces of trash. And yet here he was, chatting up another woman in the window of a bar. On the busiest street in Madison. And to think, Geneva felt guilty for pursuing Lila because she was married. Tried to talk herself out of it countless times. What a waste of energy.

An ambulance sped past Geneva as she walked, sirens blaring, possibly trying to warn her against telling Lila. Literature and history proved that the messenger was sacrificed when delivering unpleasant news. But who else would tell Lila the truth? Certainly not Alex. Not her scheming neighbor. Geneva could accept her fate if Lila said she wasn't interested. But she couldn't suffer watching Lila bury her feelings for Geneva in defense of a marriage built on lies. If cheating truly was the hiccup preventing Lila from being with Geneva, then this information might persuade her to give Geneva a chance. After all, why should Lila remain faithful, but miserable, when Alex was steppin' out? And if Lila still didn't want to be together? Geneva could take comfort in being a good friend. That was how she knew she was falling in love with Lila; she wanted Lila to be happy.

"Hey," Lila said, answering her phone.

"Listen, something happened tonight." They reached the level of friendship where they could pick up any conversation as if the last one never ended. "It might be something, it might be nothing. And I didn't know whether to call you—"

"I'm glad you called. What happened?"

"I was on my way to the Forum when I saw Alex in the window of O'Malley's," Geneva said.

"Small world."

"Small town."

"Yeah, he's meeting his partners—"

"He's with your neighbor, Shannon." Geneva paused, hating that, in the short run, she was making Lila's life worse. "They looked cozy."

"Cozy?" Something in Lila's tone reminded Geneva of Cristina. The sweetness? The naivety? The hope? *Stop thinking about Cristina! Cristina isn't Lila. Cristina is gone!* She had no place in Geneva's mind—a place Geneva evicted her from years ago—or her life.

"They weren't kissing, but I caught a mood." Geneva heard how flimsy it sounded. Except, except...she knew something was going on. She saw Alex for what he was. A smooth talker. A cheater. A man with the flexible morals of a politician. It disgusted her that he wore a Wonder Woman tie tonight. As if he was a feminist. "I'd want to know if I was you."

"Did you talk to him?"

Geneva ducked her head, shielding her face from the biting wind. "Yeah. They said they were planning the class Christmas party."

"Unbelievable," Lila muttered. "He broke the rules."

"What rules?"

"I have to go." Lila cut the call.

"Ahh!" Why was she so impulsive? Geneva earned a Ph.D., defended her dissertation to a roomful of white men looking to discredit her, commanded the attention of distracted college students on the daily. And yet, whenever she felt the slightest bit vulnerable in her relationships, she acted like Trump on Twitter, all emotion, no forethought.

She should've waited until she saw Lila. But she worried that if Alex got there first, he would spin some innocent story that Lila would have blindly accepted. Even with the warning, he'd probably end up gaslighting Lila, convince her that she's insecure and paranoid, the classic jealous wife.

Disappointment weighed down Geneva's limbs like lead. She had hoped Lila would want to talk. Open up, finally, about her marriage. Invest emotionally, if not physically, in their relationship. But Lila cut her off before Geneva could ask if she was okay.

Should I have called? Geneva asked her phone, as if it was a magic eight ball. *Outlook not so good.*

CHAPTER TWENTY-FOUR
LILA

The night after my fight with Alex, I called a therapist. In the span of a week, it became an addiction. Food for my malnourished soul. The release to get me through each day.

During my first session with Hannah, I felt weighed down, like my feelings were bricks, dozens of which were piled on my back. Once I started talking, I felt the bricks being lifted, one by one. I left lighter, making an appointment for the next day. And the next. Staying silent for nearly a year, bottling up my emotions, repressing my memories, left me with a lot to say. I met with Hannah each day around lunch, five sessions so far where we probed my memories, dissected my marriage, scrutinized this need I felt for a third child.

But today, Hannah's only open slot was at 7 p.m. I took it, needing my fix. Problem was, I wasn't ready to tell Alex I was seeing a therapist. Correction: I wasn't ready to give Alex the satisfaction of being right. I'd been paying out of pocket for the sessions to prevent him from seeing an EOB.

He was full of questions when I left the house tonight. *Where are you going? Who are you meeting? When will you be home?* I made up answers. *A bar. Geneva. Don't wait up.* Lying was a soft rebellion. He betrayed me and now I would do the same in return. But only because it was in our best interests. Childish? Yes. Vindictive? Probably. Necessary? Absolutely.

And why shouldn't I lie? I thought, as I drove to my appointment. Alex wasn't telling me the whole truth. Last Thursday, Geneva called after seeing Alex and Shannon getting cozy at a bar. Fifteen minutes later, Alex stood in the kitchen fixing a sandwich, the picture of nonchalance, as he told me how Geneva and Shannon crashed his meeting. I listened, studied his face for deception, but realized I didn't know his tell. Or maybe he wasn't lying. Maybe Geneva had it wrong. With his loosened tie, hint of stubble, and easy smile, he looked like my Alex. Not the man I had a knock-down, drag-out fight with the night before. But isn't that what he would do if he was sleeping with Shannon—tell enough of the truth to avoid questions? I didn't know what to think, who to trust, but given Alex's behavior, I wasn't keen to give him the benefit of the doubt.

"Let's talk about gratitude," Hannah said after I unleashed my frustrations with Alex. The infuriating way he acted friendly and affectionate, as if the vasectomy reversal was a phase he was waiting for me to outgrow. The unspoken assumption that *I*, alone, was the problem in our marriage.

"Gratitude." My lips vibrated as I suppressed a yawn. I had the nightmare again last night. Where I know something is wrong with the baby and rush to the hospital. I hear Milo's cries, a soft mewing, beckoning me forward. But as I peer over the bassinet, I wake up. Reality claps back. Milo is dead. Because of me.

"Don't dismiss it so quickly."

Therapy won't work unless you believe it can work, Hannah said at our first session. *Think of it like bungee jumping. The vulnerability you feel as you jump off the platform is akin to the leap you must take in therapy. It's terrifying, but there's freedom in it. An escape route from the negative thoughts and behaviors that led you here.*

Nothing else worked. Time. Avoidance. Barreling through. I drew further away from the people I loved.

"I'm listening." I sat up straight. We were sitting on meditation cushions, our legs crisscrossed like pretzels, knees nearly touching. Sitting on the ground, according to Hannah, helped people focus. Apparently, chairs made people emotionally lazy.

"Try and recognize the small acts of kindness in your world. Reasons to say thanks. Too often we get stuck in a rut and can only see the unfairness. The cruelty. The betrayals." She emphasized the last word.

"I'm struggling to see the connection," I said.

"What made you smile today?" She pulled a pen from her ponytail. Her hair was an icy blond with pink highlights swirled in. Charlotte's dream hair.

"Geneva." The answer popped out, unbidden. We covered nearly everything—Milo, the vasectomy, our estrangement, the open marriage, the kids—and yet, I hesitated here. Should I tell Hannah the truth? How Geneva's hugs felt like inhaling a batch of chocolate chip cookies, all warmth and comfort. The way she leaned in when I spoke, not wanting to miss a word. Her unmitigated desire for me. No. Hannah had enough of my problems to solve. Maybe once we made some headway, but for now, I'd apply a broad brush to the details. "She's my friend."

"I'm confused," Hannah said, scribbling on her notepad. "You say you want to forgive Alex, work on your marriage, be an active participant in your kids' lives, and yet your first thought is a friend."

The drone of the space heater filled the silence. Hannah felt more like a personal trainer than a therapist with the way she drilled into my answers. Not letting a word or emotion pass without demanding more. Instead of shutting down, I wanted to rise to the challenge. I felt angry. Unsettled. Alex issued the wakeup call the moment he asked for the open marriage, but I was finally ready to answer it. Become me again. A better me. One that stood up for herself. Set an example as a strong woman for her kids.

Just as soon as I figured out how. "Geneva saved me. I was sleepwalking through life when we met," I said, thinking back on the past year. Other than a few geographical locations—home, work, carpooling the kids—I had no concrete memory of how I spent the time. It felt like an impressionist painting, where a few details are highlighted, but the rest is a muted blur. "Being around her energy, her...joy reminded me of who I used to be. Because I used to be happy. Grateful—I promise, I'm not trying to be ironic. But I can't get there. It's like I replaced the nothingness with anger."

"What are you going to do?"

"What can I do? I tried talking to Alex, begged him to reverse it, give us a chance." Heat rose in my cheeks. A week passed since our fight, but his stubbornness still enraged me. Why wouldn't he try it my way? "He doesn't care."

"I asked about you. What are *you* going to do to change your circumstances? To find happiness?"

Happiness. It wasn't coming from Alex. Spending time with Shannon was further evidence that Alex did what he wanted, with whomever he wanted, regardless of how I felt. Could I do the same? Was I capable of cheating? Finding fulfillment elsewhere?

I felt drawn to Geneva. An inexplicable connection that grew each time we hung out. A kiss which sparked my curiosity. But while kissing was fun, sex tugged at the strings of my soul, required me to expose myself, my most vulnerable self.

Don't overthink it, Geneva said. Easy for her to say. She wasn't married. She didn't understand the invisible ties and binds that kept me committed even as Alex strayed. I swore I would never end up like my parents. Cheating. Leaving. Putting the kids last.

And yet here I was, contemplating that very act. Maybe Geneva would provide a pleasant diversion from Alex, a teaspoon of happiness, so that I could come home to the kids with renewed energy. Was that crazy? Or was I trying to justify my behavior? Maybe every cheater selfishly concluded that happy self meant happy children.

"I don't want to be sad." I heard Milo's breath, soft and insistent, in my ear. There one second and gone the next. "Always wanting something I can't have."

"Then stop," Hannah said. "It's a choice. Choose to be grateful."

I sliced my nails into my palms. "Grateful that he lied? That he destroyed our only chance of having another baby?"

"Start smaller," she said softly. "Find moments to be grateful. A smile from your kids. The feel of their tiny palm in your hand. Their excitement at discovering something new. Breathe in that moment." She inhaled, a serene smile coming across her face. "If we can shift your mindset to one of gratefulness, you'll be surprised what you can accept."

"I want to believe it could be that easy."

"Oh, it won't be easy." She laughed. "Retraining your brain might be one of the hardest things you've ever done. But, tell me, what's the alternative?"

"You're right." I shuffled on my coat, refusing to consider the alternative. *Divorce isn't an option,* I said when Alex proposed. *If you're serious, this is forever.* He agreed, probably never considering we'd deteriorate to this point. Speaking to each other with the politeness of telemarketers in front of the kids and arguing like Fox news correspondents once they were in bed. How long would he endure this turmoil? Did he remember his promise? Or would that one fall by the wayside, too?

"Go to bed tonight and ask, 'What made me smile today?'" Hannah said as I reached the door. "Wake up tomorrow and say, 'Today will be a good day.' Reframe. Your. Perspective."

I ran outside, dodging fat raindrops. Inside the car, I blasted the heat, holding my fingertips up to the vent.

What made me smile today?

I drove towards the Capital. Fingers of lightning crept across the sky, keeping me on edge. Five minutes later, Geneva buzzed me into her apartment. I rode the elevator, my heart campaigning to leave my chest.

Geneva opened her door wearing a fitted black tank-top, purple joggers, a florescent pink headwrap, and no makeup. Seeing her dressed casual sent me spiraling down a rabbit hole. One that ejected me to freshmen year of college, studying with the girls on my floor, all of us in pajamas, munching on popcorn. It was a magical two months, before the rape, before my friends shunned me, when I felt the luster of my life beginning.

Standing before Geneva, I felt like that vulnerable girl again. Could I trust her? Why would I risk what little hope I had left to fix my marriage?

Because I deserve to be happy.

"Someone asked me today what made me smile," I said, wiping strands of wet hair off my face. "And I thought of you."

Geneva reached out, her thumb brushing my lower lip. I closed my eyes, willing my body not to shake, my brain not to think of Alex. The vows we made. The vows I never thought I'd break. I let my instincts take over. I jumped.

CHAPTER TWENTY-FIVE
ALEX

I ran faster, my feet landing in puddles, spraying dirty water against my legs. The drizzle of rain when I left the house switched to an icy downpour, seeping through my climate-control clothing and needling my bones. Two days ago, it snowed, next week was Thanksgiving, and yet tonight, we had a thunderstorm. Wisconsin weather was as messed up as my marriage.

A late-night run wasn't the best idea. But when Lila told me she had plans with Geneva, I called a babysitter. I had to get out. Move. Release this awful energy inside of me that wanted to shake Lila, scream at her to wake up. Let go of the past. Forget the vasectomy already. Wouldn't that be nice? If this was an awful dream? But no. Nothing so simple could explain Lila's sudden stubborn streak. Her inability to see reason. Her unwillingness to forgive and forget.

Geneva. *Again.* It baffled me that they spent this much time together. That Lila would prefer to talk to Geneva than me. What once provided hope that Lila was emerging from her depressive state, reengaging with the world, now felt ominous. I didn't trust Geneva. I could picture Geneva giving Lila's hand a sympathetic squeeze, aghast at my unreasonableness, fueling Lila's anger with every sigh and eyeroll. But what did Geneva know? Nothing. She wasn't there in the days and weeks after Milo. The miscarriages. A decade of false starts, broken hearts, and exquisite joy.

"Alex." Someone called my name, distant and low, as if stuck inside a well. I spun around, recognizing Shannon in her Porsche Cayenne. "Get in! It's not safe."

"I'm almost home."

"I'm not leaving you here."

I flung open the passenger door. A stream of horizontal rain sprayed the seat. The cold air combined with my sweat to fog up the windshield. That's all I needed: to be caught with Shannon, parked in a steamy car, a mile from our houses. Lila would love hearing about that.

"I've been thinking about you," Shannon said, keeping the car in park. "It's been a long time since someone listened to me. Since someone was interested in what I had to say."

Her usual bravado was gone. Water ran down her face, smudging her eyeliner and making raccoon eyes. She looked strung out, somewhere between vulnerable and defeated. Or maybe it was the intimacy of the car, the privacy afforded by the darkness, the rain that set the mood for a confession, the unnerving blasts of thunder. Whatever the reason, a different Shannon sat before me.

"I'm just new, Shannon. That rush of dopamine feels exciting, but I'm not the answer."

A car passed, its headlights temporarily blinding us, making it impossible to know whether we were spotted.

"If you're worried about Brett, he won't care. I could fuck the mailman and he wouldn't notice." She laughed. "Or the neighbor."

"But you want him to notice." Beautiful women like Shannon lived for drama. They were fed a steady diet from birth: intense highs and exaggerated lows. The last thing I wanted was to accept a role in her current production of "The Lonely Housewife."

"It's not about him," she yelled, making herself heard over a ripple of thunder. "It's about me. What I want. I'd divorce him tomorrow if it wasn't for the kids."

A cramp sliced through my stomach. Her words bore too close of a resemblance to the way I feared Lila felt. Rejected. Irrelevant. And ultimately, angry. Shannon offered a glimpse into our future, one where Lila might give up on us, seek out someone new. Someone that listened, made her feel special. I couldn't let us get to that point.

"You should talk to him," I said.

She leaned across the gear shift, her nose nearly touching mine. The car felt like a coffin. Stifling. Claustrophobic. "I'd rather talk to you."

"I'm married. And so are you."

She smiled. "I don't think either of us are happy."

I turned away from her, grabbing the door handle. "I need to get home."

Shannon stomped on the gas, causing my neck to snap back. Rain assaulted the windshield like machine gun fire, steady and relentless. Just when I thought she was going to plow through my yard, deliver me to the front porch, she hit the brake, skidding up to a sideways stop. "Sometimes it feels good to do something reckless."

I wasn't up for innuendos. Or crazy women. "Talk to Brett. He might surprise you."

With that, I ran inside, paid the babysitter, and reveled in a long, warm shower. After, I grabbed a beer, flipped on the TV, and waited for Lila. Our conversations operated like a merry-go-round. Hop on, hop off. It never changed. I wanted this one to be different.

But exhaustion prevailed and I soon fell asleep, wondering, idly, what hold Geneva had on Lila to keep her out this late.

CHAPTER TWENTY-SIX
GENEVA

Geneva lay in bed on her stomach, next to Lila, unable to keep the grin off her face. The back of Lila's hand covered her eyes, as if she had a migraine, but Geneva knew the ruby red flush on her pale cheeks was due to pleasure. Lila's body trembled from the first moment Geneva touched her. She kept her eyes squeezed shut, her body a tightly coiled rope that Geneva used her lips to unwind, until Lila was as soft as putty. Now, Lila's body twitched, not quite wanting to let the experience go.

"That was...wow," Lila said, her thoughts disjointed, her voice groggy, as if emerging from a dream. "I forgot how good it feels."

"You forgot?"

Lila pulled the sheet up to her neck, covering herself. "It's been awhile."

"You've been denying Alex because of Shannon?" A wave of pleasure spread through Geneva's body—one almost as potent as her orgasm—as she imagined Lila rebuffing Alex's advances. She spent the last week debating whether she should've stayed silent about Alex. But tonight was proof she made the right choice.

"No...longer than that." Lila sat up, using her fingers to detangle the snarls in her rain-dampened hair. "It's compli—"

"Complicated," Geneva said, realizing, too late, that her pain at being excluded made her snap. "I need water."

She put on her silk robe and walked to the kitchen where she filled a glass with water, draining it. She rested her hands against the sink, breathing hard. What did Geneva have to do to get Lila to open up? How much more of herself could she give?

A memory, unbidden, flashed in Geneva's mind of the first time she had sex with Cristina. Cristina using her body to coax a vow of silence, making Geneva promise that their relationship never left the room.

The pit that formed in Geneva's stomach when she agreed, as if she polished off a bucket of greasy movie theatre popcorn.

She felt that same clawing sensation now. Lila wasn't asking for a vow of silence, but the sentiment was the same: *I'll only share parts of my life with you. Take it or leave it.*

Lila appeared in the kitchen fully clothed, clutching her purse to her side like she was afraid of pick pocketers. Geneva scraped invisible crumbs off the granite counter with her nail, her heart thudding inside her chest. She refused to roll over like she had with Cristina, accept scraps of love. Wasn't she worth more? If Lila wanted to be with Geneva, she had to trust her. Having sex was a nice first step, but not enough.

"I don't know how this is supposed to work," Lila said.

Geneva pushed a glass of water towards Lila, relieved she wasn't leaving. The glass slid across the granite like a cue ball gliding across a pool table. Lila caught it before it tumbled over the edge. "You have to talk."

Lila set her purse on the island. She twirled the glass in her hands, neither drinking nor talking. "I always wanted a big family," Lila eventually said. "Three, maybe four kids. A house filled with noise; parties, games, dinners. My house was always quiet, as if we were sitting Shiva, waiting for my dad to return."

Geneva knew all about a quiet home. Unlike Lila, she grew to enjoy it. She craved the energy of the city, loved being part of the action, but kept her home a peaceful oasis.

"The first time I got pregnant, I felt euphoric. Alive; like I was at the starting line of my life." Lila sipped her water. "We lost that baby at nine weeks. The next one made it to eleven."

"That's horrible," Geneva said.

"We moved here, and then, finally, Levi. He was perfect. I convinced myself it was the fresh air, new house, lack of commute." She sighed. "Two more miscarriages followed."

"I don't understand." Geneva grabbed a bottle of tequila and a couple sifters, but Lila declined the offer. When in doubt, drink, was

Geneva's motto. And she was in doubt now. Her friends hadn't reached the baby stage yet. "Why did you keep miscarrying?"

"The three B's. Bad egg. Bad timing. Bad luck. If I hear that one more time, I'll snap. *Bad luck.* As if my babies dying are on par with the Packers missing the playoffs."

"But then you had Charlotte. One of each." Geneva wanted to remind Lila that this story ended happily. "It's perfect."

"It happened twice more. Last October—" Lila stared at her hands, opening and closing her fists. "He was twenty-eight weeks. My Milo."

Geneva's feet stayed rooted to the floor. The anguish in Lila's twisted mouth, the raw, haunted pain in Lila's eyes rendered her immobile. Geneva recognized that look, so familiar, it might have been her own reflection.

"I'd do yoga every morning. Sit in lotus pose with my hands on my belly, feeling him kick. But not that morning," she whispered. "I thought about calling the doctor, telling Alex, but I knew what they'd say: eat something with sugar. Lay down. Wait an hour. Babies sleep. So, I waited. Kept giving it more time...but he didn't move. Milo suffocated." She bit the knuckle of her middle finger, nearly drawing blood before Geneva pulled her hand away. "Because of me. Because I waited."

Geneva held Lila's hand, trying not to shake. *This isn't your tragedy,* Geneva reminded herself. *Don't make this about Cristina.* And yet, she couldn't ignore the cacophony of alarms that sounded within her body: the arctic blast in her veins; the ringing in her ears; the numbness in her fingers. Her brain screamed at her to walk away, find someone that wouldn't push against her boundaries. Force her to be vulnerable. Confront the horrific cohabitation of love and death.

"I know how easy it is to blame yourself," Geneva said.

Lila pulled her hand away, holding it in front of her face as if blocking a blow. "Don't do that. Don't pretend you understand."

Geneva drained her tequila, enjoying the distance it put between herself and her memories. As if they belonged to someone else. "My girlfriend died." Geneva never said those words out loud before. But with Lila, it felt right. They both unwittingly belonged to the same club. The bereaved. The left-behind. "I've spent years replaying our last moments together, wondering if I could've saved her..."

"What happened?"

"It was an accident. She—" Geneva throat swelled. Turns out, thirteen years wasn't long enough. Trauma didn't give a fuck about time.

Lila walked around the island and rested her head against Geneva's shoulder. "You don't have to talk about it. Words feel...flimsy. Inadequate."

True. But if someone had sat Geneva down afterwards, explained she wasn't at fault, let her talk through her guilt, hugged her, she wouldn't be here now. Emotionally stunted, afraid of love.

"If you need someone, I'm here," Geneva said, turning to face Lila. "But don't, don't blame yourself. You'll drown in those thoughts."

"Too late." The hollowness in Lila's voice betrayed the truth of her words. "Sometimes I can hear him, gasping for oxygen."

"He didn't feel a thing." Geneva felt like a newscaster, reading from the teleprompter, all faux sympathy without any connection to the event. Anger was easier. "And what was Alex doing? While you lay around blaming yourself?"

"Getting a vasectomy." Lila's eyes narrowed. "Without telling me."

That, Geneva had not expected. "Why?"

"Alex makes every decision based on science, data, logic. Feelings don't factor. Love, apparently, doesn't factor. I have—" She hesitated. "I have a condition, APS, which makes a healthy pregnancy *more* difficult, not impossible, but all he sees is the worst-case scenario." She ran her hand down her face, her voice losing its edge. "The vasectomy felt like a death. All over again. It wasn't just my dream of another baby that Alex stole, it was our marriage. The trust I had in him. First, I lost Milo. And then I lost Alex. I couldn't take it. I shut down."

Geneva wished she had magic words for Lila. She understood the agony of betrayal. Of having someone you love, you trust, make a life-altering decision without you. Not finding you strong enough or important enough to talk to beforehand.

What she couldn't understand was why Lila stayed with him. Betrayal was part of Alex's makeup. As Maya Angelou said, *When someone shows you who they are, believe them the first time.* "You deserve better than someone who lies to you. Cheats on you," Geneva said. "If it was me, I'd have left the day he did it."

Lila stepped away from Geneva, her jaw clamped shut, her eyes hard. "I'm not you. You think monogamy's a joke. You run at the first sign of trouble."

"I didn't mean—"

"But I've invested fourteen years building this marriage. Creating a home for my children. And I'm not going to blow it up because Alex lied. I've been that child, abandoned and scared, and I won't do that to them." Lila grabbed her purse and walked out.

"Wait." Geneva chased after Lila, her breath shallow. She didn't want the night Lila took a leap of faith, both physically and emotionally, to be remembered as their first fight. A thought that should've crossed Geneva's mind before she opened her mouth.

She caught up with Lila at the elevator.

"He's allowed to cheat. Or not cheat exactly. It's complicated." Lila held her breath until her cheeks puffed out, a dragon ready to unleash a wall of fire. "We have an open marriage. A consequence of refusing to sleep with him since the vasectomy. So, let it go, okay?"

The elevator pinged and Lila stepped inside. Geneva watched the doors close, inhaling the scent of Chinese food from a nearby apartment, trying to identify why she felt like someone punched her in the gut.

CHAPTER TWENTY-SEVEN
LILA

Fifteen minutes after leaving Geneva's apartment, I stepped inside my house. The lights were on, the TV played ESPN at a low volume, and Alex was asleep on the couch. I drove home in a panic, white-knuckling the steering wheel, delusional enough to think that once I got here, everything would be okay. That I could leave my feelings, along with my actions, back at Geneva's apartment.

Watching Alex sleep, looking adorably vulnerable with one hand tucked under his chin, emotionally whiplashed me, the guilt so heavy, it took my breath away. I grabbed a blanket from behind the couch, draping it over him. His eyes opened, a lazy smile coming across his face. His joy at seeing me? Another guilt lashing.

He rubbed his eyes. "What time is it?"

"A little after midnight." I wanted to curl up next to him on the couch. Have him hold me. Reassure me that we would get through this. Instead, I knelt on the carpet and began stacking books in the bookshelf, a chore Charlotte was supposed to do before bed. Tonight, I wasn't annoyed by the mess. Anything to keep my hands and mind occupied.

"Why so late?" he asked. "Where'd you guys go?"

I took a deep breath, while the scarlet A on my chest pulsated, dripping fresh blood. "Her apartment. We got to talking—"

"Where does she live?"

"Above the Knickerbocker," I said, relieved he accepted such a simplistic explanation for the last five hours. Had I sat in Hannah's office tonight, discussing gratitude? That felt like days ago, a different person. A *better* person.

"Did you have fun?"

I dropped the book I was holding. Did he suspect? He seemed interested. Too interested? "It was okay." I pulled my hair into a bun, worrying, too late, that he might wonder why my normally straight locks looked mussed. I wanted to shower, but that too would raise suspicion.

"Come on." He crawled behind me, resting his chin in the crook of my neck. "It's been a long day. Let's go to bed."

Earlier tonight, his affection annoyed me. A pathetic attempt to gloss over our problems. But now, the way his scruff tickled my neck sent an electrical zap to my groin. After months of starving myself of pleasure, my body was alive, my hormones feasting on contact.

"You know I can't sleep if there's a mess." I felt sick with longing for him. Sick with myself for opening Pandora's box.

Alex grunted a laugh, planted a kiss on my cheek, and went to bed.

After the books, I folded the laundry, wiped the counters, and packed the kids' lunches. Still. *Still.* My mind raced. I rested my head against the island, inhaling the grapefruit cleanser, and let myself remember.

Geneva's hands exploring the topography of my body like it was a buried treasure, revered both for its beauty and elusiveness. Her lips. Magician's lips. No hesitation. No fumbling. Searching. She knew what to do. My God, she knew. Maybe it was the benefit of being with a woman, or specifically Geneva who, as she said, spent her twenties exploring her sexuality. Or because I hadn't had sex in a year. Whatever the reason, my orgasm came in such a powerful, deep rush that the rest of my body stopped functioning. My mind emptied. My sight? Gone. Hearing? White noise. A fugacious nirvana.

And then I snapped at her, stormed out like a teenager, too headstrong to see that her question about leaving Alex wasn't criticism, but rather concern. Everything about tonight—having sex, listening about Milo, opening up about the death of her ex—suggested she cared.

I walked downstairs, holing up inside the bathroom and locking the door—the furthest I could get from Alex without leaving the house. As I called Geneva, I turned away from the mirror, disgusted that I looked outside my marriage, outside of myself, for happiness.

"I'm sorry," I blurted when she answered. "I shouldn't have walked out. You were trying to help, I just..." I stopped to catch my breath. Too many thoughts courted my brain. Too many emotions plagued my heart.

"Why didn't you tell me you had an open marriage?" Geneva asked.

"As far as I was concerned, *I* didn't have an open marriage." I lowered the lid of the toilet seat and sat down. "Alex does. It's something he needs. Not me. But then you came along..."

"And you fell for me." I could hear her smile. My body flushed, remembering her tongue stroking me, while my mind tumbled down another well of regret. But can you truly regret something you enjoyed? I regretted hurting Alex, complicating my life, but, when I was in Geneva's bed, regret wasn't on the menu. "Are you going to tell him about us?"

"No!" I slapped my hand over my mouth, remembering that this was a clandestine call.

Geneva sighed. "If it's an open marriage, what's the big deal?"

It wasn't that simple. We had an open marriage, but we never talked about it. It was the elephant in the room. Bigger than that, even. Back when he introduced the idea, I was so numb, I probably would've agreed to running a prostitution ring out of our house. The thought of Alex cheating pierced my heart, but the nerve endings dulled to make it feel like a paper cut. I covered my ears and eyes—I could no more listen to him discuss sleeping with another woman than I could watch someone abuse my child. Knowledge had the power to destroy. But, as I was learning from Hannah, so does silence.

"It would hurt him," I said.

"And? Lila, he's fucking your neighbor." Her voice was soft, but the words pierced. "It's a little late to worry about hurt feelings."

I gripped the phone. Yes, our marriage was convoluted and messy. Alex's betrayal changed the landscape, changed me. Instead of enjoying each other, we hurled insults like bowling balls, aiming for a strike each time. But, as Hannah pointed out, every marriage had ups and downs.

This fractured state wasn't forever. At least, I didn't want it to be. I wanted an apology. For him to listen. Put our family first.

"This is happening too fast," I sputtered, officially freaking out. Why did I go to her apartment tonight? Why did I think I was capable of such duplicity?

Tomorrow. I'd tell Hannah everything. I had no choice now that I had sex with Geneva. Hannah needed the full picture to help— assuming I could be helped. She, rightly, might be frustrated that I took her happiness edict as an excuse to cheat. Might accuse me of self-sabotaging. But I hoped she'd have some insight that would untangle this mess. Clear my path forward.

"Telling him would make things easier for us," Geneva said. "Relieve your guilt, too."

There was no "us." This was a temporary blip, an insane spell Alex cast on our lives. This had to stop. With that thought, I nearly laughed. I was a cliché. The woman who promised to end the affair while inwardly knowing she didn't have the strength to do so. "I need to go to bed, but I wanted to apologize to you first."

"I wish I didn't have to wait until Saturday to see you," Geneva said.

"Saturday?"

"Yeah, Charlotte's party. Any gift ideas?"

"Oh, you don't have to get her anything." I dug my thumbnail into my thigh as I thought about Geneva and Alex in the same room. But how could I say no? Especially when I talked about the party all week?

"Lucky for Charlotte, I'm an excellent shopper."

Soon after, we said goodbye. I hung my head between my legs, reminding myself to breathe. I'd be busy hosting thirty guests. If I kept my wits about me, everyone, including Alex, would assume she was my friend. Nothing more.

Problem was, I sincerely doubted my ability to keep calm.

CHAPTER TWENTY-EIGHT
ALEX

Cardboard snowflakes hung from the basement ceiling, threatening to poke out an eye as I tried to escape twelve five-year old girls dressed in princess gowns and tiaras. Not an easy task. They jumped off furniture like ninjas, chasing us dads, turning us into stumbling fools. I rounded a corner—the basement was set up like two adjoining T's—only to have Charlotte, the birthday girl, raise her hands, pretending to freeze me.

I closed my eyes, trying to dull the pounding in my head, but the florescent blue fairy lights Lila and I strung on the walls blazed through my eyelids. Transforming the basement into a *Frozen* paradise after the kids went to bed last night didn't leave much time for sleep. But the way Charlotte's eyes grew to the size of quarters as she took in the snowflakes, lighting, life-sized cardboard cutouts of Anna and Elsa, and ice palace fathead, made it all worth it.

That, and the fact that Lila and I spent our first night alone together, without arguing, without making stilted conversation, in months. We talked. Laughed a fair share too, especially as the clock ticked past midnight and exhaustion turned into giddiness. Around two, I headed to bed, while Lila stayed up, her forehead covered in a sheen of sweat and flour, as she made cupcakes from scratch.

Lila raced around now, restocking food, talking to guests, betraying no evidence of a sleepless night. She looked sexy, but understated in a white T, blue scarf, skinny jeans that showcased her perfect ass, and braided hair. *Just like Elsa!* Charlotte said.

Unlike Shannon, who was channeling Julia Roberts in *Pretty Woman*, with a clingy blue dress and thigh-high black boots. She talked with a group of moms across the room, eyeing me up like a dartboard. She was the dart.

With the kids distracted, I escaped upstairs to the kitchen, reveling in the quietness. The pressure in my head felt downright explosive. I opened another beer and chugged half in one gulp. If I could have one day, one hour, one *moment*, without a headache, I would be able to see things clearly. Make better choices.

"Brett leaves for Atlanta the day after Thanksgiving," Shannon said, materializing next to me. "I was thinking about sending the kids to my parents for a long weekend."

I opened the cabinet and shook out two ibuprofens, swallowing them dry as Shannon tickled my ear with her breath, whispering words I had no interest in hearing. Words that proved she either had short-term memory loss or the never-say-die attitude of Michael Jordan.

"More Christmas party planning?" someone said.

I spun around, trying to understand why Geneva stood in my kitchen. She kept showing up unannounced and uninvited, like the Grim Reaper. "Geneva! Glad you came." I forced a smile. "Get you a beer?"

"Riddle me this. Why is everyone in Wisconsin obsessed with beer?" Geneva asked, unwinding her scarf and placing it, along with her jacket, over the back of the couch as if she lived here. She wore black ripped jeans, black lace-up boots, and a distressed grey top that looked like a thrift store find, but probably cost a hundred bucks. "What's wrong with a vodka on the rocks? Wine?"

I finished my beer with a satisfied sigh. After her snarky question about the Christmas party, I was eager to return the favor. "I love beer."

Geneva smiled. "Shocking."

"And I'm from Illinois."

She rolled her eyes. "Pray tell. What's the difference?"

"There's wine downstairs," Shannon said, gesturing with her hands towards the basement door like a flight attendant pointing out the available exits. Just then, Lila emerged from the basement.

"There you are!" Geneva said. Lila's eyes widened, telling me that she too was surprised by Geneva's presence. But then, *then*, she accepted Geneva's hug.

Bewildered, I opened another beer. Outside of the kids and me, Lila wasn't affectionate. She never hugged. No one touched her body unless she consented—and she rarely did.

"I was about to look for you, but I ran into Alex and Shannon first," Geneva said when Lila pulled away. Geneva ran her hand through Lila's hair. Or was she gesturing towards us? I blinked twice, regretting a third beer on an empty stomach. "They're working hard on that class Christmas party."

Geneva's smile lit up the room, one of those Cameron Diaz megawatt packages that hypnotized everyone to not look beyond the façade. But I wasn't fooled. Her tone suggested working was a euphemism for fucking. And I wasn't having it. "We aren't—"

"I meant to thank you Lila, for letting me borrow Alex." Shannon spoke over me, squeezing my shoulder. "He kept me company last week at O'Malley's until my girls showed up."

Lila ducked her head inside the fridge, retrieving a cake and two sheets of cupcakes, each one bearing the smug mugs of Anna and Elsa.

"If only we all had as good of friends as Alex," Geneva said.

Once again, I felt like she was trying to provoke me. But why? Was I paranoid? Perhaps Lila told her a warped version of the last year, made me out to be some egomaniac who deprived her of a third child, and was now sleeping around to twist the knife. Maybe Geneva thought Lila needed support. And yet, Geneva's pithy comments, her impatience with me, ventured further than female solidarity. It felt personal.

"Just trying to keep up with you," I said. "You see Lila, what, two, three times a week? Now that's friendship."

"Why, Alex, are you keeping track of how often your wife goes out?"

"Can you bring these downstairs?" Lila interrupted, handing Geneva and Shannon each a sheet of cupcakes. Both reluctantly left.

Lila fixed her eyes on me and marched towards the counter. "You know, I didn't believe it when Geneva told me about you and Shannon." She tossed the candles at the cake like tiny javelins, maiming

Anna's impish smile. "But seeing you two together." She bit her lip. "You promised. No one we know."

Her accusation knocked the air out of me. My instincts were right. Geneva perpetuated a lie, targeted me, wanted to drive a wedge between Lila and me. "Lila, nothing happened."

"Don't lie." A starburst of passion darkened her eyes to coal. "Lying is worse."

I gritted my teeth. "I'm not."

"I told you. *I told you* if anyone found out—" She stared outside, unblinking, her face as lifeless as the browned grass, the anorexic trees. "Never mind."

I wanted her fury. For her to make a scene. Shove cake in my face. Scream obscenities. But Lila didn't do scenes. Never had. She kept everything locked inside. Problem was, I no longer had a key. I had to wait for her to open the door.

And she had. A crack. We had arguments full of poisonous accusations and spiteful retorts that led to watershed moments of honesty. It was exhausting and frustrating and stressful. But it was progress. I'd take Lila's rage over ambivalence any day. Rage suggested she still cared.

I exhaled. My heart rate slowed, my muscles loosened to noodles, my nerves downgraded to a crackle of electricity. I had one shot to prove Geneva was lying, and I wasn't going to let the shock of the accusation sentence me without a fair fight.

"Nothing happened." I gently kneaded the knobs of her spine, trying to ground her to this moment. To our marriage. To me. "Shannon made a move at the bar, but I stopped her. Told her I loved you."

"Funny," she said, a hint of spice back in her voice. "You failed to mention that part."

"It was nothing and I didn't want you to worry. You know I'd never do anything with her."

She turned back to the cake, fixing the candles. "I don't know. That's the problem."

"She's lying to you."

"Who?"

"Geneva!" I gestured towards the door, splashing beer on the floor. "Where does she get off? Upsetting you when she had no idea what happened."

A blush crept up Lila's neck. "She cares about me."

"*I* care about you. You know my heart. You've had it for sixteen years."

Lila collapsed against my chest, closing her eyes. I pressed my lips against her forehead, burying my fingers in the valleys of her ribs.

"I wish we could go back," she whispered.

"So do I." Silence settled between us, as we ventured down separate paths of regret. While Lila wished I never got the vasectomy, I wished I hadn't been blind to her pain in the aftermath. Oblivious to the fact that I, not Milo, caused her to withdraw. Glib enough to assume that she would accept reality and move on without consequences.

"We better get downstairs," she said, rubbing her cheeks against my sweater, making no move to leave. I pulled her tighter, relishing her warmth, the hint of lavender in her hair.

"I can send everyone home."

She looked up at me, her brown eyes once again the shade of Hershey Kisses, and laughed. "And break our daughter's heart?"

"Good point."

"Grab the matches."

I tucked them inside the back pocket of her jeans, letting my hand linger. She flashed me a small smile. One hug, one touch, one smile. One night of conversation. Alone, it didn't mean much, but put together, I felt cautiously optimistic.

Thirty of us crowded around Charlotte, singing "Happy Birthday." She was unrecognizable in her blond Elsa wig, but the beatific smile that stretched to her ears was pure Charlotte. Levi exhibited a rare burst of extroversion, adding a "cha-cha-cha" between every verse. Lila tucked herself under my arm as Charlotte blew out the candles.

The moment was perfect. My beautiful family. It was all still here. Happiness rising from the ashes.

And then I saw Geneva, standing opposite us, nose raised in the air, eyes slit like zippers with only me in her sights. I met her stare. The electrical current between us worked like a defibrillator on my heart as I thought about how she manipulated Lila. She won Lila's confidence, yet she was using this position to destroy my marriage.

Her smile said she would enjoy it too.

* * *

Lila lay in bed, reading *Big Little Lies* under the glow of the bedside lamp. I undressed, threw my clothes in the hamper and washed up, thankful that tomorrow was Sunday. It had been a long day, made longer by Charlotte's bedtime meltdown. She sobbed, already depressed about having to wait another year for her birthday. I held her until fatigue brought on sleep.

"You were amazing today," I said, crawling under the sheets. The hazy blue of our bedroom walls worked its magic tonight, imbuing me with calmness, a positive outlook. Or maybe it was that Lila waited up for me. Small steps, the incremental reintroduction of a life together, gave me hope. "Charlotte was ecstatic."

Lila marked her page, set the book on her nightstand, and turned to face me. "She was, wasn't she? I know sometimes I go overboard—"

"I get it. You want to give her everything you never had."

"I'm trying."

"You're succeeding." I hesitated, not wanting to break the peaceful moment. But I also couldn't let her go on wondering about Shannon. "I hope you believe me about Shannon. Even if it wasn't against the rules, I wouldn't be interested. She's not my type."

Lila raised her eyebrows. "The blonde hair, blue-eyed, Pilates body doesn't do it for you?"

"I like brown-eyed brunettes." I grazed her freckles with my thumb, scooting fractionally closer. "Especially ones with eight freckles underneath their left eye."

"She was a model, you know."

I grinned. It was a running joke among the parents because Shannon and Brett worked it into every conversation, as if she won a Nobel

Peace Prize instead of an Abercrombie contract as a teenager. "She's not you."

I kissed her. It felt like walking through a haunted house—thrilling, terrifying, nerve-wracking—knowing, at any moment, a trap door would swallow me up.

She pulled away, her dark lashes framing the worry in her eyes. I held my breath. "Nothing happened?" she asked. "Not even a kiss?"

"Nothing," I stressed.

"Promise?"

"On the kids."

Whether it was relief, attraction, or a rekindling, Lila kissed me with her entire body. I pulled off her clothes, piece by piece, exploring, rediscovering, embracing, what I once took for granted. She raised her hips to meet me and I pressed my forehead against hers, our breath and bodies working in tandem.

The sex was perfect, achingly so. Loving. Intense. Transcendental. A physical confirmation that despite everything we endured, we still wanted one another.

After, we clung together, staring into each other's eyes, not saying a word. Both of us knew this moment was huge, too profound for words to encapsulate.

Eventually, she gave me a coy smile. "You look like you won the lottery."

"Better." I kissed her; a lingering kiss that I had to force myself to break. "I won you."

I flopped on my back, grinning like Tom Brady after adding another Super Bowl ring. The open marriage brought sex, yes, but also a heavy dose of guilt, frustration, and dissatisfaction. This. Right here. Sex with my wife. Jesus, what a luxury.

I closed my eyes, reveling in the heaviness of my limbs, the tingles that shot out of my groin, the lack of headache. To be without pain. How exquisite!

Lila's phone chimed. "Who's that?" I turned to look at her.

She bit her lip. "Geneva. Let me tell her I'm busy and then I'm all yours."

Just like that, a tapping, like fingernails against a windowpane, started above my eyebrows. A tapping I knew from experience would soon emulate Tommy Lee on the drums.

I walked to the bathroom for water. *Hydration. Hydration. Hydration,* I told my patients. And yet, I drank a lake each day and the headaches still came.

When I returned, Lila was texting. I stood in the doorway, watching, waiting for her to put the phone away. I should've let it go. Crawled back into bed. Basked in our reconciliation. But Geneva came into my house, spread lies about me, tried to wreak havoc in my marriage. And here she was again, interrupting our night. I had to say something. "Don't you think it's odd that Geneva came to the party?"

Lila set her phone down. "We're friends. And she likes Charlotte."

"Doubtful," I said. "She told me she doesn't like kids. Then again, she told you I was having sex with Shannon, so telling the truth is a challenge for her."

Lila drew a deep breath, her nose pinching from effort. "Alex."

"I'm happy you made a friend. But something's not right about her." I twirled my index finger around my temple, refraining from saying *loco* like we did as kids. "I don't know what her problem is, but she doesn't like me."

"She's crazy because she doesn't like you?" Her voice was tight. "Because everyone has to love the great Alexander Ash Cole?" She pushed past me, shutting the bathroom door firmly behind her. How did Geneva engineer such loyalty? Especially when it always resided with me.

Lila's phone chimed. It sat on the bed, pulsating with information, beckoning me to read these all-important texts. With a shaky hand, I picked up her phone. A quick glimpse, that's all.

Why can Alex and Shannon be out, but not us? Geneva wrote. A ringing in my ears sounded like a tornado warning. I scrolled up. *U looked beautiful today. Torture not kissing u.* And the kill shot, two days ago. *Woke up with the taste of u on my lips.*

The truth pummeled me. Geneva's attitude. Her false accusations. The way she fawned over Lila. She wasn't lonely, in need of friends. She was making a play for my wife.

I turned like a pitcher on the mound, torqueing my hips for maximum velocity, and threw Lila's phone against the bathroom door. The screen cracked, a bullseye fracture that would hopefully make her texts indecipherable.

Lila opened the door, staring down at her phone, bewildered, as if it was a victim of a hit and run. "What's your deal?"

"You—" My voice sounded gritty, as if I had a cold. "You fucked Geneva?"

She gasped, her lips parting at the sharp intake of breath. Enough of an admission for me.

I stepped inside my closet, pulling on whatever was closest—jeans, a hoodie, baseball cap—before marching past her to the garage. Lila followed, whispering my name like a prayer.

The wheels of my car screeched as I backed out of the garage. Lila looked like a ghost in my rearview mirror, her white t-shirt billowing in the icy wind, pale face glowing in the moonlight, before evaporating into nothingness.

An open marriage. Jesus Christ. What was I thinking? Was I thinking? Nobody fell in love while fucking someone else. Inviting a third party into a marriage destroyed the trust. It fractured the team. Instead of saying, *I've got your back, whenever, however,* the tagline becomes, *You are not enough. We are not enough.* I might as well have used our marriage certificate as toilet paper for all the respect I gave it.

And yet, was it all my fault? Lila didn't want anything to do with me! I was desperate. Confused. Exhausted at trying to reach her. We started the open marriage for *me.* She promised on the way to Chicago to let me know if she started seeing anyone. But she stayed silent. As always. A goddamn enigma until the end.

I thought because I was done with the open marriage it meant *we* were done. But I wouldn't make that mistake twice. Lila and I found our way back to each other tonight and I wouldn't let Geneva destroy that.

CHAPTER TWENTY-NINE
GENEVA

Bang! Bang! Bang!

A pounding, like a grenade splitting the earth, made Geneva jump as she drifted off to sleep. She sat up in bed, heart thrashing, as her ears strained against the silence. Growing up in Manhattan, she was used to noise. Car horns. Sirens. Garbage trucks. But this was different. Pointed. Angry. Close.

Bang! Bang! Bang!

The door. Geneva wrapped her silk robe around her naked body—the naked girl is always offed first in horror movies, say nothing for any person of color—and tiptoed out of her bedroom and towards the door. Slowly, not making noise, she looked through the peephole. A tall man in a baseball cap and a puffy North Face jacket stared through the door, as if he could hear her breathing.

Alex.

She shivered, goosebumps pimpling her skin. But she opened the door, camouflaging her fear as anger.

"We need to talk," he said, pushing past her without an invitation.

She flipped on the lights, annoyed that he made it up to her apartment without her buzzing him in. She'd have to lodge a complaint with the board—the bartenders at the Knickerbocker too often left the door to the apartment complex unlocked. "It's late."

He spun around. "Oh, is this not convenient for you?" The tips of his ears and nose were cherry red from the cold. A sheen of frozen saliva covered his lips, cracking as his mouth twisted into a spiteful smile. "You text Lila at any hour, show up at my house whenever you please, but won't give me the same courtesy?"

"Nope, see, no one talks to me that way," Geneva said. "Not in my home."

His eyes, the color of a stormy sky, scrutinized her. She tightened her robe, wishing she was wearing a bra. But who slept in a bra?

"My wife." He rested his palms face down against the island and leaned forward, his six-foot plus frame towering over her. "You fucked my wife."

Geneva filled a glass of water, slowly drinking it down. Buying time. She shouldn't have been surprised. Why else would Alex demand an audience? And yet, she felt like someone dumped an ice bucket over her head. Shock. Followed by elation.

Geneva left Charlotte's party this afternoon feeling depressed. Admittedly, she acted obnoxious, picking a fight with Alex. But when she walked into the kitchen and saw Shannon fawning over Alex like he was a pop star instead of a low-rent television personality, she lost it. Why were they allowed to be out, but not Lila and Geneva? Why was Geneva a secret? Again?

The afternoon only got worse. She felt sick, watching the way Alex man-handled Lila, steering her every move like a train conductor! Kissing her for show instead of desire. If only Lila recognized it.

But, maybe, she did. Maybe that's why she told Alex the truth. Maybe she was falling in love with Geneva. Her skin hummed, yearning for it to be true.

"Why do you care what Lila does?" Geneva said. "You wanted an open marriage."

"The open marriage is over."

She gave him a sharp look. "I don't believe you."

"Believe whatever you want, just stay away from Lila."

"It won't matter. You lost Lila long before I met her."

His eyes bore into Geneva's. "I haven't lost her."

"Oh, but you have. The moment you got snipped, you lost her."

Alex's jaw tightened, pressing his lips into a thin line, as if she yanked on a string and wired it shut. "Judge all you want. But you don't know anything about me."

"I know everything," Geneva said, her strong voice concealing her rapidly beating heart. As much as she knew falling in love with Lila was nothing to apologize for, she felt like she was seventeen again. An angry man imposing his ideas about the right and wrong way to love. An angry man slut-shaming her. Ending her relationship. "Your cheating. Your lies. The way you broke Lila's heart. She tells me *everything*."

It was a stretch—getting Lila to talk about their marriage nearly took a truth serum. But Geneva couldn't back down now. Alex came in swinging, a heavyweight fighter wanting to intimidate her with his size and power. That wasn't going to happen. Not this time. She was older. Wiser. Not easily cowed.

"You may think you have something special, that you know everything because she told you a few stories. But you know nothing. Nothing." He slashed his hand through the air. "I have sixteen years on my side. Sixteen years of sleeping with her, laughing together, listening to her worries, taking care of her. We've built a family. You? You're nothing more than a distraction."

"Get woke, Alex. If Lila wants to be with me, if she wants to fuck me—" She let the thought simmer, relishing the way Alex flinched. "There's nothing you can do about it."

"You're manipulating Lila, stirring up shit to come between us." He talked slowly, enunciating each word, tattooing every phrase on her brain. "Lila might not see it, but that's because she's a good person. She wants to believe the best in people. But she will. And then this *fling*," he spat the word, "will end and she'll forget about you. Because at the end of the day, Geneva, that's what you are. Completely and utterly forgettable."

Like an old-fashioned mic drop, he walked out on top.

Geneva felt cheated. Battered and beaten by his words. She was in control, dictating the conversation, and then she wasn't. He moved from defense to offense seamlessly, usurping her power without ever raising his voice.

She raced after him, flinging open the door. "Have you stopped to ask yourself whether she loves me?" she yelled, not caring if she woke up the floor. "That I didn't trick her. That, unlike you, I make her happy."

He turned around. "You think this is love?" His shoulders relaxed and he shook his head. It took a moment, but she realized he pitied her. He wasn't thrown by her question, didn't consider love a possibility. She was nothing more than a fly, buzzing around his head, on a suicide mission of persistence. "She chose you, Geneva, a *woman*, precisely because she could never love you."

His words brought her fears to the surface like beads of sweat. "Wait 'til she leaves you. Then you'll see."

But he already disappeared inside the elevator. She was a kid launching snowballs, long after everyone else went inside.

* * *

Alex's visit left Geneva on edge. She poured two fingers of tequila, drinking with shaky hands. History was repeating itself. She felt the same terror and loneliness as the night Cristina left. Had she learned nothing? You couldn't force someone to love you, stand up for you, brave coming out. That's why Geneva made her heart untouchable. She couldn't recover from that type of betrayal twice.

Geneva met Cristina her first day at Chapman, an all-girls boarding school in New Hampshire. She walked inside her dorm room and saw Cristina hanging a poster of Beyoncé on the wall. As Cristina reached up, her shirt crept above her belly button, showcasing a swatch of taut belly that gleamed like polished wood. With dark eyes and long dark hair, lips she treated like a snack, Geneva thought she was beautiful. Not that Cristina agreed. Cristina was shy, rife with insecurities, waiting, much like Geneva, for someone to pluck her from obscurity.

Within days, Cristina and Geneva became inseparable. They weren't the only minorities, but the feeling of being different, an outsider, cemented their bond. Not that they talked about it. Fitting in required turning a blind eye, as if they could will their differences out of existence. Cristina deferred to Geneva about everything from clothes to movies to diet tips, finding her worldly and sophisticated because she grew up in "The Big Apple." Geneva promptly told her to never use that phrase again. For the first time, Geneva felt special. Enough.

They shared everything—homework, clothes, secrets...and then, junior year, during a rainy October night spent cuddling and watching *Gossip Girl*, their virginity. Geneva felt Cristina's breath warm against her ear, inhaled the familiar smell of lavender, and it stirred her. Who kissed who? Even now, Geneva didn't know. They kissed and kissed, hands roaming, mouths gasping, clothes discarded. It was soft and wet and warm and filled her with a deep, pulsing ache.

We can't tell anyone, Cristina said after, lips mummering against Geneva's neck. Cristina grew up Catholic—gay people were sick, immoral, perverted. Her family would abandon her. Secrecy didn't sit right with Geneva, but Cristina kissed her until she took a vow of silence.

Inside their dorm room they had mind-blowing sex, soul-bearing talks, easy companionship. But outside those four walls, Cristina started distancing herself. She stopped sitting with Geneva during meals. Refused to partner with her in class. Made plans without her. Their relationship gave Cristina the confidence to soar while simultaneously injecting steroids into Geneva's insecurities. *Cristina didn't love her. Her parents didn't want her around. She would never be enough.* Geneva eventually broke down, a messy, tearful plea for Cristina to include her. Cristina accused Geneva of being needy; insisted she was only being careful. *Of course, I love you.* With these words, Geneva let the charade continue, but every little rejection was like swallowing bleach, making her feel sick and unlovable and wrong.

Ironically, Cristina's carelessness outed them. Geneva was studying in bed one May afternoon when Cristina returned from her Lacrosse game. She jumped on Geneva, kissing her, high off the two goals she scored with her parents watching from the stands.

Within minutes, they were both naked, hands and lips locked in a familiar path of pleasure. They didn't hear the knock. They didn't hear the door open. But they heard the shouts.

"Get off her!" Cristina's dad roared, his spit decorating Geneva's face more thoroughly than a sneeze. He yanked Cristina out of bed, hard enough to dislocate her shoulder. Geneva covered herself with a blanket. Later, she would feel embarrassed, but at that moment, she barely noticed that she peed herself. All she saw was his thick, sausage fingers, aching to slap her.

"I'm sorry," Cristina said, snot and tears streaming down her face, as she pulled on clothes. "I was changing and she kissed me. I didn't know what to do."

"You're lying!" he said.

"*Quemarás en el infierno*," her mom muttered, signing the cross.

Students flocked towards the noise, lingering in the hallway.

"Ask anyone," Cristina said, gesturing towards the eavesdropping girls. "It's not my fault. She's, like, obsessed with me. It's sick."

Geneva watched, speechless and horrified.

Cristina's dad pushed Cristina and her mom out the door before warning Geneva, "Stay away from my daughter."

Later that night, Geneva called Cristina, needing to hear her say she lied. That she loved Geneva. Wasn't sickened by her. But Cristina never answered.

By Monday, Cristina still wasn't back. The rumor mill targeted Geneva, but no one could have predicted the reason Headmaster York called an emergency assembly on Thursday: Cristina overdosed, dying of acute liver failure. Everyone glared at Geneva, their beady eyes accusing and vicious. Girls she laughed with, gossiped, pulled all-nighters, cried. No one reached out. *Slut. Dyke. Murderer.* Only Geneva knew the truth: Cristina would rather die than be with her, than let the world know they were in love.

Geneva didn't return for her senior year. Everyone—the school, her parents, Geneva—agreed to part ways. Her parents didn't offer sympathy. Ask whether she was okay. But they did use their connections to enroll her in an elite private school on the Upper West Side, adopting a "don't name it, don't claim it" policy still in effect today.

Thirteen years passed. Eventually, she stopped putting a microscope on their relationship, trying to figure out Cristina's true feelings, whether she meant to kill herself. But she couldn't rein in her subconscious with the same success. Geneva still awoke some days, expecting to find the warmth of Cristina. Other times, she heard Cristina's girlish giggle. Or saw a glimpse of her face in her lectures. Geneva's heart refused to say goodbye. Probably because she was never given the chance.

While her heart might never completely heal, the scar tissue served as a warning: to lust, but never love; to leave before she could be left. The plan suited her well—until now. She felt like she was driving towards a hurricane, ignoring all signs of danger—married, straight, emotionally vulnerable, often unavailable—foot pressed on the accelerator. But why? What made Lila so special?

Geneva tried ignoring the similarities between Cristina and Lila, but the more she drank, the harder it was to separate her feelings. The past from the present. Cristina from Lila. Did she love Lila? Or had she simply never fallen out of love with Cristina? Was she using Lila to fix the mistakes of the past?

Cristina was the reason she was driving into the storm. Because, unlike last time, she refused to stay closeted. Refused to accept anything less than unconditional love. Being put first.

Unlike last time, she wouldn't let a man tear her away from the woman she loved.

CHAPTER THIRTY
LILA

I stood at the dining room window, my eyes fixed on the dark street, watching for Alex's car. Despite numerous attempts, he wasn't answering his phone. Was he planning to stay out all night? Make me sick with worry? Sick with regret? Beyond apologizing, which I did a dozen times as he barreled out of the house, there was nothing I could say to appease him. And still, I wanted the chance. I needed him home, needed to assure him that tonight wasn't a lark.

My phone buzzed. Geneva. Again. Four missed calls. Or maybe five—it was hard to see through the splintered screen. But I was too distracted to talk. And, honestly? A little frustrated with her behavior today. Hannah told me to disinvite her to the party. Always conflict-adverse, I chose the path of least resistance. Chose to hope she wouldn't show. Wouldn't make a spectacle if she did. Given the amount I was paying Hannah, I needed to start taking her advice. I spent hours planning, decorating, and cooking for Charlotte's party, wanting to make it perfect. Wanting to make Charlotte feel special; an atonement for the months I phoned it in. But then Geneva showed up, not to celebrate, but to antagonize Alex. A distraction I neither wanted nor needed.

Geneva didn't like Alex; she thought he was a liar, a cheat, a phony. She questioned me today, in the annoyed manner one would confront a restaurant manager after a bad meal, why I refused to tell him about us. I was slowly learning that Geneva had no off button. She kept taking jabs at Alex, as if I was one of her students for whom she'd drill home the point: *He doesn't love you.* It hurt to know that she too, didn't think me capable of making decisions on my own.

Ironically, her pestering did get me thinking—just not the way she intended. Alex didn't sleep with Shannon. A drink? Sure. He was a social creature, magnanimous to a fault; he wouldn't have left Shannon alone at the bar. For one drink, one hour, he'd enjoyed Shannon's extravagantness. But sex? Wasn't buying it.

I felt myself softening towards Alex. Maybe it was my guilt after having sex with Geneva. Or his attitude—attentive, affectionate, fun. Vintage Alex. Or being a team again, prepping Charlotte's party. Whatever the reason, sex tonight felt like the easiest choice I'd made in months.

I closed my eyes, remembering the way his touch felt both new and familiar, electrifying and comforting. Geneva awakened my sex drive, but she could never fill the void Alex left. It wasn't a man versus woman thing. It was an Alex thing. From the moment he first kissed me outside Wrigley, I was gone. My heart was his. I had that same thought when he kissed me tonight. *You.*

The garage door opening snapped me back to the present. I ran to the bedroom and dove in bed. Our sheets were tangled and held a faint whiff of sex and sweat. What felt like a new beginning a couple hours ago now felt like a false start. A tease.

Then again, I only had myself to blame. Why did I answer Geneva's text? Why did I leave my phone on the bed? Why did I have sex with her? Stupid. Stupid. Stupid.

He stood in the doorway of our bedroom, arms hanging from the top of the doorframe as if he was about to do pullups. "Can we talk?"

I swallowed. Nodded.

"I asked for an open marriage. I brought this upon us." He perched on the edge of the bed next to me. His voice was soft, restrained. "Most nights, I think I must have been mad, but I was in a bad place. *We* were in a bad place and I didn't know how to fix it. I had no idea you were still struggling with the vasectomy. If you told me—" He shook his head. "Anyway, against all odds, I think the open marriage helped us."

"Helped...how?"

"It got us talking, got us to be honest. Not only with each other, but with ourselves." His voice gained speed, the words terse. "I'm furious with you. For acting like you were the only one that suffered after Milo.

172

For putting me in the position of having to decide whether to get the vasectomy. For checking out on the kids, our marriage, so you could hold a pity party."

I recoiled, my apology running into a traffic jam in my throat. "Pity party?"

He licked his lips. A habit which used to drive me mad with desire, but now made me want to chuck a tube of Chapstick at his head. "I gave you time. At what point does grieving become selfish when you have two healthy kids and a husband that need you? That love you?"

I took a deep, cleansing breath, trying to wade through the accusation to find the truth. But it was like diving into a swamp, hoping to find a diamond. How do you see past the grime? *Pity party.* What a horrible turn of phrase to describe losing Milo. The loss of all future children.

"After Milo died, I was...." Dying the slowest death humanly possible as I relived his last hours, minutes, seconds inside of me. But that was my burden to carry. I never told Alex that I waited all morning for Milo to move before calling the doctor. I loved him enough to spare him the what ifs. "I wasn't thinking clearly. You saw that and felt compelled to act. I don't agree with what you did," I said, hooking his eyes to mine. "I never will. But I also know you were doing what you thought was best."

Funnily enough, Hannah's gratitude exercises helped me understand that Alex didn't set out to hurt me, to betray me, destroy my dreams. He loved our family, would've loved adding Milo. From playing school with Charlotte after an early morning at the hospital followed by the clinic, to braving the freezing temperatures to toss the baseball with Levi, he relished spending time with the kids. After my shower this morning, I found him pulling my hair out of the drain like he was weeding a flower bed. *My* hair. And yet he did it, without complaining.

Gratitude. When I looked, I found bits and pieces of promise among the wreckage. But it was a two-steps-forward-one-step-back process. Acts of kindness that reminded me why I loved him, followed up by an insensitive remark that made me blind with rage. Like, calling my reaction to his vasectomy a *pity party*. Anger held me in a stranglehold, one that showed no signs of abating, despite my efforts to practice gratitude.

"Everything I do is for this family. For you," he said. "I hated getting it done. Hated—" He cleared his throat, the pause allowing hope to surge through my blood. Maybe this discussion would lead him to reverse it. "Hated knowing I was going to hurt you. I never wanted this for us, but I truly believe it was necessary to keep you safe."

A half-apology. Would he ever admit that he was wrong to go behind my back? "I still don't think you understand why I'm upset. But I also know this anger is toxic. To us. The kids. And I'm trying to work through it. I'm trying to forgive you."

"Which brings us full circle." The brightness of his smile suggested he heard me say *I forgive you* instead of *I'm trying to forgive you*. The distinction mattered. At least, to me.

"I'm confused. What circle?"

"Back to us." He clasped my hands inside his. "No more open marriage. No more distractions. Just us."

"No." I pulled away. The vehemence of my tone surprised us both.

"No?" His eyes widened as if the lids were held open by a speculum, ala *Clockwork Orange*.

I wasn't sure how I felt about Geneva, but I couldn't let him make the decision for me. Again. Every time I got close to forgiving him, he reminded me that nothing changed. Alex still thought he knew better. That he had the final word. He expected me to give him carte blanche authority, trust that he was acting in our best interests.

Maybe that worked in the past, but I no longer needed protecting. I wasn't in a funk. Thanks to Geneva, I felt more alive than ever.

"No."

This time, I would decide what was best for me.

CHAPTER THIRTY-ONE
ALEX

No. The word polluted the air like a fart, making it impossible to breathe. Lila's voice was firm, so unlike her, that it took a moment to gather my thoughts.

"I'm not ending it because we had sex," I said, fixing on what I hoped was her concern. "Truth is, I've been wanting to pull the plug all along."

Her mouth parted. "Then why didn't you?"

"I was waiting for you to tell me to stop."

"What?" She threw her hands up. "You knew I didn't want this."

"How would I know that?"

"Because we're married," she said slowly.

"But you agreed. Didn't fight me. You—" Did she need to see a transcript? I remembered proposing the idea, hoping it would make her realize how far apart we drifted. Instead, she started reprogramming the rules for our marriage like Steve Jobs. But there was no point arguing it now. "You didn't care about anything, Lila, least of all me. But lately, since Chicago, you're trying again. You're talking. Smiling. There were moments today when I felt completely in sync with you."

Lila grabbed fistfuls of the bedsheets, curling it towards her shoulders like dumbbells. Why was she angry? I thought she would be ecstatic. Relieved. I'd pardon her sins and she'd do the same for me. Which was pretty charitable, considering she stepped out without telling me.

"I need time," Lila said.

"Time? For what?"

Lila's eyes lit on mine, the inky darkness putting me on guard. "Geneva."

For a moment, I said nothing. Too stunned to speak. "Are you joking?"

"She makes me happy. Whatever changes you've seen, she's been a big part of that."

The open marriage worked. In a way. Imagining me with other women was the knock on the head Lila needed to wake up. One no amount of words accomplished. She found her voice. A backbone. Arguments followed. Arguments that were helping us rebuild our marriage. But she would never admit that. Not now, anyways. She attributed her rebirth to Geneva, as if she was Jesus fucking Christ, her lord and savior.

I stood up, pacing in front of the bed. "You broke the rules." A flawless memory, particularly one for infinitesimal details, proved invaluable when recognizing obscure symptoms in childhood diseases. It came in handy now too. "First, no sex with anyone we know."

"I didn't know her when this started."

I stopped, squared on her. "You invited her to Charlotte's party."

"She—"

"Imagine if I had done that. Brought some woman I was screwing to the house, paraded her in front of you. Let her insult you while I silently stood by. How would you feel?"

Lila buried her face between her legs, mummifying herself with the sheet. "I'm sorry." She came up for air. "I wasn't thinking. Geneva was my friend and then she kissed me—"

"Shut up! Christ, you think I want details?" Without details, I could assume it was an experiment. A drunken mistake. Temporary insanity.

"Keep your voice down," Lila said, her voice icy. "We don't need the kids waking up."

I walked over and closed the bedroom door, feeling itchy and dirty, as if I was covered in shit. That's what this news felt like, a shit bath.

"Second," I said. "We're not allowed to have sex with anyone more than three times. You've seen her what, a dozen times?"

"But we didn't—"

I cut her off. "Do you remember why you limited it to three?"

"So nobody would fall in love," Lila said.

"So nobody would fall in love." I pounded my fist against the drywall in time with each word.

The howling wind rattled our bedroom windows. The temperature would drop close to zero by morning, but the air between us already felt frigid.

"I'm not in love with her." Lila spun her engagement and wedding rings. Her fixation made my throat constrict. Was the fiddling unconscious or something deeper? Was she contemplating taking them off? "I said she makes me happy."

Semantics. Nothing short of a denial of feelings would soothe me. I felt nothing for Izzy and Ynez. *Nothing.* It was sex. Nothing more, nothing less. Exactly what we agreed. I never let feelings enter the equation. There wasn't room. My feelings were too entrenched in Lila.

"Third. No talking about our marriage. You said, and I quote, *Don't turn them into your best friend.*" I laughed, wishing my memory wasn't quite as polished. But laughing at the irony was better than the alternative: punching a hole in the wall until my knuckles were bloodied and my arm hung from my shoulder like a limp banana. "Yet Geneva knew we had an open marriage. Knew about the vasectomy—"

"Wait." Her eyes widened. "When did you talk to Geneva?"

"Tonight. I went to her apartment."

Lila froze. "What?"

"*What?* I had questions. I needed answers." I paused. "And I wanted to let her know this fling is over."

Lila raked her hands through her hair. "I wish you hadn't done that."

"Yeah, well, there's a lot I wish you hadn't done."

"I slept with one person, Alex. *One.*" She held up her finger. "It's not fair to persecute me when you did the same."

She had a point, much as I hated to admit it. "Let's move forward then. Clean slate." I mimed washing my hands of this, as if our relationship could brush off infidelity as easily. "Starting now."

She looked away. "I want time."

Cortisol skyrocketed through my veins. Geneva wasn't worth the air we were using to speak of her. "Are you a lesbian now? Is this some sort of identity crisis?"

Lila turned away. "You're not listening. You never do."

"I hear you, Lila. Loud and clear." My heart rattled inside my chest as if unjustly imprisoned there. "But I'm not going to give you the green light to fuck someone else."

"I gave it to you."

"I never wanted you to," I yelled at the ceiling. We lived on the precipice, so close to making it back to each other and yet always falling short. "I wanted you to say, no, Alex, I love you. The thought of you fucking someone else makes me apoplectic."

A sharpness, as exacting and instantaneous as an electrical current, zapped through my chest. I gasped, holding my hand against the wall for balance. And then it was gone. My heart operated at a dead sprint, rage roared through my ears, but otherwise I felt fine.

"What's wrong?" Lila jumped up from the bed and rushed to my side.

I looked at Lila. So many transformations over the past year, this latest one the most baffling. "Nothing."

"You scared me."

I grimaced. "You know if I died, you'd get all the time you want with Geneva."

Her mouth dropped open. "Don't joke about that."

I walked past her, crawled into bed, and pulled the covers over my head. My limbs were spent, depleted of oxygen from my emotionally hungry heart. "Goodnight, Lila."

The conversation swam through my mind like fish in a tank, round and round, going nowhere. Had I stopped listening? What was she trying to tell me? I refused to believe she wanted to be with Geneva, that she would give up the kids, me, our life, for that woman. But why else would she need time? What was I missing?

CHAPTER THIRTY-TWO
LILA

Overnight, our house turned into a library during finals—hushed whispers, deathly glares, a general hum of dread—as Alex silently raged about my request for time. The kids ran around like future juvenile offenders—wrestling over the iPad, name-calling, stealing candy—ignoring the turmoil between us. Maybe they were used to it, thought all parents had monosyllabic conversations.

During Monday's session with Hannah, she suggested that I answered Geneva's text in bed because I wanted to get caught. Force Alex and me to put everything in the open. Stop skirting the landmines. But that felt too easy. The harder truth was admitting that Geneva filled a void. Around her, I felt happy, heard, special—the opposite of how Alex made me feel this past year. And I wasn't ready to let her go.

I texted Geneva after my session with Hannah, asking if we could meet.

"You can't disappear like that," Geneva said, hugging me after I arrived at The Tea Room, a free-trade coffee staple on Gorham Street. "I was worried about you."

The tightness of her hug reminded me that even though she went overboard at Charlotte's party, it was because she cared. Facing Alex, having the three of us in the same room, couldn't have been easy for her, either.

I apologized for Alex's middle of the night visit, which she shrugged off, more concerned with why I didn't return her phone calls. I made my argument with Alex sound like an ultra-marathon without water, bathroom breaks, or phone privileges. "He wants to end the open marriage."

"Of course, he does!" She rolled her eyes, one of her signature full-head twirls. "Doesn't the timing strike you as odd? You find someone you care about and he ends it?"

I tucked my hands between my legs, staring out the window. "I don't know."

"What don't you know?"

"What I want," I whispered, watching a woman cross the street, walking towards us. She wore a Moby wrap strapped to her chest, the baby's blue stocking-capped head poking out the top, his limbs encased in a fleece bunting. Strike that, I knew exactly what I wanted—

Stop it! I raked my nails against my thighs. *Stop obsessing about babies!* Where has my obsession gotten me? A broken marriage. An affair. Children without the words to say what's wrong, but the feeling that something pivotal shifted in their world.

And still, my eyes trailed this baby. It was stupid. Intellectually, I knew it wasn't Milo—he'd be over a year now, walking, talking, showcasing his unique personality—but my heart used this baby as a portal into a parallel life. One where I was a good mother. One that rushed to the hospital upon waking that morning.

"Are you listening?" Geneva asked.

I tore my eyes away. Met hers. "Yes."

Geneva blew on her coffee. "I'll say this: what we have? I haven't felt—" She bit her lip. "Don't let go of us because he wants you to. Make your own choices."

"I need time." Her silence suggested she found those words as infuriating as Alex. But discussing this for another minute, another hour, wasn't going to change anything. I didn't know what to do. I left—dinner and homework with the kids beckoned—apologizing for my indecisiveness. Disappointed in myself for fulfilling both their narratives of being weak.

Thanksgiving did nothing to lift my spirits. We stayed home, mutually refusing to take this show of martial farce on the road. Alex's siblings texted us memes Wednesday night, drunkenly roasting us for bailing, while my mom threw a fit when I cancelled our weekend visit.

I'll drink, she threatened. *I can't be alone right now.* I reminded her to go to meetings, promised to call, but in the end, it was her choice. Her life. Not mine. I had enough problems.

I made a full Thanksgiving lunch. From scratch. No one cared. Levi and Charlotte combined ate a few bites of turkey, two biscuits, and a snowball of mashed potatoes. Alex looked like a baseball manager, chewing the entire meal—except no food disappeared from his plate. As for me? I played with my food like an anorexic pretending that eating didn't terrify me. Lunch lasted fifteen minutes—both of us talking to the kids, not each other—before the kids ran downstairs and Alex left to watch football. Nobody asked about dessert. I sat alone, watching the snow pile up on the window pane, trying to find something to feel grateful for.

Later that evening, I was rinsing the dishes when Alex walked in, rolling a suitcase behind him. I froze, hot water scalding my hands, too stunned to move. Too stunned to breathe. As bad as things were, I never thought he would leave. I never thought he'd give up on us.

"I'm taking the kids to my parents for the weekend," he said. "They want to see their cousins."

I shut off the water. My shoulders slowly retracted from my ears. He wasn't leaving.

"Now?" It was after six. The sky a mural of darkness. A half-foot of snow fell since daybreak. A three-hour drive to Chicago wasn't ideal. "Can't we leave in the morning?"

He looked down. "Lila..."

I took a step back, catching on too late. "You're going without me?"

"You wanted time." The offer was generous, but the softness of his voice, the sharp angle of his jaw, suggested it pained him. "I'm giving you time."

"The kids. They'll wonder why I'm not going."

He shrugged. "We'll tell them you went to your mother's. Exactly where we'd be headed tomorrow if—" He cleared his throat, emitting a slight groan. "Never mind."

181

With that, he called the kids upstairs. Alex was the "fun" parent; he roughhoused, extended bedtimes, played freeze tag during breakfast. But to practically burst out in song and dance? The kids' excitement felt a karate chop to my clavicle, puncturing my heart and spirit.

Hugs. Kisses. Goodbyes. This. Right here. Watching them go with barely a backwards glance was my punishment for the months I spent in mourning. With kids, you get what you put in. And this past year? I'd punched a time clock. Now, they were doing the same.

"This isn't easy," Alex said, looking subdued after loading the kids and luggage into the heated car.

I blew the kids kisses, but the halogen glow on their faces told me they were glued to YouTube. I turned back to Alex, the reality of this separation weighing heavy. I stood on my tiptoes, cupping his cheeks with my hands, and kissed him. Unbridled emotion—love, sadness, frustration, confusion, longing—turned our goodbye kiss into a passionate embrace.

"I'm giving you the weekend to figure this out." His lips brushed mine, our breath one. "It's killing me, thinking about what you might do. But I want to show you that I love you, that I'm listening to what you need."

I was ready to say no, I didn't need time, and hop in the car with my family. But that would only be a short-term fix. This was the first sign Alex was willing to change, that not everything had to be done on his terms. And I owed it to the kids, to Alex, and myself, to figure out what I wanted. To fall back in love with my life.

He pulled away, looking in my eyes. "When I get back, I'm going to help you remember why you chose me. Why you should choose me all over again."

One last, lingering kiss and he was gone. I ran to the dining room and watched as the rear lights of his car twinkled like stars and then faded away. Darkness. An empty street. Me. Alone.

I turned around, coming face-to-face with our wedding portrait. Alex, dapper in a navy suit that brought out his eyes. Me, elegant in a sleeveless lace dress with a scooped back. His hands squeezed my ribboned waist, lifting me to his kiss. We sparkled in the sunburst, promise and expectation glistening on our skin.

We had no idea what marriage involved, the twists and turns, the sacrifices it would demand. Back then, I thought nothing would drive us apart. Certainly not the desire for more kids. But it had. We had love in common, but used it for cross-purposes.

I walked away, unable to handle the hopefulness in our eyes, the devotion. But I wasn't safe anywhere. Levi's science notebook rested open on the living room floor, his scrawled handwriting evidencing diligent notes on gravity. Charlotte's latest family portrait hung on the fridge, our stick-figured limbs holding hands. Alex's running shoes, still soaked from his snowy run this morning, created a puddle in the mud room. Every inch of this house evoked feelings, memories, love.

I couldn't stay here this weekend, cooped up, missing the kids. Not if I wanted to get some real thinking done. Not if I wanted to have answers for Alex come Sunday. I pressed my hand against the cold window, staring at the blanket of snow in the backyard. Skiing! I would go skiing! Getting outside, breathing fresh air, would clear my head. I grabbed my iPad, looking to see whether there were any last-minute bargains for the holiday weekend.

After booking an Airbnb, I picked up my phone, debating whether I should invite Geneva. Spending the weekend alone would be beneficial, but coupling it with Geneva would solve two problems. Happiness was a puzzle, and I needed to determine what piece, if any, Geneva played in the long-term. But what should I say? How much should I divulge? In the end, I took the cowards way out and texted her. *Last minute ski trip this weekend...by myself. Want to come?*

Nerves showered my body like raindrops as I waited for her response. Were they nerves of excitement? Or fear? Fear that I might leave the weekend with stronger feelings? Or fear that I might have hurt Alex, jeopardized my marriage, over a misguided crush? I couldn't tell.

Finally, she texted, *Hate skiing, but adore u. How about I b your hot chocolate barista when u return from the slopes?*

A perfect compromise. Time alone to think on the slopes and time with Geneva. A few more texts and the plans were set. We'd leave tomorrow. An entire weekend with Geneva. I rested my head on the counter, exhausted both by Alex leaving and the weekend ahead.

I washed up, changing into one of Alex's Notre Dame cross-country shirts, as soft as cashmere after hundreds of washings, before crawling into bed. The silence made me feel hollow. No kids giggling. No whining. No feet pounding. The house felt abandoned, a foreshadowing of the future, when the kids would become allergic to staying home. At least Alex would be here.

Would he, though? It was hard to predict next week, let alone the next decade.

Tears wet my pillowcase. Nothing new. Except this time, I wasn't crying for Milo. My empty womb. I was crying because I missed Levi and Charlotte. Because everything I did this weekend would impact their lives for years to come.

I was crying for my marriage. We were not okay. And I couldn't go on pretending this open marriage was a phase, a temporary blip, instead of recognizing it for what it was, a symptom of a marriage in peril.

One would think that a cozy bed in a silent house would unlock the knots of confusion. But the longer I lay awake, only one thought broke through: if I didn't start being honest with myself, this weekend separation might become permanent.

CHAPTER THIRTY-THREE
GENEVA

Geneva lay on the bed next to Lila, watching her sleep, her body lit by the wan morning sun. She lightly traced her finger across a band of freckles that started at the top of Lila's spine, dipped beneath her tank-top, and emerged by her shoulder blade to form an L across her otherwise flawless ivory back. Nature branded her. Lila. The dark-haired beauty.

When Lila invited her on a weekend getaway, Geneva soared with optimism. Yet not even twenty-four hours into the trip, Geneva felt like it was more a farewell tour than a promising beginning.

Lila made her first mistake when she booked an Airbnb in the middle of bumblefuck Wisconsin. When Lila mentioned skiing, Geneva imagined a resort, including a spa, restaurants, shopping. A sleepy town? A one-bedroom cabin? No. Just no. Her second mistake was hitting the slopes as soon as they arrived yesterday. A few runs? Sure. All afternoon? It stank of rejection. Which led to Lila's third mistake, the one that shook Geneva: feigning to be too exhausted for sex last night.

Geneva's phone vibrated. She did a double-take. Her mother. Why was she calling, after all these months? Looking back now, Geneva could admit that she ambushed her parents by inviting Dani home. But their determination to pretend she wasn't a lesbian worked like a pair of garden shears, slowly snipping at the edges of her heart until they found an artery. She figured a shock and awe campaign, right under their intolerant little noses, would force them to accept her. Once again, she overestimated their love.

Geneva declined the call, not having the energy for a confrontation. In fact, she felt ill. The walls closed in on her. It felt like a prison—kitschy, outdated, rustic. Her skin itched from the polyester fabrics.

Her nose ran from smoky, damp air. Drinking was the only salve to combat the claustrophobia.

Or eating, her rumbling stomach reminded her. Never one to skip meals, her hunger went into overdrive when upset. She gained fifteen pounds after Cristina committed suicide, sneaking down to the corner bodega to buy family-sized bags of Cheetos and sleeves of Little Debbie powdered doughnuts. The only upside: her mother started suggesting walks around Central Park. A rare nugget of mother-daughter time. Without stepping on a scale, she knew the last week hadn't been kind. Every time she recalled Alex's words, she gobbled a muffin. A cookie. Pancakes. Needing something, *anything*, to fill the relentless ache.

Lila opened her eyes. Geneva caressed her cheek and whispered good morning. Instead of moving closer, Lila mumbled something and retreated to the bathroom. Geneva bit her lip. Not everyone liked to be touched upon waking. Some people needed space, an infusion of caffeine. It might have nothing to do with her.

A few minutes later, Lila emerged, her face glistening with lotion. She wanted to do yoga. Geneva followed her to the main room, watching as Lila spread her yoga mat on the floor. Lila stood on her right foot, wrapping her left foot around her right ankle, and bent down to a squat. All while holding her palms together in prayer. Geneva's joints burned, watching her.

"I'd like to Facetime the kids," Lila said.

Geneva walked to the window. An icy lake, snow-covered anemic trees, the sun a bruised lemon peel in the steely sky. It matched her depressed mood. Was any of this weekend going to be about them? Or was this her consolation prize? "You must miss them."

"Horribly." Lila's voice was strained as she held the pose. "Problem is, they think I'm at my mom's. So.... if you could maybe give me a few minutes alone..."

Not a prison, Geneva realized. *A closet.* Lila pulled a bait and switch, couching this as a romantic getaway when her real goal was to prevent prying eyes. If a tree falls in the forest and no one is around to hear it, does it make a sound?

"I'll work." Geneva grabbed a bagel from the kitchen, biting off a chunk so she wouldn't cry. Each little exclusion stung, but added together, it felt like a bludgeoning. "You won't even notice me."

Geneva pulled out her laptop and sat on the couch, reviewing her proposal for a new summer section entitled "Love & Marriage in Victorian Literature—Perpetuating the Myth of Femininity." Or something like that. She needed to finalize the reading list and start drafting a syllabus to submit to Professor Abrams.

When Lila's phone rang, Geneva didn't look up. Nor did she leave the room.

Initially proud of her decision—*Nobody puts baby in the corner*—she soon regretted it. Seeing Lila gush over every mind-numbing detail—A mall sighting of Peppa Pig? Flag football? French toast?—ratcheted up Geneva's insecurities. This was where Lila's heart lay. She carved out a space for Geneva, but then stuck her in the attic like Bertha Mason.

"Where's Grandma?" Levi asked.

"At the store. We're going to make cookies."

Liar, Geneva thought, banging the keys of her keyboard like Alicia Keys during "Girl on Fire." Sure, secrets can be fun. Hot under the right circumstances. She had a professor at Columbia that made a habit of late-night consultations. *Hot*. Being shoved back in the closet? Decidedly not hot.

Lila, perhaps sensing that Geneva was stabbing her with a mental voodoo doll, walked into the bedroom and closed the door.

The temperature dropped. Goosebumps raced up Geneva's arms. Her breath felt like icicles in her lungs. She felt Cristina's ghost, whispering, taunting Geneva. How did she let this happen? Geneva vowed after Cristina that she would be out and proud, never letting a girlfriend shame her, lie about her. And she wasn't starting now.

Geneva walked to the bedroom, pausing at the door to listen, determined to confront Lila when she finished. But it was Alex's voice, not the children, that stopped her cold.

"Where are you?" Geneva heard Alex ask.

"Clover Mountain," Lila answered. "I felt a sudden urge to ski."

"Clover Mountain. Geeze, that reminds me of Valentine's Day weekend. Must have been 2011? The winter before Levi was born. Remember how we got caught there during the storm?"

"How could I forget." The softness of Lila's voice killed Geneva. After everything, she still cared. In some ways, it made Geneva love her more. Lila had such a forgiving nature, such a huge capacity to love. Yet, it also infuriated her. Why was she content as Alex's punching bag? Especially when Geneva offered her unconditional love, an equal partnership.

Geneva swallowed hard and pushed open the door. Underneath her hoodie, she was sweating more than she did at her first and only spin class.

Lila sat on the bed, iPad drawn up on her knees, twirling her hair. Geneva longed to run a series of kisses along her protruding collarbone. Instead, she crouched next to Lila, whispering to appease her request for privacy, while ensuring it was loud enough for Alex to know she wasn't going anywhere. Today or in the future.

"Are you hungry?" Geneva asked. "I thought we could go into town for breakfast when you're done."

Lila's pupils darted like a couple of shaken dice. Her complexion matched the falling snow.

"*Lila*," Alex said with exaggerated patience. "Go somewhere we can talk. Privately."

Lila fled to the bathroom like she ate some bad Chinese.

Could Geneva have handled that better? Maybe. But she wasn't about to let Alex hijack their weekend. He expected Geneva to step aside, defer to his sham of a marriage. But why should she? There wasn't much of a marriage to save. They beat each other up, wore each other down. Sought pleasure in others. And yet, after weeks of bedding other women, on the same night Lila told him about Geneva, he decided to end the open marriage? Devote himself to Lila? *Pul-lease.* Geneva would pry Lila's damn eyes open with a forklift if necessary.

Alex's cockiness was his Achilles' heel. He discounted the depth of Geneva's and Lila's connection. He had history on his side, but Geneva understood what Lila needed now. She listened to Lila when Alex dismissed her. Gave her a sexual renaissance. Most importantly, Geneva understood her pain. The pain that accompanies a sudden death. The anger of betrayal. Unlike Alex, she wasn't waiting for Lila to snap out of it. *This* was Lila. And she loved her.

Geneva stood outside the bathroom door, unable to make out Alex's words above the fan, but the volume suggested yelling. All at once, Geneva knew, anger was not the way. Alex cornered the market. If Geneva demanded answers, voiced her frustrations about this half-assed holiday, Lila would leave. It would be a battle to control her temper, but Geneva had to use this weekend to offer Lila a respite from the stress of her marriage.

The shower started. Geneva took a deep breath before opening the bathroom door. It wasn't locked. A locked door would have smacked her in the face both literally and metaphorically, sending her into a rage.

"Want some company?" Geneva asked, stepping inside.

Lila spun around. Her cheeks flushed, an adorable quirk that happened whenever Geneva suggested something sexual. It was like Lila couldn't wrap her mind around the possibilities of a life with Geneva, one where she made love to a woman. Cute as it was, Geneva hoped it was a passing phase.

CHAPTER THIRTY-FOUR
LILA

Sunday morning. I got up early, before dawn, sneaking out of the cabin to hit the slopes as soon as they opened. Yes, I wanted one last ski run, but more so, I needed to be alone. Have time to think. I was still annoyed at Geneva for interrupting my call with Alex yesterday. *Purposefully* interrupting. After I asked her to give me space. We spent the day cooking, talking, watching movies, but our easy dynamic was off. My mind was on Alex, wondering what damage Geneva's stunt rued.

Alex was furious with me for going away with Geneva; furious, likely, at himself, for offering up the weekend, for putting us in this situation by starting the open marriage. But was his fury warranted? He gave me time. How I chose to spend that time, how I came to my conclusions, shouldn't matter. Should it? After a morning on the slopes, I still didn't know.

It was close to noon when I stepped back inside the cabin. Geneva rose from the couch, clad in a silky rose camisole and matching bikini bottoms. She kissed me; a plea, possibly an apology. I was tired. Both sweaty and frozen to the bone. Nervous about seeing Alex tonight. Not in the mood for sex. But I hadn't been in the mood for sex all weekend, fear switching off my sex drive the moment I watched Alex drive away. A visual reminder, a mental PSA, of everything I had to lose. So, I kissed Geneva back, making an effort to obtain the answers I sought out this weekend. That thought alone, that I was *forcing* myself, should've stopped me.

But it didn't.

Inside the bedroom, passion oozed from her lips. She ran her fingertips down my spine, teased my nipples, buried her face between my thighs—all moves that transcended me the first time. But today? I felt uncomfortable. I couldn't get out of my head. The duplicity strangled me, taking away my breath, until all I could think was no. No. No! NO!

"Stop!" I pushed her away, shivering despite the warmth in the room. "I'm sorry. I'm just—"

"Tired from fucking Alex?" Geneva's rage caught me by surprise. But it shouldn't have. After Alex's phone call yesterday, when I declined her offer to join me in the shower, tension simmered between us at a low boil. Another rejection blew off the lid. "Did you guys make up before he left?"

I flashed back to the night of Charlotte's party. His lips painting my body. Riding him. Fusing our bodies together until my nerve endings sang. My mind may have been confused, but my body knew exactly what it wanted.

"Let's not do this," I said, getting up to start packing, wishing I could fast-forward to tonight. Home. With my kids. I wouldn't take it for granted again.

"I deserve to know who I'm sharing a bed with." She pulled a pillow to her chest, squeezing it tight. "Diseases and all that fun stuff."

"Alex doesn't have any STDs."

Geneva smirked. "And you would know this how?"

Because he was my husband. A doctor. Because he would never put my health at risk. The man got a vasectomy because he was concerned about my health.

Yet none of these reasons would sway Geneva. Because Geneva wasn't worried about her health. She was used to being the center of attention, fawned over, adored. When I shone the spotlight her way, she became energetic and fun, insightful and provocative—the woman that brought me back from the brink. When I looked elsewhere, she became jealous and insecure.

"He promised to use condoms." I sounded tired. I was tired. The thought of having to spend the drive home defending my marriage made me want to weep with exhaustion. "And he's not having sex with anyone. Remember? He called it off."

She stood up, pulling on her camisole. "He's never broken a promise before?"

Geneva twisted the knife, itching for a fight.

"You're upset. I get it."

"Do you?"

"Yeah. You think I'm crazy for giving Alex another chance. But marriages are complicated—"

"I hooked up with someone on Wednesday," she said, launching the fact like a grenade, her tone spiteful and provoking. It hit, but not the way she intended. I felt rejected, yes, but mainly, I felt relief. That she wasn't looking to me to fill some undefined need. That she had other outlets. "I thought you should know. Since we're being honest."

"You don't have to explain." And she didn't. From the moment we met, she made it clear she craved sex, not commitment. Freedom to engage in new people and experiences. "I'm the one who's married."

She blinked, and if I didn't know her better, I thought she might cry. "Do you care? At all?"

I started picking up trash—napkins, wrappers, water bottles. "I don't want to think about it, if that's what you're asking."

"Then why don't you say that?" she yelled. "Why do you have to be so obtuse?"

"I'm sorry." I strangled a water bottle, unable to hide my frustration. At her. At myself. For reaching the age of thirty-eight and still not being able to express my feelings. "I'm horrible at talking. You know that."

My acknowledgement diffused the tension. She hugged me, the invisible chip-clip that held her shoulders together releasing. "Let's stay another night," she whispered in my ear. "This whole trip got messed up—we let Alex come between us."

I gently untangled myself. "I can't."

"Come on." She tugged my hand. "You know you want to."

I shook my head. "I miss the kids."

I went inside the bathroom and closed the door, resting my forehead against it. She was wrong. I didn't want to. While I had feelings for Geneva, after this weekend, I realized those feelings weren't love. At least, not the can't-live-without-you, you-complete-me, I'd-sleep-outside-your-door-in-the-pouring-rain-for-forgiveness type of love. The thought of losing her hurt, but it was our talks, not the physical intimacy, that left me empty. But that pain paled in comparison to losing Alex. Losing my marriage. My family.

Despite everything Alex put me through, his lies, his betrayals, his audacity in asking for an open marriage, I loved him. I wanted a better marriage, yes. An equal partnership. Another baby, if we could be so lucky. I willed myself to feel grateful for this dose of clarity, but fear overrode that emotion. I had no idea how he felt. Had the weekend strengthened his commitment to fix our marriage? Or made him realize we were better off apart? I hoped his heart lay with me, that he gained a willingness to compromise, as I did. But, in my gut, I knew, if the coin flipped the other way, if he let anger dictate his decisions, I would need Geneva's friendship to help me through.

CHAPTER THIRTY-FIVE
ALEX

The bright lights of the TV studio bore down on me, causing pinpricks of sweat to pool at my temples. My headache, which stalked me with low-grade pressure on the best of days, reached a crescendo once we went on-air. I struggled to stay awake. Think. Listen. Dispense advice. Normally, I prided myself on the warmth I gave to each caller. But, today? I couldn't charm the skirt off a corpse.

Rhony, the PA on *Ask Dr. Alex*, noticed it too. He unhooked my microphone when the show was, blissfully, if not successfully, over. "Thanksgiving hangover?"

"Didn't sleep much," I said before hurrying out of the studio.

That was an understatement. I drank too much after learning that Lila abused my generous offer of time. A night out with Geneva? Sure. A vacation together? Unfuckingbelievable. Whenever I managed to fall asleep—a rare feat—I dreamed about walking in on Geneva and Lila having sex. Lila's legs flapped to the sides like butterfly wings, her lips vibrating with whimpers, her neck arched in ecstasy. Geneva's head popped up between Lila's legs, her blood-red nails beckoning me. *I'll show you how she likes it.* I jerked awake each time, sweaty, yet shivering. *Just a dream*, I consoled myself. *It didn't happen.* Except it did. Some version of it. All goddamned weekend.

Rage filled every molecule of my body when I got home from Chicago last night. Lila hugged me, but she was no longer *my* Lila. I had to get away, before I said something unforgiveable. To save our marriage, I begged off with a headache and lay in bed, haunted by the Lego connection of Lila and Geneva's bodies.

Now, as I exited the studio and turned into the hallway, a sludge of lukewarm coffee splashed against my chest, snapping me out of my thoughts. A curly-haired woman stood before me, cheeks red, hand covering her mouth, too mortified to speak. The offending coffee cup lay in a puddle on the ground between us.

"You did me a favor," I said, deciding then and there to Uber it back to the clinic. Sleep deprivation was as lethal as alcohol. "I wanted to wear a brown shirt today, but it was dirty."

She laughed, a girlish tinkle that stroked the receptors in my brain. "Have we met?" I asked, dabbing at my shirt with my handkerchief.

She leaned in. "I wasn't going to say anything. You know, privacy laws."

I shrugged. My brain was too far gone to fill in the gaps.

"Bethany Warren. From Alliance Adoptions."

"Bethany." I shook her hand. Remembering. We met Bethany shortly after moving to Madison. After two miscarriages, adoption seemed like the logical step. We filled out the paperwork, underwent the home assessment with Bethany as the agency liaison, and started the waiting game when Lila got pregnant. Levi soon arrived, happy and healthy, and we withdrew our application.

"I love your segments. Such good parenting tips."

"I have two at home that provide most of the material."

"So, it all worked out then?" She sighed and smiled in contentment, as if a piece of chocolate was melting on her tongue. If by fathering two children, then, yes, it worked out. If you factored in the five miscarriages, one stillbirth, cheating, then no, I'd say everything went to hell. "I love hearing that. I always wonder about the couples that withdraw their applications." She looked behind her, then whispered, "Divorce. Difficultly having kids puts stress on a marriage."

I felt a hysterical bubble of laughter creep up my throat. "Couldn't be happier." My smile felt as false as the Joker's.

Rhony walked out of the studio, taking in my stained shirt with a bemused grin. "Your day just keeps getting better, doesn't it?"

"Nowhere to go but up."

Rhony turned to Bethany. "Ms. Warren, we need to get you miked."

"I'm filling in for my boss on an adoption segment." Bethany visibly paled. "I have terrible stage fright!"

After wishing her luck, I went to chug some coffee. It burned my esophagus like liquid bleach, the shock revving my heart and making me momentarily dizzy. I sat down, rummaging through my bag for pills. Ibuprofen was effective as popping Skittles at this point, but hopefully, combined with the caffeine, it would render me functional.

Or an amnesiac. Lila and Geneva continued to go at it in my head like a couple of coked-up porn stars.

CHAPTER THIRTY-SIX
LILA

I sat on a pillow on the floor of Hannah's office, trying to catch my breath. Feeling both at peace and jittery. At peace because I finally unburdened myself of the events that took place over Thanksgiving weekend. Jittery because, having heard the words out loud, I realized the state of my marriage was as perilous as I feared. That "taking time" might have been the death knell.

"Why didn't you tell Geneva you were upset?" Hannah asked, tightening her ponytail. Unlike me, she looked rested after the holiday weekend. Her cheeks glowed, her eyes wide and bright, and her pink hair had a sheen that I'd only witnessed in shampoo commercials. "That you felt like she ignored your request for privacy? Your boundaries?"

"Because..." I sighed. "It would've turned into a huge issue."

Hannah pressed her middle finger against her eyebrow, tracing the manicured arch. At first, I thought it was a subconscious tick, but now I wondered whether it was her subtle way of telling me I was screwing myself with my stupidity.

My only consolation: Hannah didn't do subtle.

"Sometimes letting things slide is a good trait in relationships. We shouldn't fight about every little issue. But you? It's like you took an oath of silence."

I considered this. "I'm not the only one." I glanced at my phone, wishing Alex would call. Even a text to pick up hamburger for dinner. I'd take any sliver of normalcy. Any indication we would survive this. "I spent the weekend missing Alex. Thinking about our marriage. But him? Who knows? Not one word when he came home last night. *Nothing.*"

Hannah smiled. "Why didn't you ask him how he felt? Share your thoughts?"

"He didn't give me the chance." I expected anger. Awkwardness. Best case scenario: a profession of love. But he didn't look at me. Stood rigid as he accepted my hug. It was true; indifference cut deeper than hate. "He had a headache and went straight to bed."

"You've gotten so comfortable not reacting, burying your feelings, that it doesn't occur to you to speak up—"

"I told Alex I wasn't ready to end the open marriage," I said, hoping to avoid another discussion on the genesis of my silence. Last week, we went in depth on my family history. Hannah claimed that the moment I ran after my dad's car and he didn't stop, I subconsciously learned that my voice didn't matter. That my mom doubled down on this lesson. Growing up with an alcoholic created an environment where denial, lying, and keeping secrets was normalized. I lacked stability. Became conflict adverse. Never learned how to properly communicate my feelings. It struck me as too simplistic. I doubted my brain worked in such a linear fashion. Then again, the ease with which I shut down after the vasectomy, the dozens of times I'd given into Alex to avoid an argument, my reluctance to let people in, gave credence to her theory. But I didn't want to focus on the past. I wanted to know what I could do now to fix myself, my marriage, not the broken little girl I once was.

"No. He brought up ending the open marriage," Hannah said. "After he found out about you and Geneva—another topic you stayed silent on. You *reacted* to his proposition."

"But I stood my ground."

"You did." She tapped her pen against her lips. "I don't think we ever dissected that. Why did you choose that moment to assert yourself?"

"I wanted time."

"Time to do what?"

I raked my nails across the suede pillow cover. "Figure things out with Geneva."

Hannah laughed, her blue eyes crinkling. "Lila, come on."

"What?"

Hannah's eyes drifted to the window behind me. "Here's the thing, I can't keep coddling you. Letting you lie to yourself," she said, zeroing back on me. "You need to make a choice. Be honest, be raw, even if you don't like what it says about you—otherwise, why come here?"

While our sessions were intimate, moments like this reminded me that she wasn't my friend. Hannah was a professional, paid by me, to challenge me. "I'm not lying."

She leaned forward, our knees nearly touching. "You detailed a weekend full of stress and tension. Stress because you don't know how to close the gap between the marriage you want and the marriage you have. And tension because, despite everything, you love Alex, not Geneva, and you don't know how to get out of this mess. Now." She softened her voice, making me feel like I was one breakthrough away from happiness. "Why do you want to continue the open marriage?"

Instinct. Pent-up anger with Alex for deciding our future. Again. Geneva factored, but Hannah was right, she wasn't *the* reason I asked for time.

I covered my face with my hands. "I want Alex to know what it's like to have someone make a decision, knowing it will devastate you, and do it anyways." Refusing to end the open marriage accomplished this. At least, I hoped it did. I hated hurting him but I was at a loss of what else to do. Talking didn't help. But maybe experiencing that ache would. I dropped my hands, looking at Hannah, willing her to understand. I *had* to take a stand. "Then, maybe, he'll understand how important it is that we make decisions about our future together. That his opinion can't mean more than mine. Maybe he'll change."

Hannah pressed her lips together. "It's a risk."

She was right. I hoped the weekend apart would humble him. Instead, I feared it pushed him away. "But it's fair, right?"

"Tell me this. Do you think it's fair to blame Alex for making decisions when you give him a sliver of your feelings? When you shut down instead of using your voice?"

"For getting the vasectomy? Yes, I do. He knew I wanted more kids."

She waved off my complaint like getting a vasectomy was as insignificant as getting a cavity filled. "You could've said no to the open marriage, right?"

I hesitated, feeling like I stepped into an episode of *Law & Order* and was about to be eviscerated on the stand. "Yes..."

"He discussed it with you? Asked if you had any better ideas how to fix your marriage?"

I nodded. Reluctantly.

"But instead of telling him that you were still upset about the vasectomy, you agreed." She flipped back several pages in her notebook. Blue pen filled the margins. It amazed me how much ground we covered. Then again, most people don't insist on daily appointments. "You could've refused to move to Madison, right? Alex had other job offers, ones in Chicago."

"I suppose..." Madison's pediatric critical care unit. He talked of nothing else for months. Who was I to deny him the job of his dreams?

"He wouldn't have gone without you?"

"No."

"But, once again, you buried your feelings and let Alex decide," she said. "Any other decisions he made without asking?"

"He always asks." It was impossible to explain Alex. His passion. His confidence. His protectiveness. It reminded me of the way people weaponized religion, insisting they were acting in the name of Jesus. Alex acted in the name of love, making opposition impossible. "But you're right. I deferred to Alex. Trusted him to make the right decisions. Which, clearly, wasn't the case with the vasectomy."

"I don't see a difference between the vasectomy and the rest of the decisions."

I tugged the sleeves of my sweater over my hands, suddenly cold. It felt like a betrayal, finding out she was secretly on his side this entire time. "What do you mean?"

"You guys talked about it." She spoke calmly, without malice, but the words embedded inside my heart like shards of glass. "And then he made a decision that he thought was best for your marriage, your family, similar to dozens of other decisions you've let him make."

"I told him no. That's what's different."

"That must have been frustrating, given your history, to use your voice and feel like it wasn't heard."

"He didn't listen." I squeezed my eyes shut, shaking my head. "That's a fact, Hannah, not a feeling."

"Let me ask you a question. And I want you to think before answering. Was there any part of you that wanted him to do it?"

My eyes snapped open. "No. I never—" She was baiting me, trying to get me to break through some invisible wall. But she crossed a line. "I never wanted this. I never would've given up. Ever." I grabbed my phone and stood up, refusing to spend another minute listening to her outrageous theories. "I would've kept trying for another baby until I died."

"Listen to yourself, Lila. *You would've kept trying until you died,*" Hannah said, drilling into each word. "You have two kids, whom you cherish, and yet you would've risked your life. Left them motherless. Can't you understand why Alex, who loves you, who knows you best, would've listened to you and still made that decision?"

If she punched me in the stomach, I wouldn't have felt it more keenly. I gulped for air. Everything I identified as, a good mother, a good wife, was false. Turns out, I hadn't abandoned my family on the surface, putting on a good face each day, but betrayed them at the deepest level possible.

I crumpled to the floor, my body heavy with guilt. I lied. I cheated. I wasted time. Precious, precious time, mourning the life I lost instead of enjoying the life I had.

And yet, I still wanted another baby. I'd still risk it.

"What's wrong with me?" I yelled, banging my fists against my thighs, tears sliding down my cheeks. "Why can't I move on? Forget about having another baby? Focus on now?"

Hannah rested her hands atop mine, stopping the blows. "You need to forgive yourself first."

The tears fell faster now. "How? How? Please tell me how."

"Why don't you tell Alex the truth about the day Milo died? That you blame yourself. Obsess over the hours you waited to call the doctor. Have nightmares about it. Why not share that pain?"

"It's my burden to carry." I pulled my hands away. "Not his."

"Hearing from Alex that it's not your fault might lift some of the burden."

"He can't know that. No one can."

Hannah tilted her head, assessing me. "Keeping this secret can't be easy on you."

It wasn't supposed to be easy. That was the point. That was part of my punishment. "I think the vasectomy is my comeuppance," I said. "For lying to Alex. I've sentenced myself to a life without more children."

"You're an amazing mom, Lila. You don't need another baby to prove that."

"It's not that simple." Maybe being childless herself, she couldn't fathom how each baby held your heart, even the ones never born.

"It's not that complicated, either," she said. "You feel betrayed, both by God and Alex. You feel like they stole something from you."

I grabbed a tissue, blowing my nose. "I feel incomplete."

"A baby won't complete you. It won't absolve your guilt. That's work you have to do in here." She tapped her head. "Tell him the truth."

"I can't."

"What are you afraid of?"

That he would never look at me the same. That he would agree I was at fault. That he wouldn't trust me to carry another baby.

"That he won't love me," I whispered.

When I pulled off the blinders, I didn't like what I saw. I blamed Alex for betraying me, but I was the one that introduced the culture of lying into our marriage. Lies that only beget more lies. I demanded that Alex listen. Now, I needed to tell him the truth. Whether I had the courage to do that, risk losing him not for a weekend but for good, I didn't know.

CHAPTER THIRTY-SEVEN
ALEX

"Hel-lo!" I walked inside the house, injecting joviality into my voice. After my disastrous *Ask Dr. Alex* taping, the afternoon dragged—wellness visits, flu, diarrhea, croup. Most days, I loved my job. Enjoyed the interactions, the development of relationships. I held them as pudgy-faced babies and shook their hands as college-bound adults. The diversity of personalities, talents, accomplishments, fascinated me.

Not today, though. After retreating last night, licking my wounds, I needed to see Lila. Put steps two and three of my plan into action.

"Daddy!" Charlotte jumped into my arms. Levi sat at the kitchen island, head bowed over his homework, while Lila smiled wanly from the stove.

"How was your day?" I asked, inhaling strawberries and glue as I held Charlotte close.

"Awful." She pouted. "Max sneezed on me. On *purpose.* And now I might die."

"You won't die," Levi muttered. "Tell her, Dad."

"You'll be fine." I set her down next to Levi. "Just wash your hands."

"That's what Mommy said," she grumbled, fake sneezing into a tissue, before adding it to the pile in front of her.

I ruffled Levi's hair and made my way over to Lila. "Let me take over." I rolled up the sleeves of my clean shirt, before unknotting my Batman tie and tucking it in my pocket. I gave her my most charming smile, the one that said, I love you, I will forgive you, as long as you don't share a single detail of your weekend with Geneva, unless it's how miserable you were with her. "You go change. I called Stacey to babysit tonight."

Lila's face crumpled. "Tonight?"

My plan was not off to a rousing success. Plan being a loose concept. Step one: give Lila time. Leaving for the weekend, knowing she would see Geneva, felt like taking a cheese grater to my penis. I wasn't a patient man. And I didn't like to share. Yes, I saw the irony. But time was what she needed to realize I was the one, the only one, so I endured it. Step two: apologize. Show her I listened, understood how my choices hurt her. Step three, win Lila back. A task that proved difficult if she resisted spending time together.

"What's wrong? Why not tonight?" I kept my tone friendly, even as my jaw locked in frustration. "I thought we agreed to make time for us, devote ourselves to fixing this."

"We will. I promise. But, tonight..." She sighed, looking down. "I'm exhausted."

Exhausted. Exhausted from too much sex? Work was grueling? The kids acted like thugs? She didn't say. One word. That's all it took. Lila and Geneva staged an encore in my head, trying to earn gold at the sexual Olympics.

I grabbed a beer from the fridge, not wanting her to see how much the rejection hurt. Swallowed a few ibuprofens to blunt the oncoming freight train of a headache.

"You look like you could use a night in, too." She tugged on my shirtsleeve, pulling me closer. "Are the headaches that bad? Maybe you should talk to someone."

"What?" I laughed, bitterly. "Like a doctor?"

She turned back to the stove. "Forget I said anything."

The kitchen became quiet. Too quiet. Charlotte stopped sneezing, watching us with her exacting brown eyes, while Levi stared blankly at his book. Amazing how well kids listened when you wished they'd turn a deaf ear.

I came up behind Lila, massaging her shoulders, inhaling the rich scent of lavender in her hair. "Sorry." If kids hear you fight, they needed to hear you apologize. A policy we laxed this past year. "I had my heart set on tonight. The weekend was...long without you."

Long. Miserable. Punishing. Several adjectives worked.

"Tomorrow." She leaned back against my chest. "I'll call Stacey to reschedule."

"It's a date."

A date. With my wife. We'd been on thousands, some as grand as the Signature Room atop the John Handcock building and others as cheap as Chinese takeout and bingeing *Homeland*. But tomorrow's date stood out. Never before did I have to convince Lila to trust me. Forgive me. Love me. My mind swelled with possibilities, none of which were good enough.

It wasn't until I was lying in bed that night, jacked up on caffeine, nauseated from Lila and Geneva's parade of orgasms, exhausted from the patient files that skittered around my brain like beetles, that I remembered Bethany. Without knowing it, she gave me a lifeline.

I closed my eyes and fell into a deep, dreamless sleep. Step three of my plan had come to fruition.

CHAPTER THIRTY-EIGHT
LILA

Alex leaned across the bamboo table at Zola, a steakhouse far too trendy and expensive for us. Tonight, however, Alex pulled out all the stops. He started by sending a bouquet of Calla Lilies to my office—the same flower I carried for our wedding. Then he fed the kids dinner, giving me a half-hour of uninterrupted time to prep for our date. And now, he regaled me with humorous stories of his weekend in Chicago with the kids.

"So, it's early Sunday morning and Char drags me downstairs to the kitchen," Alex said. "She pours oatmeal into a bowl, adds a dash of milk, and says, 'Daddy, I've done something for you, now you need to do something for me. Two words.' She holds up two fingers. 'Disney World.'" He threw up his hands. "Where does she get this stuff?"

I shrugged, unable to take much credit for my entrepreneurial daughter. "No idea."

"'Two more words,' she says. 'Christmas. Break.'" His impression of Charlotte was uncanny, including spot on voice inflections and facial tics to match her rainbow of moods.

"Oh, God." I laughed as the magnetic pull of Alex tugged me closer. His hand flirted with mine in the middle of the table, fingers playing my palm like a piano, soft and rhythmic.

"So, I head her off at the pass. 'Santa doesn't visit Disneyworld.'"

"Clever."

He wagged his finger at me. "You would think, but no. 'Santa visited us at Grandma's.' She was two. How does she remember that?"

"Imagine when she grows up," I said. "Negotiating skills like that."

"Our baby could run the world."

The server broke the spell, delivering the food. Two perfectly seared filets mignon atop gleaming white china, surrounded by platters of grilled asparagus, truffle fries, and steamed broccoli.

"Amazing," Alex said, chewing with his eyes closed. I remembered the first time I witnessed this, his sensual relationship with food, in the bleachers at Wrigley Field. He took a spoonful of rocky-road ice cream, closing his eyes as it melted inside his mouth. Around us, fans cheered a go-ahead hit, while I watched Alex, mesmerized by his adorable quirks.

He opened his eyes and smiled. "Perfection. And I don't just mean the food."

I felt nervous going out tonight, as if this was a first date. But Alex, much like on our real first date, displayed enough charm to put me at ease. Our conversation remained firmly planted on safe topics—Levi's intelligence, Charlotte's exuberance, the new doctor he hired—but the dynamic was so good, so *easy*, it was like being offered a glimpse into an alternate universe. One where we never lost Milo. Never stopped talking. Never opened our marriage to outsiders.

We were both pretending and yet I felt happier than I had in months.

"I've been thinking." He set down his utensils. "What if we adopted?"

The steak, seconds before sprinkling my taste buds with delicious juices, butter, and spices, tasted like rawhide. I struggled to swallow. Alex broached this topic after the first couple miscarriages, never one to mope when he could play Mr. Fix-It. Apparently, he was at it again. "Where's this coming from?"

"I love you." The candlelight flickered across his face, illuminating eyes the color of a stormy sky. Eyes that looked haunted—with pain, regret, perhaps fear. "I know some of my choices made you question that, made you feel like I wasn't listening, and I'm sorry. Good intentions can't make up for deceiving you." He pulled his chair perpendicular to me, our faces inches apart, our hands interlocked. "But I'm listening now. And I promise, I'm going to do better."

My mouth looked like a fish, opening and closing without any sound. I waited months for Alex to apologize, take accountability, listen. And here he was, doing that and more. So, why did I still feel sad? Mourning who we used to be? That narrative, the one my brain spun that cast us as equal partners, equal decision-makers, was fiction. From day one, Alex acted and I supported. With the vasectomy, it was easier to blame him, luxuriate in what if's, forget how he tried reasoning with me, than accept responsibility for my silence.

Whereas a few weeks ago, I equated forgiveness with weakness, an admission that he acted correctly, I now saw strength in my decision. Because forgiveness was a decision, as important as any he made.

"I forgive you." I sniffled as tears swelled in my eyes. I needed to say the words as much as he needed to hear them. "I forgive you."

He ran both hands through my hair, cupping my chin as he kissed my cheek, catching the first tear. "I am sorry. I thought I was doing what was best, but I went about it the wrong way. And I want to give you your dream back. Strike that." He shook his head. "I want to give *us* our dream back."

I shivered in my sleeveless black dress. "Alex..."

His eyes searched my face. "What's wrong?"

"You don't want to hear it."

"Don't do that." He pressed his forehead against mine. "Don't shut me out again."

"If you wanted to give us our dream back, you'd reverse the vasectomy," I whispered, knowing the argument was as futile as beating a dead dog. But if the second act of our marriage was going to be based on honesty, I needed to stop silencing myself.

"I disagree." He sat back. "Our dream was to have a big family; we never said that meant biological children. Imagine the life we could provide if we adopted." Alex splayed his fingers to paint a picture. "Loving parents. Older siblings. Good schools. Parks. Sports. Vacations. The list is endless."

I looked up at the exposed piping in the ceiling. Alex was right. Adoption was the safer option. We could give a child a home. A child that might otherwise bounce around in the foster system, unclaimed and unloved. If we put the argument down on paper, he'd win. That was what I couldn't explain to Hannah. The reason I deferred to him. Sat on my feelings. Because he was almost always right.

But having a child was also an emotional adventure, a rollercoaster ride, a game of Russian Roulette. The exhilaration of pushing Levi and Charlotte into this world, screaming and thriving. The devastation of witnessing blood and tissue in my underwear. The deafening silence of Milo's homecoming. And yet I'd do it again. A hundred times for a chance at another child.

I knew that was selfish. Hannah moved the fault lines, helping me understand that while my anger at Alex's betrayal was justified, pushing my marriage to the brink was not. Pushing Alex to reverse the vasectomy, when he didn't have the emotional capacity to undergo another miscarriage, proved I wasn't listening to him either.

"I need time to think," I said.

He took a long pull of his beer, assessing me. "That seems to be a frequent request."

His attitude slapped me back to reality. We weren't in a place to have a baby, adopted or otherwise. Our marriage sat teetering atop a cliff, a strong wind capable of pushing it to safety or death.

"A baby won't fix us, Alex. It's not a Band-aid. You, more than anyone, should know better."

"I wasn't using it as one. I thought I was providing a solution to end this stalemate." He threw his napkin over his half-finished plate, both of us having lost our appetites. "Every time we talk, it's babies, babies, babies. I thought you'd be happy."

I was happy. *Ish.* It was a strange feeling, one of elation and trepidation, realizing that he listened, internalized what I wanted, reflected on his own desires. Would this have happened if he hadn't found out about Geneva? If I hadn't asked for time? I didn't know. I doubted he did either.

"A little time. To work on us," I said, knowing we had bigger hurdles ahead than adoption. We needed to rebuild our trust, an impossible feat until I ended my relationship with Geneva. Impossible until I told him the truth about Milo—an admission that might render his adoption offer moot. Impossible until I figured out how to forgive myself. Parenting Levi and Charlotte this past year was like driving while sedated; I wouldn't have another baby until I felt ready to give my love as a gift, rather than an atonement. "Then we can decide together."

His face fell. A defeated look he usually only wore when the Cubs got eliminated from the playoffs. "I just...I got excited. Another baby— without all the fear."

"Adoption carries a whole new set of worries."

He squeezed my hand. "But none of them includes losing you."

I would have kept trying until I died. Alex knew this, without me ever saying it, and it terrified him. Hannah was right; the vasectomy wasn't an ego trip. He wasn't dismissing my feelings. He was trying to save me from myself. It was an act of love—albeit a misguided one. And loving him meant I couldn't ask him to suffer through another pregnancy. If we chose to have more children, adoption was the only way. It was a true compromise.

I brushed my fingers against his stubble. He tossed his razor, on a workday, for me. A subtle gesture, but one that didn't go unnoticed. "I like the beard."

He kissed me. "For you, babe, the moon."

Regardless of what we chose to do, Alex apologized. He refused to fix the past, but he wanted to create a future. One where I was happy. One where I had a say. It felt promising.

CHAPTER THIRTY-NINE
GENEVA

Geneva sat at her desk in White Hall, grading papers. Her banker's lamp filled the dark room with a green halogen glow. Snow fell in fat flakes outside her window, blanketing the campus. It wouldn't be an easy trek home; nearly impossible in three-inch Chloe booties. She needed to get over herself and invest in some winterized boots.

The office was empty, everyone using the snow as an excuse to leave early. But Geneva didn't want to face another night alone in her apartment, drinking to numb her thoughts, waiting for Lila to call. If she couldn't succeed romantically, she'd do so professionally.

She wrapped this logic around herself like a safety blanket, but it failed to soothe her. She wanted to be with Lila. But it felt like the more she gave, the less she got in return.

If she had any doubt that Lila was pulling away, their dwindling sexual connection proved it. Geneva used sex to communicate her love, not ready yet to say the words. But Lila wasn't interested in sex last weekend, going so far as to push Geneva away in the middle of going down on her. Mentally running back to Alex, if not yet physically.

The rejection made Geneva angry. She'd been patient, understanding, *calm* all weekend. And for what? *Nothing.* Geneva lashed out, insulting Alex's character, horrified at the ease with which Lila jumped to his defense. Then it made Geneva foolish. Geneva lied to procure an ounce of affection, telling Lila she hooked up with someone else. In the moment, it felt like a sure-fire way to get Lila to confess her real feelings. But Lila took it in stride, a nonchalance as lethal as a bullet to the head. And finally, Geneva humiliated herself, begging Lila to stay another night.

It pained her to remember.

Geneva's phone buzzed and her heart lurched. But it was only her mother, who, after months of silence, spent the past several days stalking Geneva's phone. Geneva answered, delighted to have a target for her frustration.

"We missed you at Thanksgiving," her mother said by way of greeting, her rich voice a time capsule, causing an unexpected sense of loss in the pit of Geneva's belly.

"I didn't realize I was invited."

"Geneva." Her mother sighed. "How old are you?"

"Old enough to know where I'm not wanted."

"This is your home. You're always welcome here."

Geneva snorted. Her mother spoke as if their apartment was a museum. During set hours, she was *welcome*. "But not my guests?"

"Must we talk about this?"

"We've been avoiding it for thirteen years and look where it got us," Geneva said, putting her mother on speaker. She stood up and closed her office door—just in case there were any stragglers. "Months without speaking."

"Thirteen years?"

Was her mother deliberately being obtuse? The memory of her mother picking her up in New Hampshire, packing up Geneva's belongings, and making the five-plus hour drive back to Manhattan in silence rubbed like a blister. Her father was either too busy or too disgusted to make the trip. They stopped once, at a diner in Connecticut, where her mother attempted to rewrite history.

If anyone asks, tell them you wanted to be closer to home, her mother said.

And forget that Cristina died? My best friend, my girlfriend—

Her mother's nostrils flared, as if the word, the very thought, smelled of raw sewage. *We never should've sent you to an all-girls school*, she interrupted. *I blame myself.* A few minutes later, they were back in the car, never to speak of it again.

Was it any wonder that Geneva was emotionally bankrupt? She was taught by the best.

"Yes, Mother. Thirteen years since Cristina died," Geneva said. "Thirteen years I've spent wondering what's so abhorrent about me, that Cristina killed herself rather than being out with me."

"Well, she certainly did a number on you," her mother said. "Then again, you've always been a little self-centered."

Geneva's head fell to the desk with a thud. Pot? Meet kettle. "You weren't there. It had everything to do with me. With us."

"When I found out what happened to Cristina—and I don't pretend to know all the details—I thought to myself: what an unstable child. What a *sad* child. Imagine the self-loathing, the extreme pain she felt being inside her own skin, to want to kill herself." Geneva wanted to argue. Cristina wasn't in pain; she was scared, scared of loving a woman. But curiosity kept her quiet. After thirteen years of harboring this secret, she needed an outside perspective. "It's never going to make sense to you," her mother continued. "Suicide is nonsensical—except to *that* person, in *that* moment." Here, she revved up, almost preaching. "But *you* didn't shove a bottle of pills down her throat. However you two left it, she made that choice. And, frankly, if you spent thirteen years trying to figure out what's wrong with you, I think that question says more about you than it does her."

Broken down into such blatant terms, Geneva felt stupid. She built a shrine for Cristina, kneeling down and praying for answers. Answers it could never give. Why had she given Cristina such power over her? As her mother said, Cristina was unstable. And yet, Geneva took the worst interpretation of Cristina's suicide and turned it into gospel. A warning against giving her heart away. A verdict that she was unworthy of love.

Child. The truth of the word, the designation, struck Geneva. They *were* children. Playacting at love. Exploring sex. Even Cristina's actions were brash—a child throwing a fit, unable to wait for the rage, the fear, to pass. To know that, one way or another, she would survive her parents' shame.

"I'm worried about you," her mother said when Geneva still hadn't responded. "You must be lonely if you're ruminating about the past."

Geneva bit her tongue. She'd admit she was broke, fired, *arrested* before she'd admit she was lonely. But that didn't make it any less true. Even when surrounded by beautiful women, good friends, she felt melancholia, like no one understood her. And how could they? She acted like she was in the witness protection program, guarding the secrets to her past as if Cristina's suicide was evidence of degenerate DNA, a fatal chromosomal abnormality, that made Geneva unlovable. For this, she had no one to blame but herself.

"I'm in love," Geneva whispered. "And I'm afraid, much like Cristina, she doesn't love me back."

She heard her mother inhale, the slightest show of hand, her hesitancy at giving her gay daughter love advice. "Tell her," she said, surprising Geneva. "What do you have to lose?"

Heartbreak. Devastation. Chronic fear of being unlovable confirmed in neon lights.

Lila, as if eavesdropping on the call, decided to put Geneva out of her misery. *Can I come over tomorrow night?* Lila texted.

Geneva took a deep, quivering breath, wiping away tears of relief. It wasn't over!

"Baby, don't cry," her mother said, misunderstanding Geneva's emotional outburst.

Sure, Geneva texted. *Drinks at Hyde Out first? @8?*

"Does Father know you called?" Geneva asked.

"He wants what's best for you."

Mother always protected him. "What *he* thinks is best."

Her mother laughed. A melodious sound that filled Geneva with joy on the rare occasion she sparked it as a child. It had the same effect now. "The prerogative of being a parent."

"And what do you want?"

"My daughter back. I'm not going to sugarcoat this, darling; your father will never allow you to bring a woman home. And I won't try to convince him otherwise. That's not my battle. But—" She paused, always dramatic. "—perhaps, next time you're in the city, I could meet this woman you love."

Geneva burst out in laughter, never having expected such a gift. Maybe her shock and awe campaign over Memorial Day weekend worked—the fruit taking months to ripen. While it wasn't everything, it was enough. For now. Her mother listened, wanted a relationship. One that allowed the possibility of acceptance.

"First, I have to convince her to give us a chance," Geneva said, watching the three bubbles appear and disappear on her text link with Lila.

"You don't have to convince anyone of anything, baby. Be the beautiful, strong, fearless woman I raised."

Okay, Lila finally texted, attaching a smiley face emoji. Normally, Geneva abhorred the use of emojis, but now she rubbed her thumb over it, as if they were Lila's lips.

She talked with her mother for a few more minutes, each second that ticked by filling her with courage. The only way forward was to face her past. Her fear, anger, jealousy, came from a place of pain, of rejection. Lila had no idea. No one did. But maybe if she told Lila the truth about Cristina, she would understand that Geneva's fears were a long-suffering attempt to never let the past repeat itself. Never feel that agony again. Having unexpectedly lost Milo, Lila would understand. And perhaps, by being vulnerable, Lila would meet her half-way, take her own risks.

She spent years on this treadmill, making sure no one got close enough to hurt her, see the real Geneva. And she wanted to stop. Lila was worth stopping for. Lila was worth confessing her secrets. Lila was worth everything. It was time to crack her heart open, expose her flaws, fears, and dreams, and hope like hell that Lila wanted to pick up the pieces.

CHAPTER FORTY
ALEX

"Watch this, Daddy!" Charlotte cried, as she swam underwater in our bathtub, pretending to be Ariel. She emerged, her long eyelashes fanned out like blades of grass, wet with dew. She was beautiful, my girl.

"Wow!" I clapped, sitting on the edge of the tub. "You might really be a mermaid."

Charlotte gave me Lila's signature stare: narrowed eyes, curled lips, flared nose. "I have legs, Daddy. I'm using my imagination."

Lila walked into the bathroom, dressed in jeans and an oversized, chunky cream sweater. "You need to rub your body with soap, Charlotte," Lila said, standing over the tub. "Not just make bubbles."

I stared at Lila, confused. Normally, by eight p.m., she was in pajamas. At least, comfy yoga pants. "Are you going out?" I asked as Charlotte kicked water in my face.

"I'm meeting Geneva. But, don't worry." She gave me a small smile before walking to her vanity. "I'll be home early."

After our date two nights ago, I fell into the most contented night's sleep since Milo died. I apologized. She forgave me—three words that now rivaled the first time she said she loved me as the biggest gamechanger in our relationship. Both of us pledged to talk through our feelings, be honest. We sealed those promises with our bodies.

The thought of her going out with Geneva, as if none of that happened, made me want to smash the mirror into a thousand pieces. What else did I have to do? What else *could* I do?

"Don't worry?" I repeated, incredulous. I stood up and grabbed a towel, drying my face. "Why would I worry?" I lowered my voice, hissing in her ear. "You're only fucking her."

Her hair brush froze mid-swipe. Her eyes skirted towards Charlotte. "Alex, not now."

"We had an agreement. One weekend. That's all."

"I know."

"And yet, here you are." I spread my hands out. "Still seeing her."

"I need to talk to her—"

"You had all weekend to talk." I didn't want her anywhere near Geneva. "Talking" was the oldest rule in the playbook: get them to meet to talk, have one more drink, come upstairs. I picked up her phone from the vanity, holding it out to her. "Text her. Tell her you can't see her tonight. Or any other night, for that matter."

Her eyes scanned the room, unblinking, while slowly shaking her head, as if I was overreacting. What did she expect? That I'd give my blessing to have an open marriage in perpetuity?

"No." Lila snatched her phone from me. "She deserves a conversation."

"She deserves?" I laughed. "That's rich. How kind of you to think about what *she* deserves." I turned back to Charlotte, pulling her out of the tub before she could complain or negotiate. "Bath time's over."

I toweled Charlotte down, rubbed lotion over her body, helped put on her PJs. Meanwhile, Lila brushed her teeth, sprayed perfume on her wrists, readying herself for a date in front of me like this was a sorority bathroom. Charlotte must have sensed the tension because she sat quietly while I untangled and braided her long curls. A first.

Ready for bed, Charlotte sprinted away, eager to finish watching *Moana*. I locked the bathroom door behind her, closing my eyes and resting my head against the wood. Bright lights flashed behind my eyeballs, fiery oranges and toxic yellows, while a tiny marching band played inside my head. I took a deep breath, searching for a level of calm and patience I didn't possess.

"Stop seeing her," I grunted at the exact moment Lila said, "Tonight was supposed to be—"

Lila pressed her knuckles against her lips. Our eyes met, a quick flick that told me the pain ran deep. Deeper than I had been able to mine. "Never mind," she said. "Why tell you? You haven't changed one bit."

I threw my hands up. "What does that mean?"

"Do you hear yourself? The way you speak to me? 'Stop seeing her,'" she mimicked, lowering her voice. "I'm your wife, not one of your nurses." She turned around, facing the mirror. Her hand trembled as she put on her lipstick, the only giveaway that this new spine hadn't completely hardened. "I don't take orders from you."

"Orders?" I tugged on my hair. "Jesus, Lila, you're cheating. Would you prefer I not care? That I let you go without a fight? Perhaps offer up our bed for use?"

She pulled the lipstick away from her mouth, defiantly snapping on the cap. "I'd prefer you trust me. Have a conversation, instead of dictating what I can and cannot do."

"I'm here. Ready to talk." I grabbed her shoulders, spun her around, bending down until we were roughly the same height. "I'll talk all night. Do whatever it takes."

"Yeah, on your schedule. Your terms. It always about what you need."

"No. It's about what *we* need. What our marriage needs to survive."

She took a step backwards, leaning against her vanity with her arms crossed, ensuring we were no longer touching. "Is that a threat?"

This woman may have looked like my wife, but she had the steely determination of a stranger. No, not a stranger: Geneva. It felt like Geneva was glaring at me. Pushing me to the brink. Goading me into saying something unforgiveable.

"It's the truth," I said, matching her aggressive posture by crossing my arms. Was it, though? Yes, it had to be. I couldn't go on like this, sharing Lila. I wasn't cut out for an open marriage. I never was.

"I thought divorce wasn't an option?"

I swallowed. "That was before you cheated on me."

Lila squatted, tilting her head down, her hair covering her face. When she stood back up, her face was flushed. "You cheated on me. Why do you keep acting like this is my fault?"

"If you're doing this to punish me, get even, you can stop," I said. "I'm already gutted."

Her mouth dropped open. "Punish you?"

"You've been punishing me since the vasectomy. First, it was not having sex, and now, it's Geneva. At least be honest."

"Still," she said, pressing her hands to her cheeks. "You don't get it."

"What? Enlighten me. What don't I understand?"

"This is about choices, Alex, not punishment. How you have the power to make them and I don't."

I shook my head. "Bullshit."

"You got the vasectomy. You opened up our marriage. You're telling me I can't see Geneva. All of these decisions, you made." Lila's voice was calm. Eerily calm. Her rigor mortis fingers, where she counted off my infractions, betrayed the only hint of stress. "But now you need to wait. Because if we're going to make this marriage work, both of us need to have a say."

The word *if* echoed inside my head, becoming more sinister with each repetition. Our marriage had become a giant game of poker, both of us upping the ante. Regardless of the cost, I had to go all in.

"If you leave, Lila, that's it." With each word, I became more and more aware that I was doing Geneva's bidding. And yet I couldn't stop. I needed Lila to stay home. Choose us. Now. "I'm done."

Her eyes widened, holding mine, waiting for a retraction. None came. She brushed past me, shutting the door behind her.

All the fight left my body as I slumped to the floor, shaking and cold despite the mugginess of the room. Nausea spread like a wildfire through my stomach, torching my esophagus. My head? Explosive.

I played my hand and lost. How much, was the only question that remained.

CHAPTER FORTY-ONE
LILA

I drove to Hyde Out in record time, frustration giving me a lead foot. This was not how tonight was supposed to go. He was supposed to trust me when I said I needed to talk to Geneva. Isn't that what we agreed to work on, trust and communication?

I imagined coming home after my break-up with Geneva, curling up in Alex's arms, and telling him I was his and his alone. Forever. Telling him the truth about Milo. Making myself as vulnerable as the night I told him about the rape, and pray that, once again, he would love me. Pray that he would forgive me.

And then Alex had to ruin it by flexing his muscles, demanding that I never see Geneva again, threatening to divorce me if I didn't kowtow to his demands.

It was still Alex's way or no way.

I screeched to a stop, finding an unexpected parking spot out front. But I was too angry to go inside. I squeezed my fists together and screamed. *Goddamn him!*

Geneva's face lit up when I walked in the door ten minutes later. With coal-rimmed eyes, nude, matte lips, and a golden headband that made her dewy skin sparkle, she looked beautiful. Impossibly, so. She jumped off her chair and hugged me, a gesture that usually comforted me, but tonight left me bereft. This was goodbye.

"You look upset," Geneva said once we were sitting.

"I'm good."

"Is it Alex?" Her voice was soft. "I know I said some awful things on Sunday, but this time, I promise, I'll listen."

I shook my head, sipping the Coke Zero she had waiting for me. That was a land mine I could see well in advance.

"Okay, then. There's something I wanted to talk to you about." She took a deep breath, giving me a bright smile. "I got an invitation to my boarding school reunion. Which is odd, because I never graduated from there."

I sat back in my chair, confused. "Oh?"

"At the end of my junior year, I was—" She tapped her blush nails against her wine glass. "—ushered out? Encouraged to explore another academic institution."

"Why?"

"My ex, Cristina—"

My phone chimed. "Sorry," I said, opening the photo. It was a selfie of Alex lying in bed with Levi and Charlotte tucked underneath each arm. Charlotte blew kisses at the camera while Levi made a peace sign. As I magnified the picture, I noticed how Levi's jaw was starting to square like Alex's. Charlotte's fingers had become long and elegant where they pressed against her lips, losing the baby pudge. I remembered how she gripped my index finger in her fist while breastfeeding, eyes locked on mine. They were growing up. I had a finite number of nights to kiss them goodnight, sing songs, read books, talk, before they closed the door on me.

And I was here. With Geneva. Missing it.

Alex accused me of using Geneva to punish him. Looking at this picture, I realized there might be some truth to his accusation. His outburst triggered me; I feared that if I gave in to his demands, we'd regress to our old power dynamics: Alex deciding, me staying silent. But, having calmed down a little, I realized that wasn't true. I put him in an impossible position—baited him, manipulated him by leaving out pertinent information—and then blamed him for failing the test.

Fear. Anger. Revenge. Nothing else could explain why I didn't insist, talk over him, to tell him the truth about Geneva.

"What's so important?" Geneva asked, grabbing my phone out of my hands. She squinted, studying the picture, before tossing the phone back, dealing it like a card. She drained the remainder of her wine, and then stood up, shuffling on her coat. "I was trying to tell you something. Something I've never told anyone."

I reached for her hand. We started as friends and I wanted to part as friends. Listening was the least I could do. "Please. Tell me."

She gazed up at the ceiling, lips pressed in a tight line. "Will you put the phone away? Promise to listen?"

I tucked it inside my purse. "Done."

"Come on. Let's talk back at my place."

Yes. I could promise a couple more hours. And when I got home, I'd wake up Alex, apologize, and tell him everything.

CHAPTER FORTY-TWO
ALEX

Charlotte found me sitting on the bathroom floor, head between my knees. "Daddy, what are you *doing*?" she asked, crawling on my lap.

I looked into her big brown eyes, identical to Lila's, searching for an answer. Lila walked out. Dismissed my pain. Dismissed me. The threat to end our marriage slipped off her tongue like a common courtesy. Her steely-eyed acceptance when I issued my own made divorce a fait accompli. But that wasn't an answer I could give Charlotte.

"Resting." I picked her up, thinking about how parenting never stops. There's no time out for emotional distress—well, unless you're Lila and just leave, assuming, once again, that I would pick up the pieces in her wake. "Come on, it's bedtime."

After tearing Levi away from the X-box, Levi, Charlotte, and I snuggled up in his bed to read Harry Potter. When I finished, I wrapped my arms around them and snapped a picture. *This*, I wanted to say to Lila. *This is why I'm fighting for us.* Or maybe it wasn't quite so altruistic. *Look what you'll miss out on if you choose her.*

In the end, I kissed the kids goodnight, sending the picture without text.

I headed to the basement, taking my anger out on the punching bag. Yes, I messed up. The vasectomy. The open marriage. But I apologized. Vowed to do better. I was doing better. Wasn't I? And yet, she still wanted to punish me.

My heart thrashed, begging me to issue a reprieve, but rage spurred me on. Okay, maybe she didn't set out to punish me. Maybe Milo's death and the shock of not bearing any more children stole her libido, but it turned into a punishment. Dante's-fucking-inferno once I proposed the open marriage.

My offer to adopt hadn't been enough to win her back. She acted like I was throwing solutions at her like darts, seeing which one stuck. But she was wrong. I wanted to create the family we dreamed up together. When Lila told me about her childhood, the way it felt cold even on the hottest of days, never brimming with chocolate chip cookies or laughter after a silly story or a hug on a bad day, I felt a desire kick in that I've never felt before: to provide. I wanted to share *my* childhood. Sure, it wasn't perfect, but I had two parents that loved me. Siblings that had my back. A home waiting regardless of the transgression. Much as I dreamed of being a doctor, when I met Lila, the dream expanded to include husband and father.

Adoption would secure our future while leaving the past behind. Not forgetting. Never. But learning, forgiving, and moving on. Yet, she forced us to stay in this purgatory. All to spend time with that woman. What was I missing?

As I took another punch, a lightning bolt of pain ripped through my jaw, rattling my teeth. Time to call it quits.

I clutched the railing, trudging up the stairs to the kitchen. At the sink, I drank straight from the tap. I rinsed water over my head, trying to cool down, slow my racing heart. Nothing worked. I gasped for air. It felt like trying to breathe at 10,000 feet—the air shallow and my lungs deprived. *Was I having a panic attack?* Absurd. But then I doubled over, clutching my chest. Shock waves of pain weaved their way across my chest, constricting my breath further.

Not a panic attack, a heart attack.

I rummaged through the medicine cabinet for aspirin, popping two pills in my mouth. Whether it was the drugs or simply a placebo effect, a straw size hole opened inside my lungs.

I grabbed my phone and called 911. Maybe it was a panic attack, but I learned in medical school to treat the most obvious cause first. *When you hear hoofbeats, think horses, not zebras,* said one attending, fond of clichés. Dr. Castor. That was his name. That man, with a watermelon-sized belly, was destined for a heart attack. Not me.

"Possible heart attack," I grunted, ignoring the 911 operator's command to stay on the line. I needed Lila. Now. But her phone went to voicemail. I called the McArthur's, grateful when Shannon said she'd be right over.

Breathing like I was on the last leg of a marathon, I made my way to the front door and opened it. I slumped to the floor as a heavy tingling sensation crawled down my left arm.

I called Lila again, leaving a message. "Please."

Please what? Please don't leave me? Please come home? Please forgive me? Please don't let me die?

Two paramedics barreled through the door, crouching beside me, saying words I couldn't make out. Blood roared through my ears like a white noise machine while they strapped me to a stretcher and started fastening nobs to my chest for the ECG.

Seconds later, Shannon appeared. Her glacial eyes widened as she took me in, her mouth opened in a silent scream.

The paramedics guided the stretcher out the door. Halfway down the front walk, I saw Levi, silhouetted by the soft light in the foyer. He sprinted after me. Tears clung to his eyelashes as he raced alongside the stretcher. His chin quivered with effort to hold it all in. Shannon pulled him back, fighting against his wiry limbs, as they shuffled me inside the van.

Black spots decorated my vision as we rode to the hospital. A lowlight reel of the past year ran through my mind. I saw the way Lila shut down, caving into herself, her voice quieter as mine grew louder, until she all but disappeared. I saw myself—selfish, oblivious, egotistical. I was so arrogant in thinking I knew best, that the question of whether I should, whether I had the *right*, to make these decisions never occurred to me. Decisions that worked to my benefit, on my timetable, that fit my set of moral parameters. Decisions that didn't engage Lila, but rather broke her spirit. Decisions, I feared, that may have cost me my marriage.

I couldn't let that happen. There was no living without Lila. No love without Lila. No family. Home. Everything we had, we created together. Partners. Lovers. Friends.

She demanded more of me, of our marriage, to communicate and work together to make decisions, and I failed her. But I would rise to the occasion. The promise sat on my tongue as an explosion of pain rippled through my chest.

CHAPTER FORTY-THREE
LILA

I sat next to Geneva on her couch, holding her hand, while my phone vibrated inside my purse—the fifth call since arriving. While I wanted to talk to Alex too, he would have to wait. This was my last night with Geneva and I'd do her the honor of listening without interruption.

Mascara-filled tears zig-zagged down Geneva's face, polygraphing her cheeks, as she recounted the tumultuous last day of her relationship with Cristina. My heart ached for her. Seventeen and confused, no one to talk to. Cristina left. Her parents too busy to care. Ostracized by her friends. The administration silent. Nobody stepped forward to tell her that she did nothing wrong. That love, in any variation, could never be wrong.

"Then I find out, no, she isn't ignoring me." Geneva dabbed a tissue against her eyes. "She overdosed..."

Geneva's words faded as my phone buzzed. Again. This felt too petulant for Alex. Could it be someone else? My mom? The kids? I had to know. I reached inside my purse, which was nestled next to my leg, and discreetly tilted the screen up.

"What's wrong with you?" Geneva said, jerking her hand away. Her face was haunted, the hurt so raw I nearly gasped. When someone lays themselves bare, you listen. You honor their courage. I let her down.

"I missed a bunch of calls." I held up my phone, hoping transparency would grant some leniency. Two from Alex, three facetime calls from Levi's iPad, one from Shannon, and another from an unknown number. "I'm worried."

"Levi probably overheard Alex and Shannon going at it," she said before sipping her wine. "You might need to have *the talk* with him earlier than planned."

I stared at her, marveling at how she turned on her rage as easily as a faucet. Having heard about Cristina, I understood its origin. The fear that she was unlovable. But those were the fears of a teenage girl. She needed to stop using a single experience as a shield and a sword.

That thought flew out of my mind when my phone buzzed. I answered it. "Hello?"

"Lila Cole?"

"Yes."

"I'm a nurse at Lakeside Vista Hospital." Images of Alex, Levi, and Charlotte flashed through my mind like baseball cards, framed and frozen in action. Alex, sweaty and smiling beneath his Notre Dame cap, running towards me. Levi, biting his pencil while solving an equation. Charlotte, mid-pirouette, arms forming an oval above her head. "Your husband was brought in complaining of chest pains. The doctors are with him now, but you should come as soon as possible."

I squeezed the phone. "Wait. Slow down. What happened?"

I heard shouting in the background. "Check in at emergency when you get here and they'll be able to tell you more."

The call ended.

"Alex's in the hospital," I said, stunned. I dealt with a fair share of adversity—an absent father, an alcoholic mother, the rape, the miscarriages—but that was the gamble we took as humans. Fate dealt me a few bad hands. So be it.

But this felt pointed, as if God watched the way I treated Alex tonight and decided to strike me down. Teach me a lesson for having the audacity to usurp His role as the judge, jury, and executioner.

Geneva rubbed my back. "Is he okay?"

"I don't know." I squeezed my eyes shut. Where were the kids? At the hospital? At home? The thought of Levi and Charlotte terrified and alone, wondering where I was, what happened to Alex, made me want to claw my nails across my face until it resembled a crossword puzzle, bloody and raw. Why had I thought I could get away with this? That I could tune out of my life like an old movie and expect the ending to stay the same?

Time was too fickle. It waited for no one.

"Come on." Geneva tugged me up. "I'll drive."

I didn't argue. Once inside her car, I pulled out my phone, staring at the red balloon hovering over the voicemail icon. Alex. He needed me. And I wasn't there.

I couldn't bear to listen to his message. Not yet. I needed to be strong. Hearing his voice would break me. And there was no time for a breakdown.

CHAPTER FORTY-FOUR
GENEVA

Geneva saw the blood red Emergency sign and drove towards the hospital entrance. Lila jumped out of the car and was swallowed up by the automatic doors before Geneva pulled to a complete stop. Lila hadn't asked her to come inside, but Geneva knew what it was like to endure a tragedy alone. Replaying the final minutes, hours, days, over and over, like CNN during a school shooting. All commentary, no answers. Geneva would stay, support Lila, help get her through the night.

Misery greeted Geneva as she walked inside the hospital. Families huddled on cheap plastic chairs, arms crossed, eyes narrowed, waiting to hear their name. Children slept on laps and shoulders. The smell of antiseptic, recycled heat, and desperation wafted through the air. Above the commotion, Geneva could hear Paul McCartney sing about the wonderfulness of Christmastime—a sentiment she doubted this crowd shared.

As she stood in line at reception, the double doors to the emergency room flung open. Without hesitating—belonging was ninety percent confidence—she swooped in behind a distracted nurse. She entered a large room with a dozen curtained cubicles on each side. A hexagon-shaped desk sat in the middle, the hub for doctors and nurses, with another set of double doors behind.

Geneva grabbed a pamphlet from the wall, using it to shield her face as she began walking the room. She knew Alex took as much pleasure from her company as an enema. And while the feeling was mutual, she didn't want an unexpected sighting to kill the guy.

She heard Lila's voice and stopped up short.

"Minor?" Lila said. The pitch of her voice suggested a recent swig of helium. "But if it's minor, why does he need surgery?"

Geneva inched forward, peeking inside the two-foot gap in the curtain. Lila sat on the edge of the bed, her body blocking Alex, while the doctor stood opposite. Geneva stepped backwards, ensuring she was out of sight, and listened.

"He has a blocked artery, Mrs. Cole," the doctor said. "It needs to be fixed. Now. Before it becomes serious. As in deadly."

"Okay...so...okay," Lila said. Nearby, a machine exploded with beeps, causing Geneva to flatten herself against the curtain as a stampede of staff trampled past. "What happens now?"

"I'll place a coronary artery stent to keep the artery from narrowing and help the blood pass through," the doctor said. "Essentially, I'll make an incision in his arm, insert a catheter with a tiny balloon into the blocked artery, insert a stainless-steel mesh stent, deflate, remove the balloon and voilà, your husband's blood will be flowing like the east river."

The doctor made it sound like he was pulling a rabbit out of a hat instead of performing heart surgery. All that was missing were jazz hands.

"Don't worry, babe," Geneva heard Alex say. His voice was brittle, weary. But he was awake. Talking. A good sign. "They do these every day."

Geneva headed back towards the pamphlet wall before the doctor left, lest he question her presence. She read up on the signs of a stroke while waiting. A few minutes later, a pair of nurses wheeled Alex away. Lila walked alongside his gurney, pausing at the doors to lean over and kiss him. A lingering kiss that suggested a much healthier marriage than Geneva witnessed.

Geneva crumpled the pamphlet, tossing it in the garbage. She should go. How many times could she put herself out there to be rejected? But when she looked at Lila, standing alone, biting her fist, her narrow shoulders caving in as nurses and doctors breezed past, any thought of leaving evaporated. She loved Lila. And love required sacrifice; the ability to put the other person's needs before your own.

While Geneva still struggled to determine where her feelings for Cristina ended and Lila began, she knew that time with Lila left her entranced. Knocked down her boundaries. Made Geneva pause, take inventory of her heart. Lila had a stillness, a quiet confidence in what she wanted out of life, that Geneva envied. She had a huge capacity for love, for forgiveness judging by her marriage, for challenging herself to grow. Geneva marveled at the way Lila made herself vulnerable, risked razing her heart. It was this fearlessness that opened her to Geneva. While she would never be a homebody like Lila, Geneva wanted more than a life spent pursuing soulless hookups. She wanted love. Someone to call home.

Summoning her courage, she approached Lila, and tentatively squeezed her shoulder. Lila turned around, eyes wide and shiny as glass. Geneva could see her reflection in the dark ember.

"He had..." Lila wiped her runny nose with her sleeve. "He had a heart attack. He, he—"

Geneva held Lila's hands. "Breathe."

"It's my fault—"

"It's not."

Lila pulled away, swatting at her tears. "I never should've gone out tonight—"

"Sometimes, bad things happen. No rhyme or reason."

"You don't understand. He was so angry when I left."

"Let's get you a Coke Zero," Geneva said, dragging Lila away before a nurse offered to sedate her. "Come on. I'll throw in a candy bar, too."

They walked through the empty hallways, Geneva listening to Lila's ragged breathing. Lights clicked on as they passed. Suddenly, Lila stopped. "I can't do this."

"Yes, you can," Geneva said. "It'll be a long night, but Alex will pull through."

"No. This. Us." She wrung out her hands, as if she could wash herself of everything. The night. Alex's heart attack. Geneva. Thank you and goodbye. "You can't be here."

Geneva blinked. Hard. Endured the slap of the words. She felt Lila pulling away ever since Alex showed up at her apartment. But feeling and knowing are different. The fear did nothing to prepare her to meet the moment. "Look, I know you're terrified. What is he, like, forty?"

"He's healthy, for Christ's sake!" Lila yelled, her voice echoing down the abandoned hallway. She never heard Lila raise her voice, swear, lose control. Geneva wanted to hold her, but Lila's eyes skittered like a trapped animal, warning her off. "He runs, bikes. Bought organic before it was trendy. Drinks these disgusting kale smoothies that make him fart—" Lila flushed and looked away.

"Keep going. I want more of you." Geneva's heart thrashed inside her chest, uncomfortable with this gamble. "At your best, your worst, whatever. I can handle it."

"I can't," Lila whispered. "Don't you see? Everything you want, I already promised to Alex."

Geneva, who refused to compromise for anything but the best, was willing to accept a half-hearted promise. A check that would most likely bounce. "But that was before you met me."

She heard the desperation beneath her words. *Love me. Let me be enough. Put me first.* She blamed this insecurity on Cristina, her death being the ultimate rejection, but this refrain played her entire life. Planted first by her parents, who made her feel like an accessory to their lives instead of the center. Affirmed at boarding school, by a gaggle of white girls who constantly required her to audition for their company. Corroborated in academia, where her colleagues dismissed her intellect and worth ethic, assuming she was a diversity hire. She learned to turn these thoughts into background music, but as she fell in love with Lila, it became a chorus. Sung loudly with a fever.

"And I'm grateful I met you," Lila said, rubbing Geneva's arms. Geneva hadn't realized she was shaking until Lila touched her. "Your friendship filled this hole—"

"I love you," Geneva said. Instinct told her to run. Shut up. Pretend Lila didn't hold her heart. But she didn't want to live like that anymore. "Don't you get it? I don't want to be your friend. I want to be with you.

Always. Even when you're moody, or tired, or preoccupied with something stupid Alex did. I may get upset, but I never want you to leave."

Lila's lips tugged into a frown. "Geneva."

Geneva pinched her eyes. Hot tears threatened to fall, but she sniffed, holding them in. "Don't."

"The way you talk about sex and relationships..." Lila pressed the heel of her palm against her forehead. "I'm sorry. I won't make excuses. I was selfish. Depressed. Fighting with Alex. Traumatized by losing Milo. And then you came along. And being with you was exciting and fun and–" She looked at Geneva. "–completely unfair," she finished. "I love Alex. I've always loved Alex. I never should've let us get this far. If I could go back–"

Lila's phone buzzed. She flinched as she read the text. "Levi's freaking out. I need to call him."

Seriously? Geneva wanted to scream. She told Lila she loved her. Words she thought she'd never say again. And Lila was going to go make a phone call?

"Whatever. Go." Lila's allegiance lay with her family. It always had.

"You deserve someone amazing. Someone that gives all of themselves to you. That just...can't be me." Lila hugged Geneva. "I'm sorry."

Geneva watched Lila walk away, the click of her boots getting softer and softer until she disappeared around the corner. The lights switched off in the hallway, leaving Geneva in darkness except for the red glow of the exit signs.

"I'm lonely," she said, the darkness giving her the courage to voice the words she feared most. It felt unbearable. She grabbed her phone, logging onto Likk. She couldn't handle being alone tonight. But as she parsed through the profiles, noting the ways each woman fell short of Lila, a choice appeared. She could find someone to get an immediate fix. Or she could sit with the feeling. Be depressed. Give herself time to heal. Refuse to budge until she found someone worthy. Someone free to give love and ask for it in return.

Something had to change. She couldn't continue treating her heart and body as separate entities. With a shaky hand, Geneva clicked out of the app and walked down the hallway, eager to get home and pour a nice, tall glass of Pino. Sitting with the feeling didn't mean she couldn't drink to help the healing process.

At the corner, she turned and saw Lila on the phone. As she watched Lila pace, her body slowly morphed into Cristina. The loping gait, the skinny frame, the waterfall of dark hair. For whatever reason, neither woman loved her. She gave and gave and they took and took. And that was no longer good enough.

Geneva pressed the button for the elevator and stepped inside, leaving Lila behind. Cristina's ghost too.

She felt lighter already.

CHAPTER FORTY-FIVE
LILA

I paced the surgical waiting room, unable to sit still, to relax my taut muscles, as the clock ticked past midnight. Dr. Lucky, whose name made me wonder if this was a joke on God's part or a fortuitous foreshadowing, said it was a minor heart attack, a minor procedure. Minor. Minor. Minor. Nothing about it felt minor. Alex could have died. He still might die. That is the definition of major. Slapping the label minor on the situation does not make it so.

They do these every day, I whispered to myself, repeating Alex's words like a prayer. He would be okay. He had to be. The alternative was unthinkable.

My phone buzzed. *He's asleep*, Shannon texted. I relaxed my shoulders, feeling one of the knots in my back loosen. For once, Shannon carried her weight as a neighbor.

Levi was frantic when we talked, crying so hard that he hiccupped between words. I reassured him that Alex would be fine, all the while scraping my nails across my stomach, making it look like I was attacked by a stray cat. The pain distracted me from my own fears. I had to be strong for Levi. For Charlotte, who slept on, oblivious.

I tucked the phone back in my pocket. There was no one I could call. No one that could comfort me. Talk me off the ledge of despair and guilt. Certainly not my mom. Her words would add a shot of caffeine to my anxiety as she dove into every worst-case scenario. No. Best to wait until the surgery was over. I already alerted Alex's parents— not that I would ever confide in them that our marriage was on the brink. And Geneva? Well, I sent her away. I had to.

The memory of Geneva's face when I told her that I could never love her haunted me. Her normally rosy cheeks held the ashy pallor of death, her mouth slackened like a stroke victim. Until that moment, I never thought she was in love with me. I knew she cared, deeply perhaps, but she sold me on it just being sex. Claimed she was allergic to monogamy. Love. But that was all an act. The jealous remarks, the pressure to tell Alex about us—I should've seen through it. But I was too selfish, too focused on my problems, to notice her heartache.

"Mrs. Cole?"

I jumped, having not heard Dr. Lucky enter the room. I searched his face for signs of relief, pride, regret, but all I saw was fatigue. Eyes run through with red, dark bags underneath that made his lean face appear concave.

"The blockage was more severe than I initially thought, but the stent was put in without complication," he said, clasping his hands in front of his stomach. "You'll be glad to know that plenty of oxygen-rich blood is flowing throughout his body."

The relief left me momentarily winded. "So, he's going to be okay?"

"Provided he makes a few changes to his lifestyle."

"I don't understand. Alex is healthy." Dr. Lucky held up his hand to interrupt, but I continued talking. "He runs, he bikes. We eat organic."

"It could be a number of things, Mrs. Cole. Diet and exercise are great tools, but they can't make up for a bad draw in the gene lottery. A family history of heart disease is one of the biggest risk factors."

"Nope." I shook my head. "At least, not his parents."

Dr. Lucky pressed his lips together, undeterred. "Have you heard the old adage that doctors make the worst patients? Knowing the symptoms and doing something about it—"

"If Alex knew he was risk, he would've done something." This was the man that had a podiatrist on a speed dial when his planter fasciitis flared up before the Chicago Marathon. He sliced off moles at the first sign of growth. He fastidiously attended his yearly physical, bragging about his bloodwork like it was a straight-A report card. He respected the profession.

But then I thought about how ibuprofen made the grocery list each week. The way he started winding down with a couple beers each night. His complaints about headaches. Not sleeping. Long hours at work.

There were signs. Maybe not of a heart attack, but signs that he wasn't well.

"And then there's stress, the ultimate masked agent," Dr. Lucky continued. "Have there been any major upheavals? At work? Home? Sometimes it takes just a single event to trigger an attack."

Dr. Lucky, the beige chairs, the ugly beige-orange-yellow swirly carpet—it all swam before me. I braced myself against the wall, certain I was going to be sick. Alex almost died. Because of me.

Why didn't I say goodbye to Geneva on Sunday? Make a clean break? One weekend away from Alex, from the kids, and I knew, in spite of all his mistakes, I forgave him. I loved him. But I was scared; there were so many unknowns.

And angry. Part of the problem with therapy was dredging up all these old issues. My dad leaving. My mom drinking. The rape. Five miscarriages. Milo. Our marriage had problems, no doubt, but my desire to take a stand tonight, make myself heard, had more to do with my history, my failures to assert myself, than his behavior.

I saw the defeat in his eyes tonight, knowing he couldn't stop me from leaving, and it invigorated me. What a rush. To have power. A voice. But I had no idea his body would revolt. No idea that my power play might send him to an early grave.

"It's my fault," I said, wanting to own up to it all.

"He'll be okay, Mrs. Cole. And so will you. Think of this experience like an alarm clock, waking you both up before something really bad happens."

Okay being a relative and useless term. Physically, yes. Mentally, no. How could I repair the damage I rued on our marriage? The trust I broke? The pain I inflicted on Alex? I learned long ago that we aren't entitled to anything—safety, health, love—but my desire for another baby, my anger at having something else taken from me without my consent, my frustration with being silenced, silencing myself, made me reckless. Stupid. And just plain heartless.

Hannah encouraged me to speak up, share my feelings with Alex, but she would be horrified by my behavior tonight. *I* was horrified by my behavior.

"When can I see him?"

"Whenever you're ready." He opened the door. "A nurse will take you up to his room."

Gratitude, Hannah's voice reminded me. *You can find gratitude in the worst of circumstances.* I closed my eyes and took a deep breath. Exhaled.

I willed myself to feel grateful that Alex pulled through. That he would live a long, healthy life. Grateful that Alex believed in us. Never stopped fighting for us. Because he knew better than me that marriage was a series of compromises. That you don't get the other person on their best day every day. Or every month. Or, in this case, a year. Grateful that I realized my mistakes. That I was willing to accept blame, admit weakness, and fix what I could. Hopefully before the habits of the past year—refusing to listen, fixating on resentments, seeking comfort from strangers—became entrenched in our marriage. Or before there was no marriage to fight for at all.

Opening my eyes, I walked out of the waiting room. Grateful that we tested each other and still love remained. Oh, how I loved that man.

I needed to find Alex. Apologize. Tell him the truth. Hold him. Promise to never let go.

CHAPTER FORTY-SIX
ALEX

I woke with a sore throat. It itched and burned, like I swallowed a handful of salt. *I'm getting a cold.* Then I opened my eyes. Looked around the sterile hospital room. And remembered. No, not a cold. A heart attack. Followed by an angioplasty. The endotracheal tube left my throat feeling like an open wound.

My brain couldn't accept it. Me. Alexander Ash Cole. Had a heart attack. Six months ago, I ran the Fourth of July half-marathon in an hour and twenty-nine minutes. I still had the six-pack abs I sported while running cross-country for Notre Dame. I could do thirty pushups with Charlotte riding my back like a horse. Was this a resume for a man with heart issues?

And yet here I was. Strapped to a hospital bed. An IV plugged in my arm. My vitals monitored with a chime that sounded like a 90s ringtone. It was absurd. My anger about having a heart attack was going to give me another heart attack.

But then I looked at Lila, curled up in the chair next to my bed, and I realized how lucky I was to be alive. If I hesitated in calling 911, convinced myself it was a panic attack, I might be lying in the morgue several floors below.

"Babe, can I get some water?"

Lila stirred, blinked and smiled before leaning over and pressing her lips against mine. My lips were chapped—it must have felt like kissing the frayed edges of a notebook. Still, she didn't pull away. She hadn't stopped touching me since I emerged from surgery, keeping vigil while I slept.

She filled a Styrofoam cup with water and held the straw up to my mouth, waiting until I finished. "I think you missed your calling as a nurse," I said.

"You just want to see me in one of those old-fashioned white dresses."

"Guilty." I smiled briefly before a spasm in my jaw stopped me short. Everything hurt. "Did Dr. Lucky stop by?"

"Earlier this afternoon. We didn't want to wake you. But he said you look great. That you should be able to go home tomorrow." She looked at the door. "He's kind of a strange one. Keeps talking about all your 'oxygen rich blood.'"

Dr. Lucky was odd, but that was fitting. From the moment I called 911, I felt like I entered an episode of the *Twilight Zone*. All my authority, the way doctors and nurses listened to me, trusted my judgment, fell by the wayside. When I told Dr. Lucky I was a pediatrician, he raised his eyebrows as if to say, *So what?* I was a patient, a number, another cow rolling down the conveyer belt towards certain death without his intervention.

"I can't believe this happened," I said.

"Did you—" She stopped, smoothed the sheet with her palms. "Were they any signs?"

Everything was a sign. I'd been operating on empty since Milo's death, overrun with work, taking care of the kids, initially compensating for Lila's depression and then later for the tension between us, that my health wasn't a priority. Stress, sleepless nights, headaches, long hours, sexual frustration, all exacted a toll.

I encouraged parents to keep a health journal for their kids. Sometimes it takes a global perspective to home in on the real issue. Other times, small issues mutate and spiral. I dispensed this advice, followed it with my children, yet dismissed its value when it came to me. Dismissed Lila when she encouraged me to see a doctor about the headaches. Instead of stopping to assess, following the bread crumbs, I popped ibuprofen and ingested liters of coffee to motor through.

Turns out my ego not only jeopardized my marriage, but also my life.

"Too many to count," I said.

"I'm sure our problems didn't help."

Should I lie? Tell her that her decision to choose Geneva over me, over us, didn't cause irreversible damage to my heart? That the threat of losing her, my wife, my best friend, wasn't a contributing factor? If not *the* factor? I never put much stake in broken heart syndrome, but after last night, I was a believer. The months leading up to it didn't help, but the surge of stress hormones when she walked out the door tipped the balance, plunging me towards a heart attack that may never have come about if she stayed home.

Was it fair to put this on her? She pushed me over the edge, but my decisions brought us to the cliff. Much as I wanted to bask in the truce the heart attack orchestrated, that band-aid would wear off. Silence infiltrated our marriage for too long. If there was a way forward, we had to go through Geneva.

"When you left last night. You broke me." I swallowed. It felt like roses were growing inside my throat, the thorns embedding in my tissue when I got emotional. "Losing friends, the babies—nothing prepared me for what it felt like to lose you."

She grabbed my hand. "You didn't lose me."

"As soon as you picked Geneva, I lost you. Can't you see that?"

"It's over with her."

The relief I expected refused to come. Her words tasted sour, like drinking from a jug of expired milk. I needed to hear those words two weeks ago. Sunday night. Last night.

I pulled my hand away, rubbing my eyes. "Perfect timing, hey?"

"It's not like that. I planned to end things with Geneva last night, before our fight. That's why I was going out. Why I needed to talk to her. Our weekend together was...enlightening." She must have caught my wary expression, because she quickly followed it up. "In the best way. I realized that I took you and the kids for granted. And I didn't want to waste another minute being depressed, holding grudges, mourning what could have been. While I care about Geneva, those feelings aren't love. You're the one I love." She ran her thumb across my cheek. "I should've ended it Sunday but I was scared you changed your mind."

"Changed my mind? About you?" I was the one that wanted to end the open marriage. Was she listening at all? "You're all I wanted. I told you that."

She tilted her head, examining me. "You said that *before* you found out Geneva went away for the weekend with me. After, it felt like something shifted. I expected disappointment, frustration...but you were so hostile—"

"Yeah." I snorted. "You were fucking her. On my time."

"No, *my* time." Her brown eyes sparkled with passion—nothing like the foggy-eyed woman that spoke to me only when necessary this past year. I'd say vintage Lila, but this woman was stronger, willing to fight to make herself heard. "You gave me the weekend to figure out how to move forward. And I used it to answer some lingering questions."

"Do you have any idea what it was like for me?" I sat up in bed...and then fell right back. I shut my eyes, taking a couple deep breaths to interrupt the fight or flight loop that had become habitual. And dangerous. "Imagining you two together?"

"Yeah, I do. You went out quite a few nights, too." She held her hands up. "But I don't want to argue, I want to explain." She looked down, directing her words at her lap. "I was lonely when I met Geneva. We lost Milo and then, when you got the vasectomy, I felt like I lost you too. The man I knew." She looked up at me. "It sounds dramatic. It *was* too dramatic. I should've talked to you, but I was struggling just to keep it together for the kids." She shrugged. "And Geneva; she didn't blame me for feeling angry or depressed. She saw me for who I was, and wanted more."

"I'll bet she did." Geneva was a smart woman. Intuitive. She recognized Lila's vulnerability. Made her feel special. And then landscaped Lila's anger, watering the seed until it bloomed into a full-blown resentment. Until, she hoped, Lila would leave me.

"You made me feel like such a disappointment," Lila said, ignoring my comment. "I couldn't move on from Milo. I couldn't have sex. I wasn't trying to be happy. Every time you looked at me, it felt like you found me lacking." She paused, perhaps waiting for me to contradict her. But I couldn't. I *did* find her lacking. I thought she gave up not only on our marriage, but on life. "And when I found the courage to tell you why I was angry, that I felt betrayed by the vasectomy, you still thought it was my problem to get over. Not yours."

Again, I wanted to argue, but she was right. Once I made up my mind about something, I never second-guessed it. As a doctor, second-guessing is tantamount to malpractice. That habit carried over to my marriage. It never occurred to me to give an inch. To imagine a different scenario, like adoption, where we both felt heard and fulfilled.

"It wasn't until you found out about Geneva, until you realized my needs were being met by someone else, that you started to listen. Reflect on your behavior."

"You had sex with Geneva to teach me a lesson," I said. It wasn't a question. It was, finally, an understanding of why she didn't end the open marriage. "This wasn't about needing time."

She shook her head. "It's not that simple. I needed time to sort through my feelings. Yes, I saw that it hurt you. And I hated that. But it was a necessary hurt." Her voice rose, pleading with me for clemency. "You needed to feel the agony of what you put me through when you got the vasectomy. To feel that helplessness. To want something and have someone else decide you can't have it."

"I never meant—" I stopped. I had good intentions for getting the vasectomy, but the end result of my actions was the same: she felt helpless. Ignored. Betrayed. Exactly how I felt since finding out about Geneva. "I was in the ambulance last night," I said. "And I saw snippets, clips from the last year. But the odd thing was, the clips were from your perspective. Delivering Milo. Days home alone while I went back to work. Finding out I got the vasectomy. Being told to see a therapist. Go on anti-depressants. Open our marriage. And it hit me." I held her eyes. "I cut you out of the equation. Not maliciously. Not even consciously. I thought I was protecting you, protecting our family, with every decision I made—even the open marriage, I convinced myself, was to sound the alarm, wake you up. And yet—" I rubbed the heel of my hand against my stubble. "—looking at it through your lens, I saw a selfish, conceited, and frankly, oblivious husband. We're different, have different skills—that's what makes us such a good team. But the moment I went ahead with the vasectomy, I fractured the team. I put me ahead of us and expected you to fall in line."

We wore matching faces of regret as we thought about all the nights we avoided talking, lying to both ourselves and each other when we said that we wanted something, or someone, else.

"Last night scared me," she said. "I walked out, not because I wanted to be with Geneva, but because I didn't want you telling me what to do anymore. I thought I was standing up for myself. And honestly? It felt good...to have power. In our marriage—in my life, really. The problem is—" She laughed sadly. "—well, there's several problems. But what most upsets me is that I wasn't honest with you about Geneva. I put you in an impossible position and then lashed out at you for fighting for our marriage. I should've understood your anger, told you everything. Instead, I let you believe I might leave you, which—" She pushed her hands together in prayer pose, pressing them against her lips, trying to hold in the emotion. "—was cruel. All I can say is that I'm sorry and hope that you'll forgive me. That you'll understand that I'm still working through how to...voice my feelings."

Her words settled in my gut like a penny fluttering to the bottom of a pond. The truth. At last. The relief I waited for moments ago began to trickle through my IV, sending a hint of warmth through my bloodstream. She didn't want Geneva. Maybe she had for a moment, but what was a moment in a lifetime together? Geneva was a distraction, a coping mechanism, a listening ear when I closed mine. My need to fix everything immediately, my ego, my fear of losing her, turned Geneva into something catastrophic.

Where would we be if I hadn't had the heart attack? How long would this charade have continued? Until we separated? Called divorce lawyers? Forged separate lives?

"I should've trusted you last night. That you just needed to talk to her." I held out my hand, waiting as she clasped hers inside mine.

"If it helps, we didn't have sex last weekend." She brought my hand to her mouth and kissed my fingertips. "Our relationship was always more emotional than physical."

It did help. Maybe my brain would finally retire the Geneva-Lila sex dream.

"I meant what I said the other night. I want to be better. I'm here to listen, always. I want to hear every thought going through that beautiful head of yours. None of these mental guessing games. No more holding back. Leaving out details."

She turned to look out the window. Flakes of snow fluttered through the air. "I started seeing a therapist," she said. "Hannah."

Why now? I wanted to ask. Why not after Milo, when I begged her to talk to someone? But at once, I knew the answer: she needed to come to that conclusion on her own. "Is it helping?"

Lila nodded slowly. "She thinks I shut down when life gets tough, because I learned as a child that my feelings didn't matter."

I remembered the vacant look in her eyes as she pushed Milo out. The impenetrable mask she wore this past year. But I didn't want my opinion to dictate hers. "What do you think?"

She took a deep breath. "After Milo, the guilt was excruciating. I couldn't breathe—"

"Guilt?" I asked, confused, assuming she meant grief.

Her eyes remained fixated on the snow growing heavier outside the window. "The truth is, I spent months focusing on your betrayal because I wasn't ready to own up to the fact that I deceived you first."

It was a bad time to joke about my heart stopping, but, with her words, I felt a pause. I couldn't handle another confession, both physically and emotionally.

"The day Milo died, he...he didn't wake me up. Normally, he did his little jumping routine, but not that morning."

"Lila," I whispered. "You couldn't have known. Babies have down times—"

"No." She bit down on her knuckle like an apple. "Please, listen. You left early for the hospital, but came in to kiss me goodbye while I

247

was doing yoga, remember?" I nodded vaguely, unable to differentiate that morning from any other. "I thought about telling you he hadn't moved, but something stopped me. I..." She wrung her hands. "I don't know. Maybe, I thought if I said something, it would become real? Maybe I believed it was nothing? I don't know. I got the kids off to school and just waited." Tears filled her eyes, but she held them at bay. "I didn't call the doctor. Didn't do anything. I froze. Hours passed. Hours that felt like minutes. Critical hours that could've saved his life." She sniffled. "And then when I got to the hospital, I lied. Said he hadn't moved for a couple hours, but the truth is, I hadn't felt him move since I got up to pee in the middle of the night. I just...I couldn't tell you the truth. Couldn't handle you hating me as much as I hated myself."

I pulled Lila against my chest, feeling the weight of her grief settle against me. She let go, sobs that shook her entire body. "Babe, it's not your fault."

"Don't—"

"It's. Not. Your. Fault," I repeated, kissing her forehead. No wonder I lost Lila; she lost herself. "You don't know when it happened. Twelve hours or one minute before we got to the hospital. Even if you went to the hospital right away that morning, he might not have survived." I believed every word. Working in medicine gave me a front-row seat to the fickleness of God. "You can't play the what-if game, Lila. It's not healthy."

She glanced up at me, giving me a watery smile. "You're not exactly in a position to lecture me on health."

I grunted a laugh. "Funny girl."

"You're not angry?"

"Angry? No. Sad more than anything." I regretted taking her depression at face-value. Probably, because I too was depressed. "I wish you would've told me the truth, trusted me to understand. Because I never would've blamed you. I hope you know that."

"I'm sorry."

The meaning of her words continued to penetrate deeper. "None of this needed to happen."

"Maybe it did." She sat back in her chair, wiping her eyes with her sleeve. "Maybe, like you said, in a weird way, it helped us. We'll be better than ever. A circuitous route to a happy ever after."

"Promise me you won't go silent again. Promise me that when life gets hard, when you feel like you've messed up, you won't shut me out."

She raised her eyebrows. "Promise me you won't make decisions without me."

I smiled. "Do you need it in writing?"

"A kiss will do."

I kissed her, silently promising that I would not kiss another woman until the day I died.

"Don't get too excited," she murmured against my lips. "Dr. Lucky says no sex for a week."

"I'll risk it."

I kissed her again. And again. And a few more for good measure.

"Alex!" My mom rushed in, wedging her way between Lila and me, pressing her cherry lips against my forehead.

"A stent, Alex?" my dad said, his six-foot-four frame filling the room like the Hulk. You want a God complex, look no further than Dad. "Someone should've called me..."

I rested my head against the pillow and closed my eyes, inhaling my mom's floral perfume, absorbing my dad's rant. It felt like listening to the best of Bon Jovi—it brought back the comfort and nostalgia of my youth. Marconi & Cheese. Summer nights playing Bloody Murder. Bubble gum inside baseball cards packets. This would only hurt for a bit. Tomorrow, everything would be better.

"...stent thrombosis...infections..."

I opened my eyes and saw a flutter of a smile on Lila's lips. Comfort in understanding. In being known. In being loved. My parents ushered in a wave of safety, but it was Lila's face that brought me home. She would always be my home.

My dance with death left me with one overriding message: I loved her. The kids we created. The life we cobbled together. Everything from the mundane to the maddening to the Kodak moments. Our life. It would never be perfect, but it's all I wanted. Why I thought different, even if briefly, was beyond me. Perhaps Dr. Lucky was right; maybe it was all that *oxygen rich blood* circulating to my brain. Because, suddenly, I felt like the luckiest guy alive.

The heart attack was giving me a second chance in more ways than one.

EPILOGUE - 18 MONTHS LATER
LILA

The heat hit the sidewalk pavement and wafted into the air like smoke from a crushed cigarette, singeing my sneakers. My ponytail was glued to my neck. Sweat trickled between my breasts. The Moby wrap didn't help. Not that I would ever complain about that.

Aurora lay sleeping against my chest with her mouth open just wide enough to encircle her middle and ring fingers. Her cheeks glowed cotton candy pink against her cocoa skin, the only hint she was aware of the heat. The sight, the smell, touch of her, as always, liquified my heart. Since we adopted her seven weeks ago, tears of joy had become such a common occurrence that Levi told people I had an eye infection.

"How much longer, Mommy?" Charlotte asked, flinging her body around the lamppost.

We stood near the finish line of the Fourth of July half-marathon, waiting for Alex. He insisted on running, despite the heatwave. If I thought he was healthy before the heart attack, I was mistaken. He took to clean living like a yogi at an ashram.

"Five minutes." I looked down the street, scanning the runners for Alex, the lake blooming robin's egg blue in the background. "Ten at the most. And then we'll get ice cream."

"I'm melting, melting..." Charlotte shrieked like the witch in *The Wizard of Oz* as she fell to the pavement. "I might die."

"You won't die," Levi said, kneeling on the cement, prodding an ant onto a stick. "It takes a few hours for heat stroke to set in. And you've been out here, what, fifteen minutes?"

Levi looked more like Alex each day, with the pragmatic, scientific brain to match. I kept hoping his good looks and intelligence would ease the teasing, help him make friends, but so far, we weren't that lucky.

I handed Charlotte my bottle. "Drink some water." I kept my eyes locked on the runners, not noticing the woman in the chic raspberry jumpsuit approaching on the sidewalk until she stood in front of me.

Geneva.

I hadn't seen her since the night of Alex's heart attack. A surprise, considering how interwoven my job was with campus life. I thought about emailing her, asking whether she was okay, but decided against it. I needed to prioritize my marriage. Knowing I made the right choice did little now to calm my hammering heart.

Geneva whipped off her aviator sunglasses and smiled. Relief tasted sweeter than a glass of ice water. She didn't hate me.

Then I realized the smile wasn't meant for me. "Who's this gorgeous creature?" she asked, brushing her fingers against Aurora's silky cheek.

"Rory," Charlotte said, announcing the nickname the kids bestowed on Aurora. They were obsessed, arguing over who got to feed, hold, and play with her. Like all gifts, the luster would fade, but for now, they revered her like an iPad. "She's my sister."

"Aurora," Levi corrected.

"Aurora," Geneva whispered, saying her name like a prayer. She stood up straight, looking me in the eyes. "She's beautiful."

"We're truly blessed."

And that was an understatement. The adoption process took an emotional toll. We were chosen on two separate occasions, only for it to fall through. Losing those babies felt like history repeating itself, but this time, I didn't break down. I focused on the kids, marveling at Levi's ability to name every bone in the human body. The fluidity of Charlotte's limbs as she ran a mile. I still cried. Spent too many sessions with Hannah working through my guilt about Milo, dwelling on my wish for a bigger family. But I didn't hide those thoughts from Alex. I let him hold me as I talked through my fears. Listened to his. We bonded over each loss. Picked each other up on bad days.

And then the call came. Shea, a high school track star with a bright future, chose us. She wanted her baby to have a loving home, a financially secure future, but she also wanted to pass on a piece of herself: her love of running. Alex's years running at Notre Dame, a picture he insisted on including in our profile, paid for more than his college. It gave us Aurora.

Our Aurora. The dawning of a new day for our family. I took a circuitous route to meet her, filled with dark days and bad decisions, but I understood now why that was necessary. I had a greater capacity for love, an appreciation for what the human spirit could endure, an internal strength that I needed to be her mother. She would grow up adopted, Black in a white family, a predominately white city. It was my job to nurture these differences, make her feel strong, proud of her roots, the star of her life. Aurora would not be a victim of circumstance. She would not be silenced.

"Can I hold her?" Geneva asked. I gently pulled Aurora out of the sling, placing her in Geneva's arms. Geneva swayed her hips, looking surprisingly adept, as she gazed at Aurora. "You're going to make me catch baby fever, little one."

"You? With a baby?"

Geneva laughed softly. "Not right now. But, maybe, someday."

She handed Aurora back, watching me closely as I shifted Aurora inside her sling. I smiled, growing uncomfortable. I'd seen that look before—Geneva was ready to get real, cut the pleasantries. And I didn't want the kids hearing anything they shouldn't.

"I'm happy for you, Lila. A year ago—" She shrugged, a gesture to downplay how much I hurt her. "But now, I appreciate what you did for me."

"I doubt that." Most of our relationship was about me, what I needed. Companionship. Courage. A break. I was too caught up in my own pain to give much to her. Geneva, Alex, the kids—they all suffered in my wake. "I wasn't a good friend to you."

She squeezed my hand, speaking with the soft authority I always admired. "You made me want more."

"Daddy!" Charlotte yelled. "Daddy! Over here!"

We turned to see Alex running towards the finish line, sporting red, white, and blue Fourth of July shorts, a Superhero Pediatrics singlet, and his trademark Notre Dame cap. He looked lean and muscular, not a hint of the pale, battered man I encountered in the hospital. His smile returned. The children's laughter soon followed. Mine too.

Alex waved and grinned, but his step stuttered as he recognized Geneva. A fraction of a second only detectable by me. Was he hurt? Angry? But then, he blew me a kiss, a non-verbal way of saying, *I trust you.* I pressed all ten fingers to my lips, blowing it back at him. *I love you.*

I was his. He was mine. Forever and always. *I choose you* had become the running joke for everything from who would make small talk with Shannon and Brett to who got up in the middle of the night to feed Aurora. Joking defused the tension, made the lowest of the lows in our marriage not quite as dangerous. But we could joke because the words held our truth, because we had done the hard work. We chose each other every day.

It would be naïve to say our marriage would never again encounter adversity. Difficulties stalked me at every stage of my life. But we would meet them together. The answers lay within our marriage. In communicating. We were stronger now than ever before.

"I'm leaving," Geneva said, interrupting my thoughts.

"I'm glad we ran into each other." And I was. At times, I questioned my relationship with Geneva. Wondered whether it was real, whether I had a bout of temporary insanity. But talking to her now, I knew, our connection was special. I was sleepwalking and she woke me up. Helped me rediscover my voice, desire, passion for life. While our tangled history meant we couldn't stay friends, I'd always be indebted to her.

"No. I'm leaving Madison. A position opened at Columbia. And my girlfriend, Gwyneth Cruz—" Geneva beamed, her happiness shining brighter than the sun. "—shoots there."

"Gwyneth Cruz from *Game Changers*?" I asked, unsurprised that the beautiful, enigmatic, alluring Geneva found someone equally magnetic. "Wow! Back in New York. Beautiful girlfriend. Dream job. You're living the life."

My perfect life included Alex at the grill, shirtless with board shorts, Aurora sucking her milk, her brown eyes glued to mine, while listening to Levi and Charlotte laugh as they flung their lithe bodies down the Slip 'N Slide. But I wanted to give this to her: a moment of awe-inspired envy. An acknowledgement of everything she'd overcome. We were both exactly where we were supposed to be.

"Mommy." Charlotte tugged on Aurora's foot. "Ice cream. Now. You promised."

I looked at Geneva, unsure what words fit the moment. As always, she made the first move, giving me a light hug before kissing Aurora's forehead. "Congratulations."

She walked away, disappearing into the crowd, sealing that chapter of my life shut.

"Let's go find Daddy." I held Charlotte's sweaty hand on my right side and Levi's on my left, firm and calloused from baseball. I bit my lip to hold back my tears. The moment felt golden, with Alex parting the crowd like Moses.

He jogged over, a smile radiating across his rosy cheeks, the brim of his Notre Dame hat shading his beautiful blue eyes. I felt dizzy, the déjà vu feeling sliding me into a time warp, ejecting me on the day we met. As I stood at the water fountain, watching Alex run towards me, I saw our life unfold. The way our limbs, breath, and hair would tangle in sleep; the vows we would take; the kids that would run down the stairs on Christmas morning; afternoons cheering on the bleachers. I did not see the lost babies, the betrayals, the grudges, the silent rages.

I didn't see those things today either. Nor did I dream of our future. I breathed in the blessing of this moment. My husband. Our kids. All of us alive, healthy, loved. He wrapped us in his sweaty arms, a bear hug for the ages. I lifted my head to meet his kiss.

Grateful.

* * * * * * * * * * * * * *

If you would like to read more of **Marisa Rae Dondlinger's** work, turn the page to read Chapter One of her forthcoming novel from Moonshine Cove Publishing *Gray Lines.*

CHAPTER ONE
PENELOPE

After wrapping a white towel around her body, Penelope opened the bathroom door and shrieked. Someone—an intruder? A ghost?—stood leaning against the wall directly opposite the bathroom. The dark hallway, lit only by the streetlight coming in through a nearby window, tripped her up for a second before the person stepped closer and she realized it was Micah. Her best friend of eleven years. More recently, her first boyfriend. Her secret.

"You scared me!" she said, swatting his shoulder.

He caught her hand, kissing her knuckles. When he touched her, smiled at her, looked at her, the rest of her world shrank. But right now, she felt hyperaware that she wore only a bath towel and they were alone. Mom was working late and her twin brother Ollie was in the basement.

"Did you win?" he asked, referring to the tennis match she played tonight.

"Six-one, six-three." She let go of his hand, tugging down the hem of the towel, which covered her to mid-thigh.

"You gave up four games?" Micah held a hand to his heart, feigning shock. His knees buckled—was that part of the act? He laughed as he reached for the wall to steady himself.

"I lost focus," she said, her anger like a switchblade, cutting through her confusion about Micah being up here, putting her back in the match. Bianca was seventeen to Penelope's fourteen, a top player from Chicago, committed to Stanford next fall—and Penelope beat her. Outplayed her, really. But serving for the second set at five-two, Penelope was broken, a case of nerves she couldn't afford against a better opponent.

"Busy thinking about me." Micah ran his fingertips from her shoulder to her wrist. She shivered involuntarily, her breath catching. "Admit it. You're crazy 'bout me."

He kissed her, sweet and slow, his tongue gently flicking hers, zapping her taste buds awake, filling her mouth with the taste of lemons.

"You can't be here," she said between kisses. His kisses drove all common sense from her mind, but the thought that Ollie could walk up here broke through. Ollie, who had no idea that his best friend and sister had been meeting up all summer. Ollie, who was too shy and sensitive to talk to girls, would feel left behind, extra, if he knew the truth. Unlike Micah, who had a new girlfriend every week since sixth grade—until kissing Penelope. "We'll get caught."

Micah's breath was hot against her lips. "There's no one here to catch us."

"Where's Ollie?"

"Don't worry, he's cool," Micah said, planting kisses on her neck.

"Meaning what?" Penelope jerked away and looked up at Micah. It was still an adjustment, looking up. She'd always been taller, but Micah recently shot over six-feet, all wiry muscles. "You promised not to tell him—"

"Chill," Micah said. "Just meant we'd hear him if he came upstairs."

Something else was at play, but, like finding Micah waiting outside the bathroom, Penelope couldn't pinpoint it. That's what being a teenager feels like: infinite feelings with infinite interpretations. No one to tell you which one was right. "I have to get dressed." She walked to her bedroom, pushing the door behind her.

Micah caught it. She turned around. "Go downstairs," she laughed, crossing her arms and blocking his way. Mom had a strict rule about no boys in the bedroom. Then again, Mom had strict rules about everything. "I'll come down when I'm done."

"I wanna congratulate you on the win." He laced his hands around her hips, backing her into the bedroom, inch by inch, a dance of sorts. He kissed her again, deeper this time, massaging his tongue with hers. Blood soared though her limbs, giving her a feeling of weightlessness. Possibility. Bliss. That's what kissing Micah felt like: diving underwater. A forehand scorched down the line. The first bite of chocolate cake. How had she ever lived without it?

Mid-kiss, Micah tripped, sending her stumbling backwards onto the bed. He fell on top of her. They both giggled.

"Damn, girl," he said, lips fluttering against hers. "Don't you ever clean your room?"

"Can't you look where you're walking?"

He kissed her again. His penis, which amazed and terrified and baffled her, pressed hard against her hip. A flutter of panic tightened her chest. Constricted her breath. She tilted her head back, disentangling her lips, needing oxygen. A great, heaping mouthful to clear her thoughts, slow him down.

"I'm worried about Ollie," she said, afraid to tell Micah the truth. That she was panicking. Throughout the summer, kissing replaced eating, talking, *being*, but he never saw her naked. She wasn't ready. Instead, they used their hands to explore each other's bodies over their clothes, a mental jigsaw puzzle she put together in bed each night.

"He won't bother us."

How could Micah be so sure? Before she could ask, Micah pressed up on an elbow, guiding her hand down to his penis, stroking it with her over his gym shorts. This, she could do. Clothes on? Okay. Soon, it would be over. And he'd go back to kissing her. Whispering. Cuddling. The part *she* loved.

He let go of her hand, hovering above her in a modified plank, his breath painting a line between her lips and eyebrows as he thrust. She continued the way he taught her, fast and tight. The smooth texture, the way it grew in her hand, his groans—she felt embarrassed, turned on, afraid, but most of all, powerful. Making him shake and shudder felt like a special talent. Along with painting the lines with her groundstrokes. Making her opponents run corner to corner. Give up. She could make Micah lose himself. Just her. *She* was his girl. The high fell short of winning a match, but not by much.

"I. Like. That," Micah grunted, but instead of moving with her hand, letting the moment culminate, he reached down, tugging his shorts and boxers beneath his hips. His penis sprang forward, rocking against her thigh, skin on skin, soft and hard. Where once three layers separated them, now there was only one, her towel. A flimsy piece of cloth that jacked higher up her thigh each time he thrust.

"Micah." A plea for him to open his eyes, look at her, realize she didn't want to do this.

"Uh-huh." His eyes were closed, nostrils flared, lips pressed with tension.

He didn't stop.

Tears of frustration sprung to her eyes. Why did he take his clothes off? That wasn't the deal. Was she supposed to like this? Was she a freak for wanting to stop? "Can we..." She didn't finish the sentence. Didn't know how to.

"I got you." He arched her hands over her head, running his tongue along her lips. "Just wait." He moved down her body, his head dipping between her thighs. She sprung backwards, her head smashing against the headboard, the surprise making her want to cry more than the pain. Why was he acting like this? Pushing her? He made varsity football a few weeks ago. Was it the older guys? Giving him ideas? Some sick hazing ritual?

"I don't like that," she said. A pit formed in her stomach the moment she saw Micah outside the bathroom. A pit that now felt like an oil spill—dark, heavy, toxic.

"Relax." He looked up at her. Eyes dark, lips glistening, he reached up and rested one hand against her cheek. "Have I ever led you wrong?"

Before she could answer—*Yes! Dozens of times! Not on purpose, but still!*—he pulled her knees apart, resuming his pursuit. She shut her eyes, bit her lip. Her muscles became rigid, her mouth dry. The certainty that this was wrong, that he shouldn't be here, that they shouldn't be doing this, made leaving her only option.

"I need to pee," she blurted out.

Micah crawled up her body until his face was inches from hers, his lips hovering, a smile playing on the corners. "That's because it feels good. You need to let go. Enjoy it."

Relieved he was finally listening, she said, "I can't."

His eyelashes tickled her cheeks as he brushed her with kisses. His elbows pressed against the curves of her shoulders, a glove, squeezing her in. Fingers splayed in her wet, tangled hair. Pulling back an inch or so, he took her in. His brown eyes were a polygraph of red. "I love you—" His voice sounded gritty, parched, aching, his breath labored. "—Penelope Mae Swanson."

Before she could process his words—Did he say he loved her???—he fused their bodies together. A hot, searing pain plunged through the depths of her core, as if someone lit a firecracker. It fizzled inside before exploding, sending shock waves down every nerve pathway.

Too late, she understood. She was having sex. SEX! With Micah. In her bed. Right. This. Minute.

She lay paralyzed as he moved above her, a shadow of himself. How did this happen? How did she *let* this happen? How did they go from kissing and touching to this? So quickly?

How could she stop him?

Before her mind could solve this riddle, Micah moaned, pressing his face against Penelope's neck. He wasn't looking at her. This summer had been about the two of them, the secret they kept, communicating their feelings through their eyes. *Kiss me. Meet me after everyone's asleep. I miss you.* And now? He wasn't looking at her! He was inside her, but she could be anyone. Nameless. Faceless. Nobody. Nothing.

"That was amazing," he said, grinning, once again the boy she knew.

"Ye-ah." Her voice broke on the word, elongating both syllables. Tears spilled from her eyes and she hated herself. Hated that she let this happen. High school started in three days. If this got out, her life would be ruined. She was a tennis prodigy. A future champion. Not the school slut. That was *not* her story.

"Overwhelming, I know." He pulled out of her, a knife drawn from a wound. No longer fused together, pain started in her center and radiated outwards, evicting all thoughts of school from her mind. "You bled some. Think that's normal though."

She turned on her side, letting the pillow catch her tears, breathing in and out, wondering if she was screaming. Or whether the high-pitched keening was inside her head.

"Being close with you," Micah whispered, laying down next to her, wrapping his arms around her waist, "felt perfect."

She couldn't feel his touch. She looked at her hands, spreading her fingers, noting there were ten, but she couldn't feel the softness of her sheets. The warmth of his body. The air in her lungs. What was this? What was happening to her?

"Me too." She was trying, desperately, to act normal.

"You're my perfect world. My perfect girl," Micah said. His words sounded like low-grade static. "I wish I didn't have to leave, but I'll be thinking about you. About tonight..."

After he left, she didn't move. She couldn't. Instead, she dove into the pit of nothingness inside her, letting it seal away the pain.

www.ingramcontent.com/pod-product-compliance
Lightning Source LLC
Chambersburg PA
CBHW031421020726
47499CB00005B/1529